The Book of Passage

A Time Travel Historical Steamy Romance

by Miranda Morrison

Preface

Time is a relentless river, ceaselessly rushing forward, swelling with moments that dissolve before they can be grasped, leaving behind ghostly echoes in the corridors of memory. We live tethered to its flow, bound by clocks and calendars that measure our days but rarely capture the complexity of the human heart's yearning. What if, beneath the measured tick of modern existence, a secret passage existed one not merely through years and centuries, but through the very essence of self and connection? What if love, that most unpredictable and fiercely transformative force, could transcend not just the boundaries of time but the unyielding walls of society and self-imposed limitation? This is the world into which you are invited in *The Book of Passage*.

From the very first turning of its pages, this story beckons you not simply to witness history but to step into its swirling vortex to feel the chill of 18th-century Bramleigh's biting winter air, to hear the creak of ancient timber, to navigate the oppressive social customs that dictate the lives of those who inhabit that world. Yet it is not merely the external trappings of a bygone era that shape this tale, but the interior landscapes of two modern souls cast unwittingly into the past, forced to perform the grandest roles of all: survival, trust, and love. Caroline Moore, a historian whose heart beats in sync with facts and structure, finds herself unmoored from certainty, drawn into a life where control is a fragile illusion. And Thomas Reed, a man whose instincts are attuned to physical reality and survival, encounters a vulnerability that challenges his very understanding of belonging.

Their story is not one of effortless romance basking in pastoral charm or grand gestures beneath starry skies; rather, it is a slow-burning fusion of tension and tenderness forged in the crucible of necessity. They are thrust together by the mysterious, unyielding will of an ancient book, a catalyst that demands their presence, their cooperation, and ultimately, their transformation. They must pose as husband and wife, a façade that demands social performance and shrewd navigation of the ever-watchful eyes of a community that prizes order above empathy. At the heart of this performance lies the raw reality of two people wrestling with their own fears of dependence, the haunting shadows of identity, and the wild, fragile seeds of trust.

Agnes Pryce, the formidable and subtle antagonist, embodies the suffocating structures that govern Bramleigh a woman whose power is wielded not with brute force but with whispered threats, keen observation, and the chilling promise of legal reprisal. She is a reminder that survival in a rigid society is about negotiation as much as it is about courage. Against her vigilant scrutiny, Caroline and Thomas's tentative alliance is tested, unraveling each thread of their carefully maintained façade until only their true selves remain beneath the weight of necessity and desire.

The Book of Passage explores themes that resonate far beyond the confines of a specific era or a portal to another time. It dives deeply into the essence of love and trust the way proximity and shared adversity bind strangers, dissolve doubt, and reveal vulnerabilities hidden even from oneself. It probes the fluidity of identity in a tumultuous world, where the past is both a literal place and a metaphor for the histories that haunt us, and belonging is a fragile gift wrested from circumstance and choice. It meditates on the duality of control and surrenders the fierce human need to master one's destiny alongside the profound necessity of yielding oneself to the unpredictable, ineffable forces that shape intimacy and connection.

Writing this novel was a journey of discovery itself, an unfolding of layers that demanded balancing the stark realities of 18th-century rural life, the customs, dangers, and social strictures with the timeless, universal truths of human emotion. I sought to craft a narrative that sweeps readers away not just with romantic heat and passion yes, there is desire here, passionate and consensual, electric and tender but with a story rich in emotional depth, where every touch and glance carries the weight of growth, sacrifice, and revelation. The romance here is not an escape from the past or from hardship; it is the flame that burns brightest because it is forged within it.

Through the shifting perspectives of Caroline and Thomas, I invite you to experience intimately their fears and strengths, their moments of doubt and daring, the sparks that fly and the silence that carries so much meaning between them. Their voices are distinct yet intertwined, illuminating not only the external hurdles of a hostile environment but the internal battles waged in the chambers of the heart. The social world of Bramleigh is vivid and unforgiving, its nuances painstakingly rendered to immerse you fully and, in that immersion, the stakes become urgent, the characters' choices vital.

As you turn these pages, prepare to lose yourself in a world where the past is not dead but alive with danger and desire, where love is as much a matter of survival as it is of the soul, and where the boundaries of time blur to reveal the enduring power of human connection. Whether you are drawn to the intoxicating allure of historical romance, the mystery of time travel, or the rich tapestry of character-driven storytelling, this book offers you a journey as unexpected and transformative as the story within it. Welcome to *The Book of Passage*. Step beyond the threshold and let the story carry you across centuries, into a world where every heartbeat defies the march of time, and love becomes the ultimate passage home.

The Unmarked Book

Sanctuary of Knowledge

Caroline Moore pushed open the heavy oak door of the Arkwell Library with a soft sigh of relief, stepping inside the quiet cavern of shelves that smelled of aged paper and polished wood. The late morning sun filtered weakly through stained glass, casting muted, kaleidoscopic patterns onto the marble floor, slow to move in the stillness. The library was a sanctuary, her sanctuary a haven where the chaotic churn of the modern world barely rained on her carefully constructed order. Here, among towering stacks of centuries-old tomes with gilded spines and cracked leather bindings, she found the comforting certainty of facts, timelines, and meticulously documented accounts. In a life too often marked by emotional unpredictability and the frantic demands of social interaction, this place was an anchor she clung to with both hands and heart. Her fingers, slender and callused at the knuckles from hours of note-taking, trailed over the spines as if to absorb the steadiness they represented before she settled at a long oak table near a window.

Caroline was resolutely a woman of reason, her mind a precise instrument honed by years of devoted scholarship in social history. Her passion lay not in the grand gestures of history's heroes, but in the quiet, often overlooked currents coursing beneath the surface the daily lives, social rituals, and the unspoken rules of human interaction that shaped entire eras. She had spent countless months poring over manuscripts and diaries from the eighteenth century, reconstructing the lives of those who moved through a world so different from her own yet tethered by universal human impulses. Yet no amount of research had prepared her for the raw sensation of being uprooted from the present and hurled into the past. That was a thought for later, if she dared entertain it at all. For now, the soft murmur of footsteps on polished floorboards and the occasional rustle of turning pages were her constants, her companions, her defenses against the uncertainties lurking beyond these hallowed walls.

Intent on locating a rare volume she'd heard whispers of among fellow historians but had yet to behold an unmarked book reputed to hold unusual knowledge about time's opaque depths Caroline allowed her gaze to wander past the familiar spines into a dimly lit, lesser frequented aisle. The shelves here were narrow, switchbacks of ancient wisdom barely disturbed in decades. Her eyes flicked over titles until a dark brown leather-bound volume with no title or author's name caught her attention, tucked discreetly between the towering tomes like an afterthought. She paused, heartbeat quickening with an unaccountable thrill. The book seemed out of place, its plainness a strange kind of invitation rather than a warning.

Reaching for it with deliberate care, Caroline's fingers brushed the cool leather cover. A faint pulse thrummed through her veins, subtle but undeniable, as if the book itself was alive with forgotten secrets. With a quiet breath of both curiosity and caution, she lifted it from the shelf, the sudden weight of the unknown anchoring itself firmly in her palms. The room seemed to grow colder, the ambient noises fading into a hollow silence broken only by the soft thump of her own pulse. As she opened the cover, the crisp pages revealed no title or author, just densely written, looping handwriting that sprawled unevenly across the parchment. Caroline's practiced eyes consumed the intricate text, the language both archaic and hauntingly familiar. Before she could decipher more, a firm, measured voice interrupted, pulling her sharply away from the book's spell.

"I wouldn't take that if I were you." Thomas Reed's presence was sudden and unyielding the stranger who had appeared seemingly from nowhere, his dark eyes steady, his stance guarded but confident. Caroline started, the book slipping fractionally in her grasp as she looked up into the handsome, angular face framed by tousled chestnut hair. His attire was unassuming yet practical, as if he had stepped out of a less formal academic context or perhaps something altogether different. His observation was plain yet carried an unspoken warning, and in this quiet sanctuary of knowledge, his intrusion felt jarring but oddly necessary.

"Why not? What's your interest in it?" Caroline's voice was cool but laced with curiosity. The last thing she wanted was to be challenged, yet some inexplicable pull filled the air between them, an electric tension neither could dismiss.

"Because it's not as ordinary as it seems," Thomas said softly, stepping closer, his fingers twitching with nervous energy that contrasted sharply with his otherwise steady composure.

Caroline felt a compelling urge to reach out and touch the book again, driven by a blend of scholarly intrigue and the need to unravel whatever mystery tethered Thomas and her to this object. Their hands brushed as they each sought the same page, and in that instant, a luminous swirl of light enveloped them, deafening in its brightness yet silent in its sweep, and the solidity of the library dissolved into a kaleidoscope of shifting colors and dizzying sensations.

When her senses returned, Caroline found herself standing not amid oak shelves but in a dim, cramped room lit by the flicker of a smoldering hearth. Her heart hammered with confusion and disbelief as the accents of the village outside filtered through wooden shutters. The dusty air smelled of peat and earth far removed from the antiseptic calm of the Arkwell Library. The book, still clutched in her hand, had imposed its first command: survive, and together. Two lives, bound by necessity and deception, compelled to pose as man and wife in a world ruled by suspicion and rigid social codes. The cold weight of this new reality settled around her like the thick woolen shawl hastily draped over her shoulders.

Caroline's detailed knowledge of 18th-century life, once an academic abstraction, now became a vital tool for navigating the treacherous social minefield of Bramleigh village. She recalled the endless hours spent tracing lines of village hierarchy, understanding how a widow like Agnes Pryce could wield quiet but formidable power, shaping fates with a mere glance or whispered insinuation. The unmarked book's pages whispered further instructions, shifting from survival to emotional openness as if it sensed the walls Caroline had built around her heart beginning to crack. The sterile certainty of historical fact, once her fortress, now seemed feeble against the immediacy of her raw, fiercely beating humanity.

Thomas, though a stranger thrust into her world, proved more than mere companion. His instincts in this harsh new landscape were indispensable, his strong arms and steady gaze offering protection and, gradually, a fragile promise of something more. Caroline, who had always prized control above all else, found herself grappling with a growing dependence on him, caught in the paradox of survival and surrender. The fireplace's flickering glow illuminated their shared struggles, threading warmth through their tentative partnership, forging a bond neither had anticipated.

As winter's grip tightened, Caroline confronted not only the external threats of Bramleigh society aggressive scrutiny, whispered accusations from Agnes Pryce, the constant threat of expulsion but also the internal battles fidelity to self and the terrifying openness of emotional vulnerability. The book's silent mandate pressed upon her the demand for honesty, for trust, for the dissolution of her scholarly armor in favor of something more elemental and true.

There, in the shadow of the external storm, Caroline glimpsed the precarious beauty of a life unrestrained by the strictures of her former world. And as she took Thomas's hand in hers, the chilling certainty of the past's brutal social codes gave way to the burning promise of shared love and the courage to claim it. In that sanctuary far from the grand library's ordered shelves, Caroline Moore found herself utterly and irrevocably changed.

Caroline Moore had always sought sanctuary amid the quiet hushed aisles of the Arkwell Library, a bastion of order and reason where the chaotic pulse of the outside world was reduced to dust motes dancing lazily in streams of pale sunlight. Her sanctuary today was no different, save for an unusual chill that seemed to permeate the air, a subtle disturbance barely perceptible but enough to prick her skin beneath the thin fabric of her blouse and settle uneasily in the pit of her stomach. Her days had grown regimented, each scheduled with meticulous precision: morning coffee at exactly nine, the steady hum of her computer, the deliberate scanning of ancient texts, and the measured solitude that she craved, all designed to keep the messy unpredictability of human emotion at bay. As a social historian, Caroline lived in the realm of facts, angles, and tangible artifacts; feelings were an unruly bother she'd long learned to sidestep.

That afternoon, as she rounded the corner of the Victorian bookcases that lined the library's oldest wing, her eyes caught a flash of something incongruous. Nestled between leather-bound tomes whose gilded titles spelled out centuries of knowledge, there was a single volume that showed no mark of age or authorship no title embossed on its spine, no lettering on its worn, unadorned cover. It was simply there, its black cover dull and unyielding as obsidian, edged with a faint iridescence that shimmered imperceptibly under the muted light. Something about it was curiously out of place, an uninvited anomaly in a meticulous collection that prized order and provenance above all else.

The insignificant little stranger caught Caroline's attention like a lodestone pulling iron filings. She hesitated only a moment before drawing it free with practiced ease, the familiar brush of cold leather against her palm sending a shiver up her forearm. The book's surface was unexpectedly frigid, far colder than the chilly ambient air of the library ever dared to be; her breath caught, misting in the sudden shudder of unease she felt as if it harbored something beyond the physical. She turned it over, inspecting it closely. The pages edged in yellowing amber revealed no title page, no introduction, only dense text written in an antiquated, elegant script she recognized only partially, its language elliptic and unfamiliar yet tantalizingly enticing.

Caroline's mind whirred as she carefully thumbed through the weighty volume, her skepticism warring against the growing insistence of curiosity that demanded she delve deeper. The coldness persisted, unnatural and uncompromising, biting through her gloves and embedding itself into the tips of her fingers despite the careful distance she maintained. Her trained historian's eye pricked to the fact that the book's bindings resisted the expected decay, the pages unwrinkled, the ink untarnished no trace of human touch had marred its surfaces for centuries, and yet this felt immediate and alive, as if it breathed and pulsed with a secret heartbeat of its own.

Her solitude was shattered in an abrupt, surprising way. A voice, low and unsure, interrupted the calm sanctuary like a sudden rustle of leaves in still air. "I see you've found it too," came the soft observation. She startled and turned, finding a man standing just a few feet beyond the bookcase, a stranger whose presence was as enigmatic as the book itself. His eyes held a quiet, questioning intensity curiosity interlaced with unease and his clothing was curiously out of place, blending indistinctly into the hushed atmosphere, hinting at a life far removed from the orderly stacks.

"Found what?" Caroline said, clutching the odd volume closer, suddenly protective. Her voice was steady, but her pulse had quickened. The coldness radiating from the book seemed to deepen under the weight of his gaze.

"The book," he repeated softly, stepping closer despite the respectful distance Caroline maintained. "That book. It's peculiar, isn't it? Not like any other here. I've spent hours searching for it... and yet it feels like it chose me."

Caroline's mind raced. Something about this man was oddly familiar, yet she could place no name or face. There was a strange resonance in the undercurrent of their unlikely encounter, as if fate had woven their paths together with invisible threads. Despite her natural reserve, she found herself responding with equal candor. "I came for refuge, for some clarity," she admitted, eyes never leaving the book as if its silent pages held all the answers she longed for. "I didn't expect to be confronted by mystery."

Thomas Reed this was the name that emerged whispered like a secret from his mouth when he introduced himself exuded an unspoken confidence tempered by vulnerability. He was a stranger, a puzzle piece that didn't quite fit into the predictable picture Caroline had arranged for herself. Yet, in this strange union of chance, something – or someone – demanded acknowledgment. He reached out hesitantly, his fingers brushing against hers as if to confirm the tangible reality of their shared moment. The instant their hands met upon the book's cover, an electric charge coursed through them, simultaneous yet disorienting, as though they were both pulled against an invisible current neither could resist.

Caroline's breath hitched, a chorus of startled thoughts detonating behind her steady facade. The room seemed to shift and swirl, a vortex of light and shadow collapsing around them. The sturdy shelves, the ancient tomes, the familiar wood scent dissolved, replaced by an overwhelming, dizzying sensation that set her senses aflame while robbing her of balance. The cold leeching from the book spread through her veins like liquid ice, locking her in place even as the world fractured and reassembled itself into a new and terrifying reality.

When the tumult ceased, Caroline found herself blinking into a dimmer, harsher light. The air was thicker, rougher, tinged with earthy dampness and an underlying chill that seeped deep into her bones. The walls around her spoke of crude timber and plaster in lieu of polished oak and embossed wallpaper. The scent of smoldering peat mingled with the faint odors of livestock and winter-gnawed fields beyond. She was no longer cradled by the comforting artificial glow of the modern Arkwell Library but transported shifted completely out of time and place to an era both alien and raw.

Beside her, Thomas was equally disoriented. His glance flickered to her, searching for confirmation that they shared this unfathomable fate, his lips parted as if to speak but hemmed by astonishment. The book, which had lain between them moments before, was nowhere to be seen; only a heavy silence hung in the air, broken suddenly by a whisper that seemed not to come from either of them but from nowhere and everywhere. The voice was cold, unmistakable, issuing forth in the form of unmistakable commands imprinted starkly in their minds. It spoke with an unseen authority, the tone neither cruel nor kind, but unyielding.

"You must remain together. Pose as husband and wife."

The command echoed with weight, like a judge's final verdict, leaving no room for argument or denial. Caroline blinked against the veil of shock clouding her thoughts, struggling to summon reason amid the surreal clarity of the instruction. Pose as husband and wife: the demand was as simple as it was devastating. Social laws of this time bore savage consequences for those who dared tread outside their rigid boundaries, and the mere hint of improper conduct could render outsiders unwelcome, if not worse. Survival here was no longer a question of intellect alone but of performance, of navigating a perilous social theatre where every step was scrutinized.

Thomas looked at her his eyes dark pools reflecting uncertainty and something deeper, a flicker of resolve barely betrayed behind the shock. His jaw clenched, an unspoken commitment forming in the space between them. Caroline felt her meticulously constructed walls begin to erode under the pressure of this shared exile and sudden dependency. The urge to control, to anchor herself in fact and logic, buckled under the raw force of necessity. Here, knowledge could inform but no longer shield. Here, survival mandated trust, cooperation, and the willingness to become something neither of them had been prepared to be.

In those first moments, the cold, unyielding book became less a guardian of hidden knowledge and more the harbinger of their ordeal. Caroline felt a fragile, flickering ember of defiance kindling deep within her an ember that whispered of endurance, of adaptation, and of love yet to be born in the crucible of hardship and time. The strange volume might have transported them here, but it was their choices thereafter that would define their passage through this perilous landscape, threading a delicate path between history and heart, between control and surrender, between strangers and something far more profound.

As the raw wind swept through the village outside, carrying the faint strains of distant life voices calling, horses' hooves clattering purposefully on cobblestones, the low murmur of everyday struggle Caroline wrapped her arms around herself, seeking warmth she could neither find in the chill nor in the presence of the man beside her alone. The book's unspoken challenge loomed overhead, a silent sentinel binding them with invisible chains. Somewhere deep inside, amidst the swirling uncertainty, a single certainty crystallized: their fates were intertwined, irrevocably, in this strange new existence. They would march forward side by side into the unknown, bound by necessity and a promise to each other that none dared yet to speak aloud to stay together through the coming trials, in body and in heart, until the final choice revealed itself.

The unmarked book, cold to the touch and inscrutable in its silence, had been only the beginning.

Collision of Hands

Caroline had always found solace in the vastness of the Arkwell Library, a sanctuary of order and knowledge where the chaotic pulse of the outside world dulled to a gentle murmur. It was a refuge for a woman who prized facts over feelings, whose life had been meticulously arranged like the rows of books lining those time-forgotten shelves. Here, among the scent of aged parchment and polished wood, she could bury herself in history, tracing the patterns of human follies and triumphs without ever becoming entangled in their messy emotional realities. It was a place of certainty, a tether to the rational foundation upon which she had built her existence. Yet, on this gray, overcast afternoon, even the library's quiet comfort seemed insufficient against the gnawing anxiety clenching her chest.

Her footsteps echoed softly as she wandered deeper into the labyrinth of knowledge, eyes scanning row upon row of leather-bound volumes. Despite centuries of dust and decay, the Arkwell held treasures forgotten stories, secrets wrapped in faded ink waiting to be uncovered by a discerning archaeologist of the mind. Caroline's fingers trailed affectionately along the spines as if greeting old friends, seeking the perfect installment to accompany her afternoon.

That's when, in the shadowy alcove nestled between history and folklore, an unmarked book caught her eye. Unlike the meticulous titling of every other tome, this one seemed deliberately anonymous, its cover worn almost to a near-translucent glaze of pale leather. The edges, though fragile, beckoned with a faint, almost imperceptible pulse, like a heartbeat that belonged not to the past, but to the present moment. Intrigued and uncharacteristically timid, Caroline reached out, the bridge between skepticism and curiosity narrowing to the touch of her fingertips on the delicate cover.

At precisely that moment, another

movement stirred the stillness. From the corner of her eye, she detected a shadow of a man, tall and broad-shouldered, with an intensity in his gaze that was as commanding as it was weary. His steps were purposeful, measured, as though the library itself should make way for him. She watched, half-alert, as he too extended a hand toward the very same enigmatic volume.

The collision of hands was unexpected, electric. Their fingertips brushed, a jolt that traversed both anatomy and mind, like a spark between two dormant circuits snapping to life. For a moment, the library's grand silence was ruptured by the quiet gasp escaping her own lips, and she caught the sharp arrest of his breath mirrored in his deep-set eyes. There was neither irritation nor surprise but something else an unspoken recognition, a binding thread that tangled their fates irrevocably.

Neither withdrew. Instead, a gentle pressure held their palms together, as if the book demanded this union that their connection was the key to whatever secret it sheltered. Caroline tried to strip her eyes away, to reassert control over the scene, over herself. It was an intrusion upon everything she guarded: the boundary between the known and the unknown, the line between her safe solitude and the chaotic realm of human entanglement. But her fingers remained locked against the stranger's, skin reluctant to separate.

Then, before either could comprehend the unfolding beyond their grasp, the world itself seemed to tremble. The edges of reality blurred, the air thickened with a potent swell of energy, and suddenly the familiar sanctuary of the Arkwell Library dissolved like a fading reverie. The steady hum of fluorescent lights was replaced by the whispering symphony of rustling leaves and the distant bleating of a sheep. The scent of leather and musk succumbed to the earthy tang of damp soil and smoldering hearth fires.

Caroline's breath hitched. She opened her eyes to a sky painted in bruised purples and steel blues, a chill breeze weaving through strands of loose hair, and a landscape that felt painfully foreign, yet excruciatingly vivid. Beside her, the stranger Thomas, she learned his name moments later shifted with a similar disorientation, eyes scanning the unfamiliar horizon. The ambient sounds of a bustling village life filled the air, with the distant clatter of wooden carts on cobblestones and the murmur of voices speaking in a dialect just beyond her full understanding.

A small piece of parchment fell from the open pages of the mysterious book onto the hard-packed dirt at Caroline's feet. With trembling fingers, she retrieved it, smoothing the delicate paper as the first chilling commands scrawled in archaic ink revealed themselves: "Remain together. Pose as husband and wife."

Her pulse thundered in her ears at the gravity of these words. It was not merely a demand but a mandate woven into the fabric of her new existence here, a sinister rule that left no room for error or defiance. The implication of survival hinged on a performance, on a deception that could easily unspool into ruin if discovered. She glanced sideways at Thomas, whose expression was a stratagem of calm underwriting an unmistakable thread of uncertainty and resolve.

For all her knowledge, Caroline was awash in a torrent of disbelief. Her reason struggled to strain against the surreal veil that had yanked her from a world she understood into one governed by social codes sharper and more merciless than any footnote in her historical tomes. The weight of centuries pressed down upon her like a suffocating shroud, threatening to unravel the meticulous architecture of her identity. Control, that ever-present guardian, now seemed a broken shield.

Yet, in this enforced proximity to a man she barely knew, a stranger who embodied both a puzzle and a promise, something began to stir. An unspoken alliance was born in that shared, trembling contact of fingers a fragile bond forged in the fire of unexpected destiny. Neither could bear the vulnerability alone. In this collision of hands upon an ancient text, they had not only touched a relic but the threshold of a new world, where history and humanity converged, where survival demanded surrender as much as strength.

The village of Bramleigh awaited them, its narrow lanes and rough-hewn cottages promising trials as merciless as the icy wind that whispered through the skeletal trees, and it was there, amidst the shadowed glens and watchful eyes, that Caroline and Thomas's journey would begin. For beneath the weight of the book's cold commands lay an uncharted landscape of emotion and courage an invitation to reshape their fates, to claim love and belonging in the most unlikely of circumstances.

And so, hand in hand, beneath a sky ancient and eternal, they stepped forward into history's cruel embrace, the boundary between past and present irrevocably shattered by the simple, profound collision of hands.

Arrival in Bramleigh

A New World

The air was crisp, tinged with the earthy scent of damp soil and freshly turned hay, carrying the gentle murmur of a village awakening beneath a soft dawn sky. Caroline's eyes fluttered open, the blurring shapes around her gradually resolving into a landscape that belied every expectation her logical mind could muster. Rolling hedgerows divided plots of farmland sprawling beneath a pale sun that had barely risen, its light casting long shadows over the dew-speckled grass. Beyond the meandering dirt paths lay neatly thatched cottages with smoke curling lazily from chimneys, wisps dancing upwards into a sky slowly blooming from cool silver to soft, inviting blue. The stillness was both soothing and disorienting, a world utterly unlike the quiet bustle she was accustomed to in the modern city, yet alive with a subtle pulse that hinted at life's unyielding persistence.

Caroline blinked as the sensation of cold,

rough linen beneath her fingers grounded her in this bewildering reality. Her clothes coarse and unfamiliar clung oddly to her skin; gone were the sharp lines of her contemporary attire, replaced by layers of homespun fabric that robbed her of the comfort of modern design and its promises of ease. She turned her head, heart quickening as she found Thomas a few feet away, his own expression a mixture of confusion and guarded wariness etched in the furrow of his brow. His eyes met hers, searching, as if trying to piece together a puzzle neither of them comprehended fully yet.

They had arrived here inextricably linked by a force neither could explain a mysterious, unmarked book whose touch had thrown them through time, depositing them amid this pastoral tableau that existed centuries before their own realities. As Caroline sat up slowly, brushing stray strands of hair from her face, the weight of their predicament settled over her with a chilling clarity. The village lay quiet but watchful, and beneath that silence floated a current of invisible rules and expectations, whispered warnings encoded into its very essence, shaping every interaction and gesture they might attempt.

Thomas rose, his body language alert and protective as he regarded the landscape and then turned his steady gaze back to her. His practicality and instinct for survival were already at work beneath the confusion, a stark contrast to Caroline's analytical mind racing to assemble fragments of knowledge from history texts she had poured over countless nights. But knowledge alone was no shield here. This place demanded conformity to rules that, from their modern vantage, seemed archaic and suffocating laws that forbade outsiders the freedom to act without suspicion, to walk unknown paths without the weight of judgment bearing down.

They exchanged a glance wordless yet laden with the mutual understanding that lingered between strangers forced unwillingly into alliance. The book's decree wasn't merely a strange edict; it was a lifeline, cold and pragmatically binding them to a survival tactic none could question. To walk these ginnels and market squares as anything less than bound by the sanctity of matrimony was to risk exposure, dangerous scrutiny, and expulsion from a world that had no mercy for those who stood outside its rigid order.

Caroline's mind grappled with the implications. The notion of pretending to be Thomas's wife felt alien, a charade that collided violently with the independence and self-possession she had nurtured all her life. Yet as her gaze drifted over the village's orderly rows of homes, the women tending their gardens, and the men leading horses to pasture, she comprehended the fragile fabric of this society. A single misstep, a misread gesture, and the welcoming smiles could turn sharp with suspicion, the minute an outsider's secret was unearthed. Privilege here was measured by pedigree and social conformity, not by the ideals she had been raised to cherish. Freedom was an illusion, tethered tightly to the performance of accepted roles and the weight of community enforcement.

Thomas's hand brushed against hers, a subtle but grounding touch amidst the swirl of uncertainty. He spoke softly, voice low yet firm. "We don't have the luxury of questioning it yet, Caroline. The people here they'll watch us, judge. That book's instructions aren't arbitrary. If we want to survive, we must play the part."

Her mouth opened to protest, to argue the fallacy of surrendering identity to such constrictive norms, but the sight of a village elder emerging from behind a copse of trees, her sharp eyes flickering with cautious appraisal, stilled her words. The woman's presence was commanding, a living embodiment of the society's relentless gaze. Caroline felt the weight of that scrutiny settle firmly on her, an invisible noose tightening with each heartbeat.

The necessity of their shared masquerade became painfully clear. Each step they took would be under watchful eyes; their every gesture dissected for authenticity. The village's social laws could not be broken or bent lightly virtue and reputation held the power to shield or condemn in equal measure. This was a world where alliances were forged not by affection but by survival, where trust was a fragile commodity and deception a daily necessity. Caroline swallowed hard, wary of the vulnerability the book's command demanded, and yet beginning to recognize that surrendering control might be their only hope.

The fields stretched out endlessly, golden and green under the morning sun, yet within their picturesque borders lay a cage of unyielding expectations. The village of Bramleigh was no utopia; it was a living organism bound by history's chains, where every outsider was both fascination and threat. Caroline's historian's mind cataloged everything the attire of passersby, the structure of the cottages, the spoken dialect echoing faintly on the breeze. But this knowledge brought no comfort. Instead, it deepened the awareness that assimilation required far more than mere observation it demanded immersion, performance, and, most dauntingly, trust between two people who were until now strangers.

Thomas took a tentative step forward, his gaze sweeping the road ahead. "If we're married, we need to act like it. Not just for show, but for us. There's strength in unity. And maybe... maybe we can find something real in this." His words held an unspoken hope, a delicate flicker of possibility amid the fog of uncertainty.

Caroline looked at him, an unexpected softness touching the edges of her guarded heart. The cold, impersonal historian was giving way to something more fluid, an openness tinted with cautious optimism. Together, they began to walk down the dusty path leading toward the cluster of houses, shoulders squared against the unknown, yet tethered inexplicably to each other by the strange, binding force of the book and the raw human need for connection.

The journey ahead was daunting and fraught with peril, but the pastoral calm of Bramleigh belied the undercurrent of threat woven into its gentle rhythms. For Caroline and Thomas, the path to survival was clear they would build a life in this new world, with all the compromises and courage it demanded. In the mingling scents of hay, hearth smoke, and morning dew, a convergence of past and future, reality and desire, was quietly unfolding, a passage neither had sought but both would navigate together, bound by fate and the fragile promise of love yet to be born.

Reading the Book

The room settled into a thick silence, the only sound the faint crackle of the dying fire in the stone hearth. A fragile peace filled the cramped space, flickering shadows dancing across the roughly hewn wooden beams overhead. Caroline sat rigid on the edge of the narrow bed, her fingers trembling slightly as they hesitated over the unmarked book that had both ensnared and confounded them. The heavy leather-bound tome, worn yet undeniably ancient, rested on her lap, unnervingly out of place amid the rustic austerity of the cottage's sparse furnishings. The faint scent of must and ink emanated from its fragile pages, curling upwards like whispered secrets begging to be heard.

Thomas stood by the window, gaze lost but attentive, peering out at the landscape that stretched beyond their temporary refuge. The patchwork of hedgerows carved the countryside into tiny geometric holdings, the village of

Bramleigh punctuating the distance with the cluster of low, thatched cottages and the slender spire of the church. Overhead, a pallid winter sun fought through slate-grey clouds, casting muted light over frost-nipped fields that lay fallow and weary. It was a stark tableau, both beautiful and desolate, resonating with an unspoken hardship that mirrored their own uncertain plight. Neither of them spoke, as if the gravity of their shared predicament demanded reverence.

Finally, Caroline's eyes shifted back to the book, the surface of the page catching the light to reveal ink that had not been there earlier. Fresh and sharply inscribed, the words seemed to pulse with urgent vitality amid the faded script. She blinked, drawing closer, and the mystery became command. The ink spelled out new instructions, terse yet laden with implication. "Remain together. Assume partnership as one. Act as husband and wife to preserve life and livelihood within the village bounds. Outcasts suffer dire consequences. Obedience ensures survival." Her voice broke slightly as she read aloud the stark advisories, the weight of each phrase anchoring the room in a sudden, almost suffocating reality.

Thomas moved swiftly to her side, his brows furrowed in concern and disbelief. "What sort of laws have they spun here?" His tone was low, steady, but the unease threaded beneath was undeniable. Neither of them had anticipated such an exacting social gauntlet, and the realization cut deeper than the chill seeping through the cottage walls. Caroline met his gaze, and in that moment, the world outside the window seemed to shrink to this single shared truth: to survive, they must become others, play roles forced upon them by an invisible but ruthless hand.

The words echoed in Caroline's mind as she attempted to reconcile the knowledge she had amassed as a social historian with the stark demands of this living nightmare. She had written sometimes about the rigid hierarchies and unforgiving customs of 18th-century rural England, the delicate dance of appearances that governed survival especially for those deemed outsiders but theory and practice lay worlds apart. Understanding had never required the sacrifice or the intimate exposure this moment demanded. The subtle artifice of marriage, a social contract so often romanticized or relegated to the status of a mere formality in her previous life, now loomed as a vital, breath-stealing necessity. It was no longer a choice but a lifeline tethering them to a precarious existence.

Thomas exhaled audibly and shook his head, frustration mingling with reluctant acceptance. "We can't just pretend. Not with everyone watching." His voice lowered, heavy with the tension of unspoken dangers. "There's Agnes Pryce. If she suspects anything... she'll see to our ruin." His words summoned images of the widow's austere gaze and the whispered judgments that clung like shadows to every village gathering. The power Agnes wielded was subtle but absolute, a reminder that survival here required more than avoiding physical threats; it demanded navigating an intricate web of social expectations where one misstep could mean expulsion, or worse.

Caroline's hands tightened around the book as she absorbed the weight of their new existence. What had once been a mere curiosity an unmarked book unearthed from the recesses of a grand library had become the script for their survival, inscribed in fresh ink that bore the weight of a cruel and uncompromising past. She glanced back at the window, where skeletal branches scratched against the dull sky, a quiet testament to the harshness awaiting them. The hedgerows framed not just fields but the invisible barriers of their confinement, the village not merely a home but a cage, each stone and furrow charged with the vigilance of those who guarded its fragile order.

The notion of marriage, cloaked in layers of obligation and expectation, suddenly took on a dual meaning: it was their shield and their shackle. For Caroline, whose life had been built upon the pillars of control and factual certainty, the concept was suffocating. To be bound to another in such a forced intimacy ravaged her sense of self where was the freedom in such an arrangement? Yet, beneath her resistance, a nascent understanding flickered. This was a performance, yes, but one upon which their survival depended a precarious dance choreographed by the invisible laws of the land and the watchful eyes of its people.

Thomas's gaze softened as he regarded her turmoil, the muscles in his jaw flexing beneath the stubble of the morning's growth. His natural instincts leaned toward protection, toward the tangible act of sheltering Caroline from the unseen threats that lurked as much in whispered conversations as in the biting cold. Yet even he was not immune to the confusion threaded through their new reality. His world, previously defined by straightforward physicality and instinct, was now shadowed by roles and expectations that required subtlety and performance as their currency. The forced proximity seeded a tension neither could ignore, a mixture of wariness and a reluctant reliance that expanded with each passing moment.

Caroline closed the book gingerly, as though afraid the magic ink might vanish if handled too roughly. "We have to convince them," she murmured, almost to herself. "Not just with words, but with everything how we live, how we move, how we interact. If we fail, they'll see right through us. Agnes will know. And then..." Her voice faltered, the specter of their expulsion perhaps worse looming like a gathering storm. The room's stillness deepened, the cold pressing in closer, as if the walls themselves awaited the outcome of this silent deliberation.

Out the window, the village life went on obliviously women carrying baskets across the frost-bitten path, children's laughter echoing faint from the central square, the distant clatter of hooves on cobblestones. Yet beneath these ordinary sounds simmered the rigid social order that brooked no outsiders. The whispers of gossip, the pointed glances from weathered faces, the unspoken rules etched into every exchange they would have to navigate all with care, wearing the trappings of a union neither chose but both must embody.

Thomas's hand brushed against Caroline's

knee in a tentative gesture, grounding them in the present despite the surging chaos within. His voice, when it came, was steady but quiet. "We can do this. Together. If the book commands it, then that's our path." The conviction in his words was neither boast nor bluster but a simple promise anchored in necessity and something almost like hope. It planted a seed in her guarded heart, a fragile possibility amid the bleakness of their predicament.

Caroline inhaled deeply, the cold air prickling her lungs, clearing the fog of panic that had threatened to overwhelm. She had built walls around her emotions for years careful and rigid defenses born from experience and disappointment but here, now, those defenses showed fissures. To survive in Bramleigh meant more than playing a part; it meant stepping into vulnerability, forging trust where there had been none, surrendering control for a shared future not yet written. The unmarked book was no longer an enigma to be solved but a living guide, its insistent script illuminating the path ahead, however treacherous.

As the afternoon waned and the shadows lengthened across the uneven floorboards, Caroline and Thomas settled into a fragile accord. They would wear the guise of husband and wife, not merely as a shield but as a tentative bond forged under extraordinary circumstances. It was a union born not of love but necessity, threaded through with uncertainty and the raw edges of fear. Yet within that uncertain frame lay the potential for something new a partnership both perilous and resilient, shaped by the harsh social laws of a time long vanished yet startlingly immediate.

Outside, the world awaited, indifferent to their fate. But inside the small cottage, amidst the flickering candlelight and ancient, whispering pages, two souls began the slow, tentative journey toward understanding, companionship, and survival. The book had spoken, the village had set its rules, and Caroline and Thomas stood at the precipice of a transformation that demanded more than knowledge it demanded surrender, courage,

and the tentative hope of a future shared against
all odds.

Understanding the Stakes

The morning sun filtered weakly through thick gray clouds, casting a muted silver light over the thatched roofs and winding dirt streets of Bramleigh. Caroline and Thomas stood at the crest of a low hill, the hedgerows framing their narrow view, the village unfolding before them like a meticulously crafted diorama from centuries past. The air was crisp, carrying the faint scent of damp earth and wood smoke, a constant reminder of the encroaching winter. Caroline's gaze swept over the clustered cottages, their small windows shuttered or curtained against the cold, the smoke rising from chimneys in lazy spirals. Beyond, fields segmented by drystone walls and erect hedges stretched well into the countryside, their brown and green patches a patchwork testament to human toil and nature's quiet claim. It was a landscape deeply rooted in tradition, in rules and roles older than time, and now, acutely, Caroline realized, it was a place where they were glaring anomalies.

Thomas shifted beside her, his stance low and watchful, but even he could not mask the uncertainty in his eyes as they took in the scene. The reality of this sudden transport into the eighteenth century hung between them like a thick fog opaque, dense, and impossible to ignore. Words spoken the previous night as they fled the library's unnatural portal ricocheted back in their minds, underscoring the simple fact that survival here was dependent on understanding forces far more complex than mere geography. What at first felt like an odd and disorienting curiosity had now begun to seduce them into a profound and pressing truth: the laws that governed this village and its denizens were as unyielding as the stone walls lining the streets; bending them even slightly could mean instant ruin.

As they descended the hill toward the village, Caroline's historian's mind began piecing through everything she had gleaned already from snatches of overheard conversations, the furtive glances the locals cast, even the way women crossed themselves subtly as they passed the old stone church. The yoke of the past, with its tightly woven social fabric and suffocating conventions, was formidable. Her memories of eighteenth-century England, painstakingly researched and cataloged before because she preferred facts over feelings, suddenly shifted from abstraction to urgent necessity. Among the most pressing revelations was the existence indeed, the enforcement of vagrancy laws. These laws were designed precisely to exclude and expel those deemed outside the accepted social order: the homeless, the unemployed, the wandering strangers with no family or place. The very fact that she and Thomas had suddenly appeared, unmoored from any known lineage or roots, placed them on the razor's edge of suspicion and danger.

Thomas's voice broke the complicated silence, low and edged with concern. "Vagrants, eh? So we're basically unwelcome by default," he said, his tone pragmatic but tinged with something harsher frustration, perhaps fear. "That's not just about begging in the street, is it? It's about survival losing your name, your rights hell, losing your life if you're caught long enough." He eyed Caroline, gauging her reaction, searching for affirmation or refutation in her calm scholarly exterior. But Caroline, despite her controlled façade, felt an internal churning. She understood in a visceral way that the rules here were far more than bureaucratic barriers; they were weapons wielded quietly, and cruelly, to enforce conformity and control. To be branded an outsider, an unclaimed soul, meant exclusion on a fundamental level a slow social death.

She nodded, the weight of the realization settling heavier on her shoulders than the frosty morning chill. "Yes. The vagrancy laws were brutal. Punishments included public whipping, forced labor, even imprisonment. It's as much about policing identity as about controlling movement. The village relies on everyone knowing their place, their family ties, their obligations. Strangers disrupt that order. And our mere presence here is enough to invite scrutiny." Her voice was steady, but inside a storm of unease had begun to breed. She could feel the urgency even as she tried to remain composed the necessity of disguise and conformity forced upon them like chains. It was no longer about mere survival, but about becoming someone else entirely, someone credible to these wary eyes.

Thomas tightened his jacket around him, glancing down to the small leather-bound book unmarked, enigmatic that had pulled them here. The object felt increasingly like both their salvation and their sentence. "And that's where the… uh, marriage charade comes in." He hesitated, watching Caroline's reaction carefully. "We're not just pretending to survive; we're pretending to belong. In this place, a married couple has security, respect, protection. Single strangers, especially women or men traveling alone, are immediately suspect. We have to convince them we're... rooted." He trailed off, the implications settling over them like a thick cloak.

Caroline drew a slow breath, realizing the magnitude of that forced intimacy. The idea of posing as husband and wife, of forging a bond out of necessity rather than choice, was a bitter pill. Her entire life had been a testament to control and rationality; now, survival demanded vulnerability, trust, pairing with a stranger in a way that challenged everything she instinctively guarded. The rigid social architecture of Bramleigh was merciless to those who did not conform, and it did not look kindly on ambiguity or independence. Real or not, their marriage would become their shield, their excuse for proximity, their only defense against suspicion.

As they edged closer, more details of village life emerged small clusters of villagers moving purposefully about their routines, children trailing behind butter-laden carts, an elderly man leaning heavily on a cane, his face etched with hardship but also the quiet acceptance of a life framed by rigid expectations. It was clear that any disruption to the social order would threaten the delicate balance that held Bramleigh together. Caroline noticed too the subtle signals: furtive whispers behind small cupped hands, the sudden quiet when they passed, the glances heavy with unspoken judgments. Agnes Pryce, the widow who ran the local apothecary and held subtle but undeniable power through her connections and knowledge of legal codes, came sharply to mind as a symbol of this surveillance an enforcer cloaked in civility, ready to pry and press for faults among newcomers.

Caroline's mind flicked back to the notes she had jotted in the library, recalling descriptions of vagrancy laws designed not just for punishment but as tools of social engineering. These laws existed alongside poor relief statutes, the parish system, and the intricate web of parish tithes and dues, each governing movement, labor, and social expectations with unforgiving precision. The idea was clear: enforce order and eliminate threats to property and hierarchy by excluding those who failed to fit the mold idlers, wanderers, the unemployed. "Outsiders who can't prove their place were often imprisoned or labeled as vagabonds, making their existence nearly impossible. There was no safety net for us here," she explained, voice low with dawning dread.

Thomas absorbed this, his brows knitted.

"So it's about more than just getting by day-to-day; it's about avoiding not just suspicion but outright persecution. And we can't trust anyone. No inns, no lodgings without a reference, no work. We're trapped in a cage made of rules we don't understand yet." His gaze flicked back to hers, searching. "Which means we're dependent on each other, whether we like it or not."

Caroline felt a flicker of reluctant acknowledgment. Every instinct screamed for independence and control, but here, relying on a stranger was a lifeline. The book's mandates, strange and inexorable, had decreed their union and now, surrounded by the unyielding reality of their predicament, the logic was undeniable. Their survival hinged on the illusion of belonging, the performance of marriage, the careful negotiation of social roles that, for her, implied surrendering a piece of autonomy she had fiercely defended all her life.

As they stepped down into the village proper, the cobbled path crunching underfoot, Caroline noticed the deliberate stillness with which villagers watched their approach. The unspoken rules of observation were clear: any display of ignorance or discomfort would be weaponized against them. The old chapel bell's toll echoed faintly, signaling midday prayers or meeting times, perhaps community rituals where failure to participate or improper conduct would quickly expose outsiders. Their presence was a threat, a catalyst for suspicion that even the warmth of a firelit room couldn't fully obliterate.

They reached the small square where a few market stalls, though sparse in goods, were arranged beneath the frozen branches of a large elm. Here, Caroline and Thomas paused, absorbing a sharper taste of the social order. A woman in a molted wool dress eyed them coldly before turning away her glance was unmistakable, a blend of challenge and warning. Caroline instinctively pulled her shawl tighter, instinct clashing with learned awareness of the vulnerability such a gesture implied. Thomas, sensing her discomfort, stepped slightly forward in unspoken protection, though both knew that no physical strength alone could secure their place in this community.

The enormity of the challenge pressed on them. They were not merely visitors from another time; they were outlaws in the eyes of the community by virtue of their very existence here. Rules without mercy, enforced with quiet but absolute precision. The village was not just a place but a living system of control and surveillance, where bonds of blood and reputation guarded thresholds against transgression and difference. Their survival depended on mastery not just of physical needs but of social understanding a gauntlet Caroline felt ill-prepared to navigate.

Yet, beneath the dry facts and cold social analysis, a flicker of something warmer began to grow the recognition that their mutual survival necessitated cooperation, trust, and perhaps, in time, something deeper. For now, that simmered beneath layers of fear and uncertainty, a fragile ember that might yet kindle into something sustaining. But for that to happen, they had to learn to live within this imposed hierarchy, embrace a role not chosen but assigned, and play it with such conviction that Agnes Pryce and the watchful eyes of Bramleigh would be none the wiser. The stakes were nothing less than life itself, and failure meant exposure and with it, exile or worse.

As the afternoon wore on and shadows lengthened over the village, both Caroline and Thomas understood that the road ahead was not merely about survival in the physical sense but about mastering the ruthless social architecture of eighteenth-century Bramleigh. Their forced marriage was not simply a cover but a lifeline woven out of necessity, deception, and the tentative hope of acceptance. Only by inhabiting their roles fully could they hope to weather the scrutiny, the cold judgment, and the unrelenting demand of a society that valued conformity above all else. The challenge was daunting, and the consequences terrifying, but there was no turning back now. The book had delivered them here, and in its inscrutable demands lay the faint promise of salvation if only they could understand the stakes fully and embrace the precarious dance between control and surrender that fate required.

First Steps in Survival

The cool, damp air of Bramleigh curled around Caroline and Thomas as they stepped through the narrow, unassuming gateway that led to the village's cluster of cottages. The path they tramped upon was uneven and muddy from the recent rain, each step sinking slightly into the earth, forcing them to move cautiously lest they soil the worn fabric of their coarse linens or lose their footing altogether. The sky above, a tapestry of slate gray clouds piled thick and low, threatened to burst again, casting the afternoon into a muted, somber light that seemed to press down upon the low, thatched roofs and leaning chimneys with a quiet weight. It was not the idyllic pastoral scene Caroline had romanticized while poring over history texts, nor the quaint image her imagination had painted in the time before the places she had studied from behind the protection of spotless pages and distant perspectives but something raw, tactile, and unrelenting.

Their temporary home awaited them on the far edge of the village, a small, weathered stone cottage, no larger than a single-room space, patched over the years with bits of wood and wattle, its crooked chimney coughing faint smoke into the gusting breeze. The windows were glazed with uneven, rippled glass that caught the minimal daylight and fractured it into uneven shards, while the door hung slightly ajar on creaking iron hinges, as though it barely wished to admit them. Caroline, ever the historian despite the shock of their predicament, was hit with a sudden, sharp realization of what such a dwelling truly meant a world away from the comfort and cleanliness of her modern life, where dust clung like a second skin and privy facilities were no more than a dark corner behind the barn.

Thomas, with his broader shoulders and practical sensibilities, moved quickly to close and fasten the door behind them, his hands firm and purposeful as he surveyed the cramped interior. A modest hearth took up one corner, its grate cold and blackened from disuse, the floor patched unevenly with rough boards that creaked under their weight. There was a single narrow cot pushed up against the far wall, its straw mattress lumpy and covered with a coarse, faded blanket that smelled faintly of smoke and damp. The room doubled as a sitting area and kitchen; a wooden table scarred from years of use sat beneath a small, dusty shelf hosting a handful of earthenware jugs and pots. The only sign of any comfort was a handful of dried lavender tied with string hanging near the hearth an attempt to mask the omnipresent odor of stale smoke and wood mold.

Caroline's gaze flickered nervously over the spartan surroundings. Here, in this dim, confined space, their ruse would unfold this one bed, cold and unforgiving, would be the stage upon which they were to pretend the intimacy of marriage, an act so foreign and deeply unsettling to her practical, fact-bound mind. Becoming "husband" and "wife" was more than a charade it was a necessity, a safeguard against suspicion, but beneath the surface, it convulsed her very sense of self and privacy. The warmth and softness of genuine connection were beyond this room's drafty walls and musty corners, yet she knew her survival, and Thomas's likewise, hinged on convincing everyone, including themselves, of the legitimacy of their bond.

Thomas squeezed her shoulder gently, a silent reassurance that softened the tension coiling in her chest. He began unpacking the meager bundle of belongings they had managed to bring with them: a few shifts and undergarments, a worn leather-bound journal, and the mysterious book that had been the conduit for their passage. The ritual was forced, but in the simplicity of their shared actions, a thread of warmth began to weave through the cold stone this tiny space was suddenly more than bricks and mortar; it was a crucible for trust, a fortress against the unyielding demands of a time that neither of them truly belonged to.

Their first challenge was the performance of domesticity demanded by the codes of 18th-century village life. Caroline found herself tied to the tasks she had only ever cataloged from a distance the hard physicality and quiet endurance of maintaining even the most basic household. Fetching water from the village well, chopping kindling for the hearth, and preparing simple meals with the austere ingredients available tested her resolve and transformed her understanding of the hardship concealed behind historical narrative. Thomas lent his shoulders to tasks requiring strength, his familiarity with manual labor evident as he worked alongside her, not as a stranger, but as a partner bound by necessity and gradually by something more tender and unspoken.

Outside this tiny chamber, the villagers' eyes tracked them keenly, like hawks circling wary prey. The village was no place for the weak or the naive, and Caroline and Thomas had quickly learned that their mere status as outsiders invited suspicion and speculation. Each glance and whispered word could unravel their delicate guise. Thus, when the following Sunday arrived, they donned the modest, well-worn garments borrowed from the landlord and made their way to the village church, an imposing stone structure with stained glass windows that threw prismatic patterns across the worn pews. Here, they moved together with tentative grace, hands barely touching but never quite separated, each step syncing their movements in the dance of assumed marital unity. It was a strange baptism, this public performance, swallowing their individual identities beneath the collective role imposed upon them.

Inside the church, the congregation was a blend of wary villagers who measured Caroline and Thomas with keen scrutiny. Caroline, sitting stiffly beside Thomas, felt the weight of countless silent appraisals pressing upon her, the polity and doctrine of the 18th century laying heavy over every whispered prayer. The sermons, fiery against sin and transgression, underscored the thin tightrope they walked. In those stained glass shadows, surrounded by flickering candlelight, the boundary between performance and reality began to blur. Caroline sensed it in the way Thomas caught her eye during the reverent silences a shared acknowledgment of the impossible situation that had thrust them into this past, this fragile marriage only fated to be sustained by their mutual acquiescence.

As days settled into weeks, the rhythm of village life, harsh and unrelenting, began imposing itself on their existence. The cottage walls, once cold and daunting, gradually warmed with their presence. The simple rituals of shared meals, whispered conversations in the embers' glow, and the slow discovery of one another shaped a tentative intimacy. Caroline's usual veneer of control cracked, letting in vulnerability that she recoiled from but could not deny any longer. Thomas, too, revealed a softness beneath his rugged exterior a protective tenderness that was difficult to feign. Their hands, once reluctant to brush, now sought each other in the darkness, fingers exploring the lines and scars of a stranger who was becoming so much more.

Yet, even as their connection deepened, the reality of 18th-century life refused to ease its hold on them. The village imposed its laws not mere civil rules, but social edicts encoded in suspicion and tradition, strictly guarded by figures like Agnes Pryce, whose gaze lingered too long on their interactions, whose whispered cautions traveled swiftly through the village grapevine. Every interaction became a subtle negotiation, a delicate dance to avoid provoking suspicion while affirming the facade of domestic normalcy. Caroline caught herself scripting conversations in her head before uttering them, aware that a misstep could bring their fragile respite crashing down.

The harshness of winter crept steadily, its chill seeping through the thatched roof and unyielding walls of their cottage. The fire in the hearth, once an occasional necessity, became their lifeline, an ember of warmth in an otherwise biting world. They stored their clothes by the fire to thaw, shared the threadbare blankets at night, and held each other close against the creeping cold not solely for warmth but something more profound, an anchoring presence amid the relentless storm of uncertainty. Caroline's heart, which had guarded itself fiercely against dependence, thrummed now with a palpable need that was as foreign as it was undeniable.

Night after night, they recited the vows they had no choice but to believe, words spoken under the gaze of a communal necessity rather than a heartfelt promise. Yet, beneath the charade, something genuine festered, subtle and unnameable a silent understanding growing between two souls battling the impossible. The tight confines of the cottage no longer felt like a cage but a haven, the humble hearth a witness to moments of laughter and quiet confession, the soft rise and fall of shared breathing a rhythm that defied time itself.

Each dawn brought with it new challenges a scarcity of provisions, the prying curiosity of neighbors, the omnipresent threat of Agnes's legal machinations but also small victories. Thomas's ease with the land and its labor complemented Caroline's knowledge, turning survival into a shared assertion of their new reality. They learned the nuances of village etiquette, the subtleties of greeting and avoidance, mastering their roles with a finesse that surprised even themselves. Confidence flickered alive where once only fear had resided, and amidst the hardship, the façade of their marriage began to feel less like an act and more like the first fragile threads of a life newly woven.

Here, in this cramped, weathered cottage on the edge of Bramleigh, amid the harsh bite of the winds and the glow of an uncertain future, Caroline and Thomas planted the fragile seeds of belonging. No longer merely passengers in a narrative forced upon them, they began shaping a shared story one carved from necessity but tending toward the irrevocable, where the boundaries between performance and truth blurred, and where two hearts, once strangers, found the precarious beginnings of home.

The morning weighed heavy with mist as Caroline drew the coarse woolen shawl about her shoulders, the threadbare fabric biting into her skin in contrast to the modern comfort she had so recently known. The weight of an unfamiliar world settled around her in the cramped, one-roomed cottage she and Thomas now shared, each movement deliberate, careful not merely of physical coordination but of perception. Their marriage, a façade imposed by the enigmatic book from an era far removed, demanded performance above all else. And today, as mandated by the invisible script that tethered them to this strange past, they would step into the public eye, into the village church, and blend with the inhabitants of Bramleigh like any other couple bound by the solemnity of custom and faith.

The morning air was thick with the scent of damp earth and woodsmoke, rising in spirals that mingled with the low murmurs of the waking village. Caroline's eyes flicked nervously to Thomas as he adjusted the threadbare waistcoat over his rough shirt. He appeared steadier, more at ease in garments that might have been pulled directly from some dusty history tome she had studied under the glow of a library lamp. His hands, broad and calloused, moved with unaccustomed tenderness as he helped her fasten the small brass clasp holding her shift in place, the smallest gesture a promise of support in this foreign ordeal. Whatever remnants of their previous lives awaited them beyond the church's heavy oak door, within this moment, they were an inseparable unit husband and wife. The book had no choice but to accept their pledge.

Navigating the winding dirt path through fields fallen fallow and dotted with stout hedgerows, Caroline's noble-born sensibilities wrestled with the realities of rural 1770. Cobblestones replaced pavement; wagons laden with produce rattled past, and the occasional rural child zipped eagerly ahead, wide-eyed and innocent. The villagers observed them cautiously at first, yet their stares were soft with curiosity rather than cruelty. Here, survival was a delicate dance of appearances and whisperings, where any misstep could unravel carefully woven alliances. Caroline's historian's mind raced to catalog and categorize; the tactile immediacy of the world, the weight of every glance, every murmur, broke through scholastic detachment.

The church loomed before them, austere in its simplicity yet filled with the richness of communal life. Its grey stone seemed to absorb the dampness of the morning sky, and its steeple thrust a silent accusation towards the heavens. Thomas grasped Caroline's hand a silent reminder of their bond as they stepped through the heavy door. The scent of aged wood, beeswax polish, and faint incense wrapped around them as they were swallowed by the pews' orderly rows. The murmur of gathered voices ebbed and flowed with the rustling of bonnets and the creak of wooden benches, a choir of whispered prayers and gossip alike.

Caroline's heart thudded unevenly beneath

her bodice as they claimed a place near the church's center, positioning themselves deliberately amidst the farming folk and tradespeople, their simple attire blending just enough. The act of sitting shoulder to shoulder in silent communion was itself a test of their resolve; the closeness forced by limited space reminded Caroline of the truth behind their charade. Thomas's presence was no longer a mere convenience, but a tether both physical and emotional. Within these walls of faith and tradition, their survival hinged upon the delicate performance of married life.

The vicar emerged, a stern figure cloaked in threadbare black, whose sharp gaze swept the congregation with practiced discipline. His voice, raised initially in the hymns, was rich with conviction, carrying upwards to meet the rafters and return steeped in reverence. The congregation's voices intertwined in a fervent, unyielding tapestry of devotion some roughened by labor, others soft from generations sheltered in faith. Caroline, unsure at first of the proper cadence, gradually found herself caught in the rhythm, the words rising and falling like ocean waves, each phrase a shared ritual cementing the social fabric they were desperately trying to inhabit.

Beyond the sanctuary's walls, the realities of 18th-century village life began to seep under the veneer of ritual. Neighbors exchanged knowing glances; whispers traveled between huddled figures like tendrils of smoke, invisible yet potent. Caroline noted each glance, each small smile, carried the weight of social currency, and Thomas, more attuned to this delicate calculus, shifted imperceptibly to present a united front. His seasoned instinct against hers scholarly suspicion created a fragile yet balanced defense against scrutiny.

As the service progressed, Caroline's fascination with the hidden dynamics intensified. Here was the heart of Bramleigh's collective soul, laid bare in quiet reverence and subtle hierarchies, where the village's pulse throbbed beneath the veneer of faith. She recognized the unspoken language the way certain faces lit with warmth in recognition of status, how others, like Agnes Pryce's keen eyes, pierced the sanctuary for any sign of impropriety. Agnes sat in a commanding pew, the widow's austere presence radiating control under the guise of pious devotion. Caroline's pulse quickened at the memory of their encounters; Agnes's smile had never reached her eyes, and here, in the hush of the gathering, that cold appraisal stoked a simmering fear. Agnes's whispered warnings, her influence cloaked in churchly authority, lingered like a shadow over Caroline and Thomas's precarious existence.

The ritual of communion came, and Caroline's fingers trembled as she watched Thomas discreetly pocket a small piece of the consecrated wafer, his eyes steady despite the sacredness of the act. Their imitation had to be flawless any hint of ignorance or disrespect could unravel the fragile trust they sought to establish. As Thomas leaned in to softly murmur a whispered recitation of the Lord's Prayer learned in haste the night before, their shared vulnerability deepened. Caroline lowered her gaze, swallowing her burgeoning panic, aware that this ritual was more than religious observance it was a promise, a contract with a society that demanded conformity.

Outside, the churchyard rustled with the stirrings of a world still bound to the seasons and cycles so foreign to Caroline's modern sensibilities. The sharp chill of early winter nipped at exposed skin, and smoke from hearths mingled with pungent compost of manure and rich soil. Children darted between adults, their laughter breaking through the somber tick of time, while elderly figures bent beneath the weight of years and expectations. As the service drew to a close and the congregation began to stir, the murmur of conversation swelled into murmurs steeped in gossip and social maneuvering. Caroline and Thomas remained intertwined, a unified front amid the slowly dispersing crowd, acutely aware that every step beyond the church's threshold was a return to the precariousness of survival.

In the bustling village square, the air thick with the scents and sounds of daily life, Caroline's mind churned with observations that challenged her academic preconceptions. Here was the unyielding grit beneath historical narrative, the lived texture that no book could capture. Thomas's comfortable movement within this world suggested a lifetime's worth of tacit knowledge she lacked, from gauging the tone of a passerby's glance to the practiced modulations of speech that deflected suspicion. He offered her steady reassurance a solid anchor against the tide of disquiet. Their forced marriage was more than a social performance; it was the Fortress holding at bay isolation and peril.

The villagers approached and greeted them with varying degrees of warmth and suspicion, their interactions laced with ritual greetings and subtle assessments. Caroline's heart thudded heavily as the reality of their adoption into this community unfolded: they must navigate layers of custom and unwritten law, adopt mannerisms etched by centuries, and suppress modern reflexes that, if revealed, would mark them as outsiders galling to the fragile social fabric. The weight of expectation pressed against Caroline's chest; she who had ventured here in quest of knowledge now fought for acceptance, for belonging.

Together, amidst the common folk, Caroline and Thomas held fast, a new and fragile constancy amid the uncertainties. Their shared performance of marriage, at once a deception and an evolving truth, bound them to Bramleigh and to each other in a way Caroline's orderly mind had never anticipated. As the village square thrummed with life and whispered judgments, the church bells tolling softly in the rising dusk, Caroline felt the first stirrings of surrender not to the past she had known but to the uncertain, intoxicating present where love, trust, and survival intertwined beneath the enduring gaze of history.

The morning light sifted through the narrow, leaded panes of the cottage window, casting long, uneven shadows upon the wooden floorboards worn smooth by years of bare feet and hurried footsteps. The air was thick with the faint scent of smoke lingering from the hearth's embers, and a faint mustiness that spoke of neglect yet offered a strange comfort in its authenticity. Caroline stood near the patched table, her fingers tracing the coarse, splintered surface absentmindedly, while Thomas paced quietly by the crooked doorway, a brooding figure framed by the early dawn. Though the cottage was humble to the extremes of modern sensibility, here they were, forced into this cramped existence by the impossible transported back nearly two and a half centuries, burdened with a book that demanded they perform a marital role to survive.

Earlier, the reality of their predicament had

forced itself upon them with brutal clarity. The notion of a shared surname, shared quarters, shared lives it was not only social convention; it was a lifeline in Bramleigh, a village tightly bound by its unwritten but inviolable codes. To step outside these unyielding norms was to risk suspicion, to invite prying eyes, gossip, accusations, and for outsiders like them, possibly even banishment or worse. Caroline's mind, so accustomed to cataloguing data and dissecting history from the calculated distance of dusty tomes, found itself wrestling with a living, breathing manifestation of those social laws, far less forgiving than the records she revered.

Their first forays into village life had been punctuated by a series of bracing lessons in restraint and observation. Agnes Pryce's ever-watchful gaze lurked like a storm cloud behind every whispered conversation and sideways glance. The widow's power, subtle yet pervasive, weaved itself through the fabric of Bramleigh's daily rhythm. Her approval governed the tacit consent required to exist here without peril.

Caroline's initial assumption that her scholarly knowledge might grant her an advantage was naïve; the lived experience, the instinctual understanding of nuance, deference, and unspoken codes were a language entirely new to her.

It was not merely about dressing the part, although clothing itself was a declaration of identity a delicate balance of humble modesty and visible respectability. Arriving at the market in unseemly garments would invite judgement; failing to participate in communal labor, a fatal sign of arrogance or idleness. Embodied in the stiff-limbed corsetry and woolen skirts that irritated her skin and constrained her movements was the reality of submission to social expectation. Thomas, with his broader shoulders and unpretentious strength, moved more easily in the thrifted clothes they had scavenged forged in this new existence but even he was not immune to the disapproval that simmered beneath the polite greetings exchanged in the village square.

Their first Sunday at church was a baptism

of social immersion, a crucible where the performative aspects of their marriage became tangible to the community. They stood side by side, Caroline clutching the hem of her worn shawl, fingers clenched to steady the tremor that threatened to spill over. Thomas, tall and steady, impenetrable in his calm, bore the burden of their charade with a stoicism that grated against Caroline's ever-analytical mind. The church, with its musty hymnals and wooden pews smoothed by generations of devout parishioners, echoed with the soft murmurs and practiced piety that bound the villagers in shared purpose. It was here that freethought must yield to collective expectation, where the law of God and man converged.

The rules of conduct in Bramleigh were not laid out in printed decrees but rather whispered in the corridors of gossip and affirmed through the silent, watchful approval of the community. Caroline learned swiftly that their survival depended on mastering the art of unobtrusive conformity. At the market, villagers scrutinized their interactions for signs of 'impropriety' a term broad enough to encompass everything from overt flirtation to the smallest breach of etiquette. Public displays of affection were forbidden; to touch a spouse in anything but a socially prescribed manner invited suspicion. Thomas's easy, protective touches, meant to reassure in the privacy of their cramped quarters, had to be extinguished before stepping beyond their doorstep.

Mealtimes, too, became lessons wrapped in ritual: dishes were shared sparingly among a table of modest size, conversation was moderated to avoid offending sensibilities, and deference was owed to the eldest or most respected at the table. Caroline, unused to such cautious negotiation of daily life, found herself rehearsing polite speech and strategic silences as if they were incantations that might ward off disaster. Thomas mirrored her adjustments, his once sharp modern instincts reined in by an ingrained need to survive that transcended eras. Even their internal monologues, usually bubbled with contemporary references and jargon, had to be filtered through this new lens, suppressing the urge to question overtly or express frustration.

One afternoon, as the chill of an approaching winter gnawed at their bones, Caroline ventured cautiously to the bakery, clutching a few coins that felt incongruously heavy in her palm. The bakery was a bustling place, fragrant with the sweet warmth of baking bread and the tang of fresh butter. Yet beneath the inviting aromas lay a battlefield of social mores. Every exchange was a potential misstep. The village matrons, eyes sharp and tongues sharper, listened intently to phrasing and tone. Caroline discerned subtle tests in casual inquiries about 'her husband' the volume of their voices, the timing of their smiles, the registered weight of their glances. She realized that her half-hearted, book-learned responses fell short of the nuanced fluency required to pass unnoticed.

Thomas accompanied her whenever possible, a silent sentinel whose mere presence seemed to ease some of the tension but also drew attention, remarkable for its unexpected ease considering their short time among the villagers. While he possessed a natural comfort navigating physical environments and social subtleties in his own world, this new reality honed his instincts differently. He learned quickly that the appearance of confidence was as vital as actual skill. A slight nod here, a measured glance there, and the performance of a united front became an unspoken language between them a fragile bulwark against the prying and the scornful.

The social calendar of Bramleigh unfolded like an intricate dance, punctuated by Sunday services, market days, and the occasional village gathering that tested their ability to blend in seamlessly. Each event brought fresh challenges: engaging in conversations that skirted controversial topics, furnishing answers to idle questions that balanced truth and invention, suppressing the modern shades of their personality that might reveal their anachronism. Caroline marveled, though not without a touch of bitterness, at how much energy was expended not merely surviving but performing survival consistently aligning external behavior with expected norms to avoid casting shadows over them.

Even the language posed hurdles. Though their English was the same, the cadence, idiomatic expressions, and certain words carried an 18th-century inflection that Caroline found fascinating yet daunting. They practiced "thee" and "thou," adjusted their pronunciation to avoid jarring slips, and refined their body language to appear natural rather than rehearsed. Their script, once informed by collar stiff with formal academic tone and proprietary modern brusqueness, shifted to measured deference and openness, though it was often an effort of sheer will. Caroline sometimes felt as though she wore an invisible mask, the contours of which were drawn by the expectations of a society she had only read about.

In the evenings, when the village drifted into darkened windows and the only sounds that filtered through the thatched roof were the crackle of fire and the murmurs of night creatures, Caroline and Thomas met in the small back room, their temporary sanctuary, to debrief and strategize. They pored over the book's shifting commands and their growing understanding of Bramleigh's ways, piecing together the gaps left by Caroline's bookish knowledge. She observed with mounting awe how Thomas's intuitive social sense adapted dynamically, his readings of human nature tuned to the smallest tells hidden beneath polite smiles. Her own mind, while slower to embrace the emotional undercurrents, began to acknowledge the necessity of flexibility and vulnerability.

Their nightly conversations bore the weight of their double lives. They navigated not just the practicalities of survival but the mental toll of inhabiting roles they neither desired nor understood fully. Caroline confessed to Thomas the exhaustion of playing a part so alien to her nature, the fear that any misstep could unravel the fragile security they had established. Thomas's response was steady and simple a promise to stand beside her, to shoulder the risks together, transforming performance into partnership. It was from these moments, forged in whispered supplications and shared silences, that the first fragile tendrils of genuine connection began to weave between them.

Each day's lessons in Bramleigh's rules of conduct etched themselves into their beings with relentless clarity that trust, though tentative, was essential; that survival required a balance of intellect and instinct; that the performance of marriage was not mere mimicry but a complex negotiation with fate. The village, with all its stifling restrictions, nevertheless offered a mirror in which Caroline and Thomas glimpsed parts of themselves long suppressed or undiscovered. Through imposed roles and hard-won acceptance, they began to unravel the convoluted tapestry of identity, belonging, and desire.

And as winter tightened its grip, cloaking Bramleigh in biting winds and deepening shadows, Caroline felt the cold gnaw not only at her bones but at the barriers she had so meticulously constructed around her heart. The knowledge that beyond the walls of their shared cottage, Agnes Pryce's gaze never wavered, and the stakes of their survival remained perilously high, sharpened their understanding of just how intertwined their fates had become. The rules of conduct, once mere guidelines on thin parchment, were now the lifeblood of their existence, demanding obedience but also offering an unexpected path to connection, resilience, and the slow blooming of something painfully beautiful within the constraints of time and tradition.

Challenges of Village Life

Physical Trials

The dawn broke with a dull amber sky, casting a pale light through the narrow window of their cramped Bramleigh cottage, awakening Caroline to the sharp scent of damp earth and wood smoke that clung to the air like a stubborn second skin. The chill seeped into her bones despite the thin wool of the blanket, a reminder that in this time, comfort was neither swift nor sure. As she rose carefully, mindful not to disturb the fragile peace of their shared quarters, the reality of their predicament a relentless series of physical demands, far beyond the ease of her modern life pressed heavy upon her. The floors creaked beneath her bare feet, darkened by years of grime and hard use, emblematic of the toll this place exacted on all who dwelled within it. The morning ritual of fetching water, kindling warmth for a fire, and preparing meager sustenance was already underway as she joined

Thomas at the hearth, where his presence was a grounding constant amidst the uncertainty.

Thomas moved with practiced efficiency, his hands skilled and purposeful as he worked split logs into manageable kindling, his broad frame a formidable silhouette against the dim chamber. The effort was strenuous, but it revealed a deep resilience that Caroline, despite her scholarly detachment, admired quietly and relied upon more than she cared to admit. In these early hours, their partnership transcended pretense; the performative veneer of marriage gave way to an unspoken understanding forged in shared toil. She observed how he wiped a sheen of sweat from his brow, muscles taut beneath the loose linen of his shirt, a contrast to her own frailty. It was as if the modest physicality of 18th-century life demanded a surrender of body and spirit she had never anticipated a surrender Thomas met with neither complaint nor hesitation. His labor shielded her from the brunt of hardship, a bulwark against the unforgiving environment and the ever-looming threat posed by their status as outsiders.

The day unfurled in a relentless dance of necessity and endurance. Thomas took to summoned tasks as if born of this era, laying sturdy fence posts to protect their limited land from wandering livestock and curious eyes, each hammer strike echoing like a heartbeat in the quiet countryside. Caroline shadowed him at times, fetching tools, repairing threadbare hems on their scant clothing, learning in these acts to exist not merely as a spectator of history but an active participant in its rough textures. The physical exertions left her limbs trembling with unexpected fatigue, muscles unfamiliar with such demands tightening and loosening through repetitive motions. Yet Thomas, ever mindful, tempered his strength, careful not to overwhelm but always ready to intervene should danger arise. His protective instincts were no less vital than his brawn, scanning the horizon with a hunter's acumen, noting suspicious figures or the subtle shifts in village watchfulness that threatened to unveil their charade. Each whispered report of Agnes Pryce's inquiries cast a shadow longer than the evening twilight, as the village's unyielding scrutiny pressed on them like a storm cloud ready to break.

Between the grueling labor and the guarded glances from neighbors, Caroline's internal defenses began to falter against the creeping realization that survival hinged not only on their cleverness but on their evolving reliance on one another. Thomas's steady presence was a balm to her growing unease, a tangible link to safety amid the unfamiliar rhythms of this era. His familiarity with outdoor tasks whether mending a broken cart wheel or securing the worn door with a hastily crafted latch was indispensable, his competence a quiet declaration of strength and stability. When a sudden squall descended, violent and unpredicted, it was Thomas who bailed water from their fragile roof with frantic urgency, while Caroline gathered their scant belongings and sought the warmth of his side for shelter from the storm's fury. The closeness was no longer endured solely for performance; it became an instinctual refuge, the line between pretense and truth blurring in the heat of shared adversity.

Their interactions grew textured with new layers of meaning: a touch extended under the guise of passing a tool, a brief glance lingering longer than circumstance permitted, and moments when heavy silence gave way to confessions whispered against the crackle of their hearth fire. Caroline found her heart thudding not merely from exertion but from the stirring of emotions long subdued by her intellectual rigidity. Thomas, too, revealed vulnerability beneath the hardened exterior a flicker of doubt in his eyes, a tentativeness born of a past shaped by lost belonging. The physicality of their existence in Bramleigh demanded a surrender to the immediacy of need, yet within this surrender bloomed a tentative trust, a shared recognition of the stakes that bound them beyond the charade of spousehood. The laborious days forged a rhythm that carried them through the isolation, knitting their lives in unspoken ways and eroding the walls each had built around their hearts.

Outside, the village remained a place of watchful eyes and veiled menace. Agnes Pryce's presence loomed like an unseen predator, her whispers and inquiries a constant threat that tightened the noose around their fragile cover. It was in this crucible of labor and surveillance that Thomas's protective fervor became most apparent. On more than one occasion, his posture shifted from companion to guardian, his gaze narrowing as he intercepted rumors or blocked suspicions with measured charm and calculated displays of familiarity. The physical trials of the day melded with the social dangers that shadowed them, each challenge intensifying their dependence on shared strength her knowledge and his instincts. Caroline's meticulous understanding of the era's customs offered guidance but little defense against Agnes's subtle manipulations, making Thomas's tangible protection all the more essential.

Their nights were equally a battleground of exhaustion and connection. After the labor drained their bodies, they were left with the fragile warmth of their hearth and the silent pull of companionship in close quarters. Caroline's fingers shook as she mended Thomas's worn coat by the flickering candlelight, her hands learning the delicate artistry of stitches and seams small acts of care that spoke volumes beyond words. Thomas watched her with a mixture of admiration and longing, the physical tasks of the day giving way to the emotional trials that lay beneath. The cottage, though humble and often cold, transformed in these moments into a sanctuary of shared vulnerability. Their proximity cracked the walls of solitude they had both constructed in their separate pasts, revealing raw, tender spaces that neither dared name directly but both felt smoldering beneath the surface.

Despite the harshness of their circumstances, there was an undeniable beauty in the way they adapted and grew toward each other. The labor that might have once been a source of alienation for Caroline became a crucible that tempered her spirit, urging a surrender of control that had defined her modern existence. Thomas's strength, once merely physical, unveiled dimensions of emotional depth and a fierce devotion that softened the edges of her resolve. Together, their bodies and hearts forged a rhythm not dictated by time or place but by necessity and newfound affection. In the struggle to meet the demands of a world that was not their own, they discovered an unexpected sanctuary in each other's presence a sanctuary built on sweat, effort, and the quiet promise of protection.

The trials were unending, and yet with each strenuous day and guarded night, the invisible threads tethering them tightened into bonds of something impossibly close to love. The past's harsh demands became the crucible in which their connection was forged, proving that even amidst the grueling physical trials and mounting dangers, the heart could find warmth, and the body strength, to endure and perhaps even to flourish.

Caroline's Expertise Tested

Caroline had always believed her knowledge was her greatest armor against the unknown. A social historian by discipline and a skeptic by nature, she had spent years weaving through archives, understanding the rhythms and routines of eras long dead, piecing together the lives of those who had dwelled in times far removed from her own. Her expertise had been her sanctuary, a place where facts reigned supreme, where dates and customs wove together to form a tapestry she could trust. Yet, as the chill of the 1770 English countryside seeped through threadbare walls and into her bones, she discovered, with a mounting sting of frustration, that knowledge alone was a fragile shield. It was not enough to simply understand the social customs or memorized laws; survival demanded more intuition, endurance, and something more elusive: presence, an unflinching engagement with the harsh realities of a world that refused to bend to her expectations.

The cramped cottage they had taken refuge in was a far cry from the lofty halls of the Arkwell Library, yet Caroline found no comfort in the contrast. The small hearth cast flickering shadows against the rough-hewn walls, warmth as fickle as the brittle flame itself. Caroline busied herself with the small tasks she could manage   chopping kindling with an uncertain hand, fetching water from a well whose depths seemed bottomless and foreboding. She approached even these acts with the precise rationality of a scholar, cataloguing sensations and reactions, attempting to overlay her modern sensibilities with the grime and grit of eighteenth-century labor. But every movement came with a cost, her muscles unfamiliar with strain, her palms raw and blistered. The errors she made   a slash too close to the knuckle, a careless misstep on uneven stones gave silent testament to her helplessness, a language of pain Caroline had never learned to speak.

Thomas proved a stark reminder of the demands this age required. His hands were strong and sure, moving with an ease born from a life attuned to physical hardship. She observed him carefully, her mind hungry to absorb the subtle cues of his movements   how he held the ax, how he maneuvered through the cramped village lanes without losing his footing. His confidence contrasted her faltering steps, a constant encouragement but also a bitter admission of her own inadequacy. In moments of exhaustion, when confidence faltered and her vision blurred with weariness, she found herself leaning into him, an impulse that surprised and unsettled her. The modern Caroline, the woman who had prized control and independence, was being forced into a coexistence dictated by necessity   one that demanded reliance and, ultimately, trust.

Their relationship, once defined by polite distance, began to shift under the weight of their shared predicament. They were no longer two strangers abruptly torn from the twenty-first century, but partners thrust unwillingly into a 1770s village that measured worth by conformity and suspicion. The book's command that they pose as husband and wife was more than a subterfuge; it was a mantle that carved into their identities, binding them in performative proximity while reality gnawed at the edges of pretense. Caroline felt the weight of their precarious façade each time they ventured beyond the cottage's meager shelter. In the marketplace, wary eyes followed their tentative steps; in the crowded tavern, whispers spun webs of distrust that tightened with every glance. Agnes Pryce was ever-present in the shadows   her scrutiny a spectral threat whispering the price of failure. The widow's subtle manipulations and statuesque presence underscored the village's rigid social strictures, a reminder that survival required more than knowledge; it demanded dexterity in the unspoken rules that governed behavior in a community like Bramleigh.

Caroline's historical insights, while invaluable in theory, faltered against the living mosaic of prejudice and pragmatism. She understood the class distinctions, the expectations for widows, for young mothers, for travelers yet, she quickly learned that knowing was not the same as navigating. When a local man's gaze lingered too long, laden with unsavory intent, it was not a fact from a dusty ledger that shielded her but Thomas's firm intercession, a protective posture both physical and social. The need to embody her role convincingly to respond with the appropriate airs of a respectable wife placed a strain on the measured detachment she usually maintained. Each forced smile, each careful phrase uttered before wary neighbors, deepened the hunger she had learned to resist: to be seen, truly seen, and accepted, not as an aberration or an outsider, but as someone who belonged.

Yet, the physical hardships were perhaps the most unrelenting challenge. The damp that clung to the cottage walls seeped into the marrow of their bones, and the cold gnawed relentlessly, especially in the pre-dawn hours when Caroline would awake shivering beside Thomas, her breath a fragile mist in the dim light. She had never fathomed how exhausting it was to simply exist in a body unaccustomed to such deprivation, where every task demanded a toll far beyond what she had known in her modern, climate-controlled life. Illness lurked in every shadow, and poor shelter bred a subtle but insidious weariness. Caroline found herself counting breaths, sweating feverishly under thin blankets, fighting against the fraying edges of her composure. Thomas, too, bore his invisible wounds, mornings when his face bore the softened hardness of a man pushed beyond endurance, his jaw clenched in quiet resilience.

Within this crucible of suffering and uncertainty, their dependence on each other became not just necessary but deeply human. When Caroline fainted one bitter evening after a day spent hauling firewood, Thomas caught her without hesitation, holding her with unexpectedly tender concern. His touch, firm yet gentle, was an anchor in the swirling instability of their existence. She heard the subtle catch in his breath, the rapid beat of his pulse beneath rough skin, and for the first time, felt the fragile heartbeat of something unspoken blooming between them. The walls she had constructed around her emotions cracked beneath the weight of proximity and proximity's demands. It was not knowledge or historical insight that brought them close, but the shared reality of vulnerability   a defiant, unyielding need to protect and to be protected.

Yet danger always lingered just beyond the hearth's slender warmth. Agnes Pryce's quiet vigilance was a shadow that lengthened with each passing day. The widow's sharp eyes caught nuances invisible to others, and Caroline sensed the slow coiling of suspicion that threatened to unravel their precarious existence. One afternoon, while fetching water, Caroline overheard Agnes speaking in hushed tones with a grizzled elder. Their conversation was laced with insinuation, hints that outsiders like Caroline and Thomas were liabilities, threats to the village's fragile order. The realization gnawed at Caroline's confidence, a stark reminder that all her preparation, all her knowledge, could not shield them from the multifaceted dangers of a world ruled by observation, gossip, and unyielding rules.

Even within their fragile home, tension

crept in like an unwelcome visitor. The strain of constant vigilance wore thin their patience and exacerbated their differences. Caroline's habitual need for control often clashed with Thomas's instinctual pragmatism. In moments when she sought to plan with precision, to dissect and anticipate, Thomas pushed back, advocating for adaptability and action over endless deliberation. The tension between them was not born of anger but the natural friction of two wills tempered by circumstance a friction that flared and settled, that shaped the raw edges of their evolving partnership.

In the quiet of the evenings, when the village slumbered and only the wind whispered against the windowpanes, Caroline lay awake wrestling with her fears. She questioned whether her reliance on Thomas was a surrender of autonomy or a recalibration of strength. Was this dependence a brittle concession to survival or a deeper acknowledgment of interconnectedness that had always eluded her? The modern lone scholar had been stripped bare, revealing an unfinished, vulnerable self beneath the armor of facts. Her mind revisited the volumes she had poured over in the library: the stories not just of grand events but of ordinary lives shaped by endurance, by love forged in the crucible of hardship. It was in this mirror of history that Caroline began to glimpse a possibility   that knowledge, while incomplete, could be a seed for empathy, that survival demanded more than detachment, that trust was a currency more valuable than any learned fact.

Thomas, for his part, endured his own battles with identity and belonging. From the moment of their arrival, he had been an enigma to Caroline

a man of few words but decisive action. His early reticence had slowly given way to glimmers of something deeper: humor that slipped through cracks in formality, tenderness disguised beneath the harshest pragmatism. He navigated the physical tasks with a dexterity Caroline envied, yet she sensed his own struggle to reconcile this forced existence with the life he had briefly left behind. Their shared journey was not merely a passage through time, but a voyage through shifting selves, where the boundaries between pretense and truth blurred, where each touch and glance unwound old fears and rewove new connections.

The relentless demands of the era extended beyond the physical; social survival exacted a toll that gnawed invisibly at their spirits. Every encounter carried unspoken tests did their gestures convey the authenticity of marriage? Did Caroline's poised yet cautious responses face the scrutiny of village matriarchs without faltering? The absence of modern protections no instant communication, no legal safety nets left them exposed to the worst whims of gossip and suspicion. Here in Bramleigh, reputation was a fragile thing, and for outsiders, it could shatter with a single misstep. The knowledge Caroline had painstakingly accumulated about the era's social structures offered some guidance, but the lived experience was an altogether more brutal tutor.

One particularly harrowing evening crystallized these truths. A village gathering at the tavern, intended as a gesture toward acceptance, instead unraveled into whispered warnings and sideward glances. Agnes Pryce was there, her presence like a cold breath across the back of Caroline's neck, her eyes conveying silent judgment. When a stranger questioned Thomas's place in the village, the atmosphere thickened, suspicion blooming palpably. Thomas's measured defense and Caroline's guarded composure barely masked the gnawing fear that all their efforts might come to naught. In that moment, Caroline understood that their survival depended not just on knowledge or strength but on a fragile dance of perception a performative truth they had no choice but to enact.

As days blurred into weeks, Caroline embraced a new reality. Her role had shifted from detached observer to active participant, from scholar to survivor. Every challenge chipped away at old certainties and bred a profound empathy for those who had endured such hardships before her, their stories etched not just in texts but in lived pain and resilience. The passage of time within Bramleigh was marked not merely by the turning seasons but by the gradual shift of Caroline's own inner landscape a transformation seeded by shared struggle, by the slow bloom of trust, and by a burgeoning recognition that knowledge without courage was an empty vessel.

Night after night, as the hearth's glow wavered and the wind carried whispers from the past, Caroline and Thomas drew closer, their dependence evolving into a connection neither had anticipated. What began as a necessity to survive the brutal social and physical environment grew into a delicate, fierce bond forged in the crucible of adversity, strengthened by vulnerability, tempered by shared secrets and stolen moments. Caroline's expertise had been tested beyond the realm of bookish certainty; it had been stretched, shattered, and reforged into something alive and breathing.

In the crucible of a world that demanded everything, Caroline learned that knowledge was a map but never the terrain itself. Real dangers could not be outwitted by intellect alone; they were endured, navigated, and sometimes transformed by the human heart. And in this transformation lay hope the promise that even in a time of stone and shadow, the fragile flame of trust could ignite, illuminating the darkest hours and guiding them forward into uncertain tomorrows.

The brittle chill of dawn seeped through the cracked panes of the tiny cottage, threading cold tendrils around the worn edges of the hearth where a reluctant fire struggled to catch life. Caroline stirred beneath layers of coarse wool, the hard reality of the morning pressing down with unforgiving weight. Her muscles ached a soreness unfamiliar yet undeniably clear in its language. The very air of Bramleigh was different, thick with a grit that clung stubbornly to skin and meaning, demanding endurance where ease had once been granted. She rose with a measured breath, attentive to the creak of floorboards and the muted stir of Thomas beside her. Their shared silence in the early hours was no longer merely a courtesy but a fragile bridge between two worlds, two selves still trying to meld into the tenuous façade they now wore like armor.

The village beyond the narrow window was

waking with a slow reluctance, wagons creaking along muddy thoroughfares and the punctuated clatter of horses' hooves on cobblestones threading through the dusky quiet. It was an existence carved out of sturdy necessity, one that brooked no waste of time, of resources, or of personal vulnerabilities. Caroline's fingers brushed the rough-hewn wooden table, tracing the grain with a scholar's yearning, understanding that here history was something they lived within, breathed, and battled against not merely studied from a distance. Yet, it was in this place of rigid tradition that they found themselves painfully vulnerable, two strangers marked by their otherness, attempting to cloak themselves beneath the brittle guise of a husband and wife.

From the first day they had arrived, the suspicion that flickered behind the villagers' eyes had begun to solidify into a slow-burning haze of watchfulness. It was Agnes Pryce, with her jutting chin and eyes like steel traps, who set the tone a quiet sentinel of social order whose gaze swept over the pair with an unyielding gravity. Caroline had caught the widow's piercing scrutiny on more than one occasion, each glance a silent accusation wrapped in polite civility. Agnes embodied the village's collective wariness, a living embodiment of its customs and fears, dispensing judgment as if it were personal creed. Each whispered word behind closed shutters, each lingering glance over a market stall, seemed to echo the same question: Who were these intruders intruding upon tradition, and what danger might they represent?

Thomas, more attuned to the physical rhythms and unspoken codes of the 18th century, had become Caroline's unexpected anchor in these moments. His steady presence beside her, the subtle adjustments he made to their shared narrative, spoke of an instinct honed by hard experience rather than academic knowledge. The physical demands of their new life were unrelenting each chore, from gathering firewood to hauling water, pulling at the sinews of their bodies in ways Caroline's modern sensibilities had not prepared her for. Yet it was in these shared labors, the grit beneath the fingernails, the ache in their limbs, that their dependence deepened, quietly forcing them beyond the brittle shell of pretense toward a reluctant trust.

The cottage, cramped and fraying at the edges, became both sanctuary and stage, a crucible where their forged alliance could be tested against the rigid world outside. Their footsteps, once confident, had grown measured, layered with caution as they moved through the village, aware that every misstep might unravel the fragile acceptance they had stitched together. Caroline's knowledge of history lent them some timeless insight, but it did little to shield her from the raw social power Agnes wielded. Every interaction, from the exchange of goods at the market to the veiled remarks from neighbors, was steeped in an undercurrent of control the unspoken rules by which Bramleigh demanded obedience and conformity.

The villagers' watchfulness was a slow accretion of collective suspicion, faint yet undeniable. At the market, the eyes of women hardened as they observed Caroline's hesitant attempts to navigate unfamiliar customs, the careful avoidance of certain topics, the quickness of her repartee tinged with a peculiar modern cadence. Men in taverns exchanged knowing looks, their conversations dipping into hushed speculation about the newcomers who did not quite fit the village's worn patterns. Even the children, with their unfiltered honesty, seemed to sense the breach in the social fabric, whispering questions that lingered like shadows. The tight-knit community, bound by generations of shared history, regarded the pair as fragile anomalies, threats against a well-ordered narrative they guarded fiercely.

Despite the growing pressure, Caroline found herself wrestling with an unfamiliar cocktail of emotions fear tangled with an unexpected flicker of exhilaration. The challenge of this alien world urged her into a surrender she had long resisted, the slow melting of her carefully constructed walls. Thomas's quiet strength fortified her, his touch a salve against the cold, his laughter briefly disarming the relentless tension. Yet even in moments of reprieve, the specter of Agnes's approval or lack thereof loomed large, a reminder that their survival depended on far more than mere appearances.

Each day wound tighter the noose of social conformity, weaving an invisible thread that pulled at Caroline's resolve. The masquerade of their marriage demanded endless vigilance, an exhausting performance that left little room for genuine connection. Yet paradoxically, it was through this very pretense that their guarded facades began to crack, revealing glimpses of something deeper beneath the surface. Private conversations, stolen moments by the dim glow of the hearth, unveiled vulnerabilities that words alone could not contain. Caroline's usual reliance on intellect faltered before the raw necessity of emotional intimacy, her breaths hitching under the weight of confessions shared and fears voiced. Thomas, too, shed the rough exterior that had once kept him at arm's length, revealing the tender hope that resiliently tethered him to a future they could not yet name.

As the winter deepened its grasp, the physical hardships intensified, the landscape turning stark and unyielding, mirroring the social scrutiny that kept them under relentless siege. Frozen mornings bled into long, cold nights, punctuated by the distant howl of wind threading through skeletal branches. Food grew scarce, fires hard to kindle, and the vigilance required to maintain their fragile roles demanded a fortitude neither had anticipated. Yet, in the crucible of deprivation and proximity, the invisible bond between them strengthened. They became each other's refuge, a solitary island of warmth and understanding amid the relentless storm of suspicion.

Agnes's subtle machinations shadowed every interaction, her fingers deftly threading legal threats alongside social coercion, a quiet war to be won through intimidation and compliance. Caroline recognized the danger that lurked behind the widow's calm exterior a danger born not only from personal grudge but an institutionalized fear of the unknown, the other. Each threat whispered under breath, each summon to the magistrate's office weighed heavily on their choices, eroding their confidence but never quite breaking their will. In this battle for existence, the lines between foe and ally blurred, and survival took on a deeper, more intimate meaning.

Among the villagers, alliances shifted and reformed like the unpredictable wind. Some sympathized but dared not interfere openly, while others embraced Agnes's vigilance, fostering a climate thick with quiet judgment. Caroline noted the subtle exchanges the tightening of lips, the averted gazes that spoke volumes of an unspoken consensus. It was a world ruled by performance and perception, where a single misstep spelled exile or worse. The harsh reality of life in Bramleigh enforced strict adherence to social mores, and Caroline began to understand, with a mix of dread and awe, how tightly control was woven into the fabric of survival here. To navigate this intricate dance was to sacrifice parts of oneself, to become a creature molded by necessity rather than inclination.

Yet amidst the watchfulness and whispered suspicions, a strange tenderness blossomed between Caroline and Thomas. The enforced closeness of their shared hardships dissolved earlier reservations, the fragile trust they granted each other evolving into an unspoken promise. Caroline's precise mind struggled to categorize these emergent feelings, her scholarly detachment giving way to a startling vulnerability. She found solace in the warmth of Thomas's presence, a shield against the encroaching cold, both of weather and heart. Their interactions, once constrained by the fear of exposure, began to carry a different weight a tentative intimacy threaded with stolen glances and subtle touches, as if their bodies understood truths their words dared not speak.

The physicality of the era imposed itself relentlessly upon them a constant reminder of the world they inhabited. Every task demanded endurance and strength, transforming their days into cycles of toil and small reprieves. Caroline learned to set aside her modern fragility, discovering an unexpected reservoir of resilience within. She watched Thomas navigate the demands with a seasoned grace, his survival instincts an unspoken guide that steadied them both. The weight of manual labor, the ache of muscles unaccustomed to such strain, and the simple but rigorous requirement of bearing their roles without faltering forged a bond steeped in shared struggle.

Yet, despite their growing cohesion, the village did not relent in its scrutiny. Caroline sensed the tightening noose of collective suspicion in the furtive conversations that ceased when she approached, in the shift of posture among market-goers, in the pointed glances that lingered too long. Agnes remained a formidable presence at the heart of this pressure, her insidious surveillance a constant reminder that their charade was tenuous at best. Caroline knew that it would take more than careful mimicry of social customs to secure their place; it would require the courage to confront the watchfulness head-on, to assert their right to exist in this world on their own terms.

Inside the small cottage, the flickering candlelight cast long shadows upon the walls, illuminating the lines of worry etched into their faces. Here, away from prying eyes, Caroline and Thomas confronted the weight of their circumstances in earnest. Words spilled forth, tentative at first, then with greater urgency, unraveling tensions that coiled tightly from days of restraint. Thomas's steady voice cut through the heavy silence as he reminded Caroline that in their union though initially forged from necessity there was a potential for something real, something worth fighting for beyond mere survival. Caroline responded with equal candor, acknowledging the shattering of her carefully constructed defenses, the fearful but hopeful recognition that vulnerability might be their greatest strength.

Their growing dependence on one another was not merely a practical matter but an emotional imperative, a lifeline in a world where trust was scarce and betrayal often hid behind the most courteous of smiles. The social watchfulness that enveloped them was a crucible, a trial by fire that revealed the depth of their resilience and the fragile beauty of their burgeoning connection. In this relentless scrutiny, every glance, every whispered suspicion, became both hazard and catalyst, binding them closer even as it threatened to undo them.

Outside the humble walls of the cottage, the village moved inexorably forward, a steady current against which they struggled to stay afloat. The social fabric of Bramleigh was strained by the presence of these outsiders, and in the warp and weft of daily life, the tension became a living thing visible to those who cared to see, palpable in the air they breathed. Caroline found herself increasingly aware that integration required more than mere endurance; it demanded transformation, a reshaping of both identity and desire, a surrender to the uncertain mercy of a hostile world.

And yet, as the days stretched into weeks, the oppressive weight of suspicion began to shift, imperceptibly but surely. There were moments when villagers offered tentative smiles, when

Agnes's cold gaze softened just enough to suggest a begrudging acceptance. Small kindnesses emerged, fragile and fleeting, like fragile shoots breaking through winter's frost. Caroline and Thomas clung to these glimmers, their hope a fragile flame flickering against the storm of watchfulness.

In the quiet moments between hardship and hope, Caroline understood that their greatest challenge was not simply the physical demands or the hostile scrutiny it was the internal battle to reconcile who they were with who the world demanded them to be. The performance of their marriage was more than a survival tactic; it was a journey into the heart of trust and surrender, a passage through fear into the tenderness of connection forged under fire. And in this passage, amid suspicion and strength, they discovered that even the harshest watchfulness could not quench the fragile bloom of love growing quietly between them.

Agnes Pryce's Gaze

Widow of Influence

The cottage sat snugly beneath the leaning eaves of Bramleigh's narrowest lane, its thatched roof sagging like the heavy breath of an old beast settled into slumber. Here, shadows stretched longer as dusk conspired with the chill creeping over the village, a tangible reminder of the time both in season and in history held firmly in its thrall. It was into this dim and heavy atmosphere that Agnes Pryce moved with the quiet surety of one born to navigate such worlds, of a woman for whom the dominion of social order was a breath as natural as the air she wove through the small, gossipy town. Ageless but unyielding, she bore the mantle of widow with a precise blend of dignity and steely resolve, a role that granted her influence over Bramleigh's fragile equilibrium in ways far more potent than simple wealth or station. Agnes was, in every whispered conversation behind curtained windows and every downward glance cast over crossed arms, the unseen hand that held the textile of village society tightly knit.

To understand Agnes Pryce was to delve beneath the veneer of civility she so meticulously maintained. She was not a woman of explosive temper or glaring brutality; rather, her power lay in control that required neither force nor fury, but an arsenal of subtle manipulations wielded with the delicacy of a violinist and the precision of a surgeon. Her eyes, a pale and penetrating gray, missed nothing a glance, a slip of the tongue, the flicker of defiance or desperation in a visitor's posture. Those eyes scanned the cobblestones and faces of Bramleigh as a hawk scouts the fields, always seeking, always weighing. Yet Agnes cloaked this surveillance beneath a manner as genteel as the lace handkerchief she pressed to her lips when speaking of troubles that did not concern her, and as gracious as the perfectly brewed tea she offered to those she deemed acceptable. Such contradictions made her intimidating and inscrutable; she was the village's guardian of propriety, its silent enforcer of norms woven so tightly that breaking one was akin to treason.

Her role as a widow was itself a mantle of unique power. Agnes's late husband, a man of modest wealth and respectable lineage, had left her enough property and standing to elevate her position beyond that of most women in Bramleigh, especially in the rigidly patriarchal society of 1770 England. Widowhood conferred upon her a peculiar form of autonomy a liminal space where a woman, devoid of a man's direct oversight, could articulate, enact, and enforce social order with a ruthlessness tempered only by the need to maintain her elevated status. Agnes exploited this rare liberty masterfully. She had inherited not only land and title but a vast network of connections, spanning the gentry and the village's merchant class alike. These contacts were her invisible tapestry of influence, stringing together whispers and information channels that reached into every hearth and hand.

Through gatherings at her modest but richly

appointed home afternoons thick with the scent of beeswax and infusions and formal parish meetings where her voice carried measured authority, Agnes perpetuated the village's unspoken laws. Often, these were less about the letter of the law than the weight of tradition, the ethics of appearances, and, crucially, the maintenance of social harmony as defined by those few who understood its delicate functioning. Where others saw only quaint customs and humble villagers, Agnes perceived a complex chessboard of alliances and rivalries, debts and favors, fears and hopes. To disrupt this order was to invite chaos not merely social inconvenience but the potential ruin of lives, livelihood, and long-held respect. Agnes stood vigilant, a sentinel who allowed no trespassers beyond the invisible thresholds she guarded.

Into this tightly controlled world came Caroline Moore and Thomas Reed, strangers dislocated from their own time but irretrievably ensnared in the brutal strictures of 18th-century rural England. Their very presence, unexplained and unaccounted for, sent ripples through the fabric Agnes was sworn to protect. It was not merely their foreignness that unsettled her but the dangers their ambiguity posed. To be an outsider in Bramleigh was to wear a mark as visible as any brand on a livestock's flank. The village had mechanisms to detect and expel such threats systems of suspicion and accusation quietly mobilized behind polite smiles and well-mannered inquiries. Agnes, as the chief arbiter of these convulsions beneath the surface, found herself compelled to observe and, when necessary, intervene.

She had first encountered Caroline and Thomas when they appeared at the local inn two strangers whose ease, or lack thereof, in the world around them betrayed a veneer barely concealing unease. Agnes watched from a distance, noting Caroline's sharp gaze and meticulous attention to detail, traits that spoke of education uncommon among most village women, and Thomas's cautious but confident bearing, as if his muscles were ready for a fight he hoped to avoid. It was their interaction, their mutual dependence, that piqued Agnes's interest but also sounded alarms. Marital cohesion was sacred here, but it was also strictly regulated by proof, witnesses, and a community's tacit consent. Posing as husband and wife without the bounds of legal recognition or local sanction was a dangerous game, one that Agnes knew could unravel the careful social order if left unchecked.

Her methods for dealing with such anomalies were as intricate as the village tapestry itself. First, she initiated a regimen of observation softened by outward civility. Agnes made point to invite Caroline to parish meetings and tea gatherings, positioning these seemingly casual hints of inclusion as both a test and an entrapment. Every word spoken in such settings was designed to probe, to reveal cracks in the facade the pair tried so valiantly to maintain. Agnes's questions were never direct accusations but rather pointed inquiries edged with concern or curiosity questions about family, employment, parish loyalty, and adherence to community norms that

Caroline, with all her historical knowledge, found draining and pathological in their intrusive insistence.

Beyond mere conversation, Agnes employed her network with subtle thoroughness. Letters were dispatched under the guise of innocuous correspondence but carried undertones that could unsettle even the steadiest nerves. Local shopkeepers, the parish parson, and other key figures discreetly fed her information regarding Caroline and Thomas's habits, expenditures, and interactions. Silent glances exchanged at market stalls, the stifled conversations behind lace curtains, the shudder of disapproving whispers all these were threads Agnes wove into a net designed to contain and ultimately control. It was a strategy born of pragmatism, for outright confrontation would risk scandal and community division, outcomes equally detrimental to her carefully balanced dominion.

Yet Agnes's pressure extended beyond surveillance to include veiled threats underscored by an acute understanding of power dynamics in a village where reputation could build or destroy with equal ease. When Caroline allowed herself a moment's slip a too-modern phrase, a gesture that betrayed a lack of ingrained deference, or a glance that spoke of defiance Agnes was there, offering advice couched in gentle tones but carried with the weight of consequence. "Such matters," she would intone, voice smooth as silk, "must be handled delicately. The eyes of Bramleigh are not as forgiving as one might hope. Reputation once tarnished is a stain that no washing can remove." In these exchanges, the edge of menace was ever present, a reminder that Agnes did not wield law as many imagined but social acceptance the far more insidious and enduring weapon.

For Agnes, control was as much about psychological maneuvering as it was about social formulae. She understood that Caroline's initial reliance on knowledge and logic made her resistant to emotional manipulation, yet this, too, was a field ripe for cultivation. Agnes watched as Caroline's body and spirit battled with the depriving conditions of the past, as the historian's need for order was slowly eroded by cold, hunger, loneliness, and the unrelenting scrutiny of village life. Agnes's interventions were designed to aggravate just enough to fracture this armor, to force Caroline into acquiescence or at least visible submission. To yield was survival, to resist risked exile or worse a measured lesson Agnes sought to imprint through subtle social sanctions enforced with an unapologetic firmness.

Thomas, with his physicality and pragmatic instincts, represented a different challenge. He was less susceptible to Agnes's verbal and psychological stratagems but more vulnerable to isolation and suspicion. Agnes's networks whispered rumors of a stranger without clear profession or allegiance, stirring unease among the male villagers whose skepticism toward outsiders was an unspoken ritual. Agnes knew that by sowing these seeds, she could press Thomas into conformity or fracture the fragile alliance between him and Caroline. The divide-and-rule tactics were cold but effective. Agnes's skill was not brute strength but a mastery of what people feared most: the loss of their place, their community, their dignity.

Beneath the polished veneer of her genteel exterior, Agnes's motivations were a tangled amalgam of personal history, duty, and survival. Widowhood was not merely a social position for her; it was a crucible through which she had been forged, a life neither softened by grief nor corrupted by bitterness but hardened by the necessity of control. Agnes had witnessed the fragility of social networks when unchecked passions, disgraced conduct, or ill-timed defiance tore communities apart. She perceived herself as the last bulwark against such chaos in Bramleigh, the stern matron who would bear the burden of unpleasantness so others might enjoy peace and prosperity. Her actions, though often ruthless, were never without purpose or consideration of larger consequences. In this, she held a perverse form of compassion, though it was compassion expressed not through kindness but control.

Her presence lingered like a storm cloud

over Caroline and Thomas's tentative new life, a constant reminder that their façade was under scrutiny not merely by strangers but by a force integral to the village's very heartbeat. For Agnes, their survival depended not on escape or defiance but on submission to the roles assigned them performing their marriage as scripted, obeying customs without question, and never threatening the structure she so assiduously preserved. Her gaze, sharp and unblinking, was both shield and sword, watching over Bramleigh's social order with iron resolve, ready to snuff out any ember of dissent before it could kindle into flame. In this relentless monitoring, the undercurrent of menace was always present, pulsing beneath the civility, shaping every interaction and sealing Caroline and Thomas's fate in the unforgiving web Agnes had spun.

The heavy curtains of dusk draped Bramleigh's narrow streets in a soft veil of grey, but even the fading light could not conceal the sharpness of Agnes Pryce's gaze as she perched beside the narrow window of her parlor, her hands folded neatly in her lap, the faintest hint of a smile betraying nothing yet suggesting a growing amusement beneath her composed exterior. To the casual observer, Agnes was simply a refined widow residing in one of the village's larger cottages an estate acquired through prudent management and a marriage curtailed too soon by fate's cruel hand. Yet beneath her polite facade and the carefully coiffed hair dusted with powdered white, there was an unwavering sentinel, a guardian not just of propriety but of the fragile social lattice upon which Bramleigh precariously balanced. Where others saw village life as quaint or mundane, Agnes perceived a delicate ecosystem, fraught with potential disruptions that, if left unchecked, could crumble the cohesive order she so assiduously maintained.

Her attention had long since fixed upon the newcomers Caroline and Thomas whose arrival had stirred whispers beneath the breath and sideways glances nestled in gatherings at the market and the chapel. Agnes's methods were neither blustering nor overt; she wielded influence with the precision of a needle threading unseen stitches. The village's social dynamics were her theater and her tools were subtlety, inference, and the calibrated application of pressure. Every conversation she engendered, every acquaintance she nurtured, was part of an intricate web of observation and influence extending well beyond what was visible inside her walls. Through the network of servants, market vendors, and the local clergy individuals ever keen to curry favor and maintain standing Agnes gathered the slivers of information necessary to construct a mosaic of the strangers' daily habits, their small weaknesses, and their interactions with the local populace.

What lent her efforts an almost chilling

effectiveness was the art of silent observation. Agnes employed a meticulous patience, often positioning herself at communal points the edge of a gathering, a discreet shadow behind a well-worn fence where she might watch without inviting notice. She knew the cadence of village life intimately: the cadence of morning chores and the tempo of evening reprises, the ebb and flow of light and dark, sound and silence. She was a woman who could discern more in a single glance than others might in hours of chatter. Whether it was the way Caroline's eyes lingered on curious shop signs or how Thomas's gait betrayed his tension when they passed under the scrutiny of a watchful passerby, Agnes cataloged every detail. To outsiders, it might seem an over-attentiveness born of idle gossip or personal animus, but the truth was far more strategic a protective mechanism shielding Bramleigh from the chaos that strangers, unmoored from tradition, could potentially unleash.

Her tactics were not limited to mere watching. Agnes interwove herself into the fabric of their everyday existence to gently remind them of their precarious position. Invitations to parish gatherings where she presided over seating arrangements that ensured observers were never out of earshot delivered with the civility of a hostess yet laced with unstated expectations. Casual remarks during community dinners that, beneath their congenial tone, hinted at the consequences of transgression. The deliberate spreading of minor rumors, subtle enough to seed doubt yet easily disprovable if needed, functioned as warnings rather than accusations, a means to destabilize without provoking direct conflict. Agnes understood the power of reputation in a village as tight-knit as Bramleigh; a single whispered suggestion of impropriety could lead to isolation or calls for removal. Her mastery lay in wielding social pressure as effectively as any official decree, directing the currents of communal judgment with deft, unseen hands.

There were moments when Agnes's tactics extended beyond social maneuvering into the realm of surveillance enforced through proxy.

Trusted villagers would be dispatched to subtly trail Caroline and Thomas's footsteps, reporting back with careful descriptions and interpretations. These agents of observation were chosen not only for their discretion but because they understood the stakes and shared Agnes's desire to preserve order. Unlike the brashness of a magistrate's warrant or the clamor of public denunciation, these quiet eyes maintained a suffocating presence that eroded the strangers' confidence, breeding wariness and second-guessing. Agnes was fully aware that control often stemmed not from confrontation but from the ability to make those watched feel perpetually observed, vulnerable in their most private moments. This invisibility of surveillance was perhaps her most potent weapon.

Yet Agnes's vigilance was not born solely from intolerance or suspicion; there was a pride in stewardship threaded through her watchfulness. She perceived herself as a custodian of Bramleigh's legacy, a sentinel safeguarding the mores and manners that had entwined generations of villagers. To her, the sudden intrusion of

Caroline and Thomas represented not just outsiders but destabilizing variables capable of unraveling the invisible contracts that bound society. Agnes's own life was steeped in the traditions she sought to protect widowed early yet formidable, she had spent decades honing the delicate craft of influence, shaping outcomes not with brute force but with the quiet persistence of a fiercely competent governess ruling her dominion. Her respectability was both shield and sword, an identity she wielded deftly to uphold laws that in other hands might have seemed petty or oppressive.

Her observations were recorded not in ink but in memory, stored in mental notebooks cataloging every nuance of body language, every hesitance in speech, every borrowed phrase or gesture that might betray Caroline and Thomas's unfamiliarity with local customs or their growing attachment to one another. Agnes noted how Caroline's intellectual curiosity usually a strength set her apart, exposing her to inadvertent slips in decorum or misinterpretations by villagers wary of difference. Thomas's manner, at once cautious and assertive, revealed a protective instinct that could either endear or alienate. Through these insights, Agnes plotted her quiet interventions, designed to steer their relationship within acceptable bounds, or at the very least, to expose vulnerabilities that might justify punitive measures should they resist assimilation.

There were evenings when Agnes sat by the fire in her sitting room, hands cradling a porcelain cup of chamomile tea as the flickering flames illuminated the sharp lines of her face, pondering the balance of mercy and severity needed to contain the newcomers without fracturing the village's fragile peace. She was aware that open hostility risked rebellion or ruinous scandal, but a measured combination of surveillance, social pressure, and the occasional pointed reminder of the law had, so far, kept Caroline and Thomas compliant. Agnes's mind choreographed these moves like a seasoned player in a prolonged game of chess, watching the subtle shifts in posture or mood as pieces danced across her imagined board.

Her tactics evolved with the seasons, adapting as the harsh winter set in and the village's social rhythms shifted indoors. Public spaces diminished in importance, replaced by the intimacy of homes and the close quarters of communal hearths. Agnes responded by increasing the frequency of visits, her presence cloaked beneath the unpretentious guise of a concerned neighbor or a benefactor bearing gifts of food and yarn. Each smile concealed a calculated assessment, each inquiry carefully phrased to elicit confessions or admissions without provoking outright resistance. It was this veiled scrutiny that steadily, imperceptibly chipped away at Caroline's steely self-reliance and tested Thomas's resolve to protect their façade.

Agnes's most formidable strength lay in her unwavering conviction that order must be preserved, that the survival of Bramleigh depended upon the subjugation of chaos and the strict adherence to social roles. In her eyes, Caroline and Thomas were disruptions wildcards whose presence was a threat not only because they were outsiders but because they represented the possibility of change, of uncertainty, of challenges to authority that could not be left unattended. Her watchfulness was more than mere enforcement; it was an act of preservation, a sentinel's vigil over a world she deemed delicate and deservedly safeguarded. And yet, beneath this resolve, beneath the surface of control and determination, there lingered the faintest trace of something resembling admiration an acknowledgment, perhaps unspoken even to herself, of the resilience and defiance embodied in the very subjects of her scrutiny.

This intricate dance of observation and influence set the undercurrent of tension that ran like a subtle current beneath every interaction in Bramleigh. Whether Caroline appeared in the village square with books clutched tightly to her chest or Thomas escorted her along the unfamiliar paths, Agnes's eyes followed, unblinking and unrelenting. Her watchfulness was a quiet but insistent reminder that their survival hinged not only on their ability to navigate the rigors of 18th-century life but also on their capacity to endure the invisible, insidious gaze of a woman who embodied the village's collective will to persevere. Every step they took was measured, every word carefully spoken, because beneath the polite society, beneath the veneer of neighborly concern, Agnes Pryce held sway a silent observer who ensured that order was never truly out of reach.

Gathering Evidence

The chill in the air had deepened as autumn bled into the bleakness of early winter, wrapping the village of Bramleigh in a muted, restless haze that seemed to seep into every stone and timber of its ancient buildings. Caroline Moore, newly tethered to this world through fragile threads of necessity and adaptation, felt the oppressive weight of unseen eyes more acutely with each passing day. It was not the coarse judgment of strangers that unnerved her after all, she had long been trained to observe rather than absorb but the methodical vigilance of Agnes Pryce, the village widow whose unassuming presence belied a keen and relentless capacity for control. Agnes's reputation as Bramleigh's moral arbiter was whispered in the same breath as reverence and unease, and Caroline now understood just how formidable that duality could be.

What made Agnes especially dangerous wasn't raw force, but the surgical precision with which she wielded influence. Like a spider drawing invisible threads across the parish, she spun an intricate web of social connections that extended beyond idle gossip into a weaponized network. Agnes was masterful at marshaling this web, using veiled insinuations and cultivated relationships to turn neighbor against neighbor, suspicion into supposition, and hearsay into actionable threats. Caroline and Thomas's arrival and their ostensible marriage already set them apart, a prickly anomaly in an insular community fiercely protective of its own. Agnes understood deeply the power of appearances, and she had sensed, almost immediately, that beneath their polished veneer lurked uncertainty, vulnerability anything less than perfection could be exploited.

Agnes's campaign of subtle intimidation began with the church, that hallowed seat of authority and tradition around which Bramleigh's social order revolved. The parish priest, Reverend Halliday, was a man of steady countenance but limited vision, gladly reliant on Agnes's counsel in maintaining discipline among the flock. Agnes presented herself as a devoted parishioner, attending services with unwavering punctuality, her hand never failing to clutch tightly the embroidered prayer book that marked her as a woman of devout standing. In conversations with the reverend, Agnes spoke in measured tones about the newcomers, her words laced with the insinuations of impropriety despite the surface civility. Caroline, ever alert, discerned that Agnes's repeated inquiries about their origins, their behavior, and the particulars of their so-called marriage were less about curiosity than the calculus of social surveillance.

Behind the tall, narrow windows of the church office, Agnes would sit with Reverend Halliday, poring over parish records, subtly steering his attention toward any discrepancies or minor lapses in Caroline and Thomas's participation in village life. The churchwarden's role extended beyond spiritual oversight; the church was the heart of communal judgment, and

Agnes held the pulpit's ear like a savvy political operative. Caroline guessed, correctly, that not a word was forgotten or forgone in these clandestine consultations, where Agnes's sharp eyes traced patterns and potential breaches so easily overlooked by others less vigilant. The reverend, constrained by his own sense of decorum and deference, seldom challenged her, feeding on her unrelenting presence to shore up his authority in the village's intricate hierarchy.

Outside the church's austere walls, Agnes extended her surveillance through the ever-watchful community she nurtured with calculated charm. It was in the marketplace, the communal well, even the cramped interior of the tavern, that her influence flourished. Here, amidst the chorus of barter and gossip, Agnes's network mobilized with a subtle but palpable energy. The village women, fieldworkers, and servants those whose daily routines intersected with Caroline and Thomas relayed details with an air of casual normalcy that masked the sharp edges of espionage. Caroline, who prided herself on her analytical mind cultivated by years amidst archives and history, found the scope of Agnes's social machinery both vast and intimate, working through loyalty, fear, and the complex tapestry of village bonds.

One afternoon, as frost glistened on the leafless branches and a low sun cast long shadows over the muddy roads, Caroline noticed the familiar figure of Judith, the baker's wife, lurking near the edge of the village square. Judith's sharp eyes caught Caroline's gaze momentarily before she turned away, her expression unreadable but charged. Caroline knew better than to dismiss such encounters; Judith was a known conduit in Agnes's network. Her role was unassuming a simple basket carrier, a helpful hand but beneath her affable demeanor lurked the practiced caution of one who fed tidbits back to the widow. When Caroline ventured out later, she observed Judith in polite conversation with other villagers, her discourse subtly weaving the threads of suspicion and alarm through the marketplace. The baker's wife was skilled in the art of gathering information without raising overt concern, a living extension of Agnes's silent inquisition.

Even Thomas, less susceptible to the subtleties of village politics, felt the tightening grip of Agnes's gaze. His instinctive wariness sharpened, especially as he noticed the frequent presence of strangers at their humble lodging's periphery neighbors who lingered just long enough for a whispered word, eyes flickering like wary animals when caught. Thomas's protective nature bristled against the invisible fences creeping around them, threatening exposure and ruin. The sense of being perpetually observed gnawed at the fragile trust blossoming between him and Caroline, forcing their conversations indoors, whispered in the dim light of the hearth where shadows danced and secrets held breath.

Agnes's methods carried a veneer of respectability that rendered confrontation perilous. She never raised her voice, never overtly accused, but her pointed remarks and carefully orchestrated appearances sowed an undercurrent of doubt so potent that it spread like a slowly infecting chill through Bramleigh's social veins.

Caroline's meticulous mind cataloged these maneuvers not as isolated incidents but as strategic assaults, part of a broader plan to unmask and expel them. Agnes was a maestro of the social dance, choreographing suspicion and enforcement with the finesse of a seasoned tactician.

Behind closed doors, Agnes cultivated her informants with precision. She lent an attentive ear to the grievances of the women who felt threatened by the newcomers' presence, to the servants uneasy about unfamiliar faces disrupting routine, to the elders unsettled by any change to established norms. Her gifts of homemade preserves and thoughtful gestures disguised a purposeful intent, encouraging confidences that would otherwise remain guarded. Agnes's hospitality was a thin mask, beneath which simmered a relentless campaign to dismantle the facade of Caroline and Thomas's fictitious marriage. Her influence transformed village informers into agents of social enforcement, turning everyday interactions into potential reports delivered with hushed urgency.

The churchyard, with its weathered stones and gnarled trees, was yet another stage for Agnes's subtle assertion of power. Here, under the watchful eye of the congregation gathered for Sunday hymns or the solemn quietude of funerals, Agnes moved with the unchallenged grace of one who had carved her place through decades of social navigation. She used these moments, ripe with communal emotion, to reinforce narratives about order and purity, gently reminding others of the consequences that befell those who defied the established rhythm of Bramleigh life. Her quiet admonishments and pointed prayers were suffused with a double meaning, understood perfectly by those attuned to the language of power cloaked in decorum.

Caroline, increasingly ensnared by Agnes's orchestrated pressure, found her own attempts at asserting autonomy thwarted not merely by direct confrontation but by the ambient tension coursing through every interaction. Doors that once appeared open now seemed to close subtly with polite nods, opportunities shrank under the weight of whispered doubts, and the ever-watchful eyes of Agnes's network cast long shadows over every plan. Thomas's practical efforts to counteract this through displays of confidence and social engagement met with varying degrees of success, as the village's intricate web of loyalty and suspicion proved welded tightly around the pair.

Yet, amid the rising tide of surveillance and control, Caroline detected in Agnes not just calculated malice but a deep-seated fear the kind that arises from a desperate need to preserve identity in a world threatened by change. This realization complicated the once-clear image of Agnes as merely an antagonist. In moments when Caroline observed her quietly tending to her late husband's grave or speaking with reverence to the reverend about the sanctity of tradition, the widow's stern façade fractured, revealing the human frailties beneath. This understanding did little to alleviate the immediate peril but added layers to the unfolding drama a testament to the complex interplay of power, fear, and survival etched into the fabric of Bramleigh society.

As the days shortened and the grip of winter tightened like an iron clasp, Caroline and Thomas's existence became a delicate performance, choreographed by the intimate knowledge Agnes wielded like a sword. Every movement, every whispered conversation was subjected to invisible scrutiny, each gesture weighed against the harsh doctrines of an unforgiving era. The unyielding social networks and church authority converged into a suffocating force, a gauntlet that challenged both the will and the heart. And yet, in this crucible of tension and threat, the fragile ember of their growing bond glowed brighter, defiant against the shadowy realm Agnes sought to cast upon their lives.

It was within this web of subtle menace and veiled observation that Caroline resolved to navigate with both caution and courage, aware that survival depended not just on knowledge and appearance but on the courage to forge connection and trust in the most unlikely of places. Agnes's gathering of evidence was relentless, her tendrils woven deep into the marrow of village life, but so too was the determination of two strangers bound by fate and the unspoken promise of something far more powerful than mere survival love.

Growing Closeness

The fire had long died down to a faint ember glow, casting a warm but fragile light across the cramped room where Caroline and Thomas found themselves confined. The cramped cottage, with its rough-hewn beams and single narrow window, offered little sanctuary from the biting winter that pressed relentlessly against its weathered walls. Tonight, as the chill crept into their bones despite the meager blankets, the smallest details of their forced proximity seemed to weigh heavier than ever. The shared bed rough, narrow, and far too small for two had become the most paradoxical place in this alien time: a refuge offering both solace and unrest, a fragile stage where the complex dance of their uneasy partnership played out in quiet desperation.

Between the coarse linen sheets and the hard straw mattress, Caroline felt raw nerves tauten with a confusing mixture of longing and restraint. The warmth of Thomas's body beside her a presence she had avoided acknowledging too fully during the day was suddenly undeniable in the quiet shadowed hours before dawn. Yet, as much as that warmth invited closeness, it also exposed a cavern of vulnerabilities she had never allowed herself to explore, even in her most private reflections. Her mind churned restlessly, grappling with the odd intimacy born not of desire but of necessity, a closeness imposed by circumstance and maintained by the constant, delicate balancing act of control and surrender.

Thomas lay rigid, staring at the weathered beams above, muscles held tight as though bracing against the invisible weight that pressed not only upon his frame but upon the fragile boundary between them. Their bodies curved tentatively towards each other, mindful of space yet haunted by the invisible cords of tension woven from unspoken fears and unacknowledged hopes. A few careful inches separated them enough to maintain a veneer of propriety in this unforgiving era, yet minimal enough to make the ache of proximity and withheld touch all the more acute. Each breath he took was a soft reminder of his nearness, each rise and fall of his chest a siren call to a yearning Caroline refused to name aloud.

Their days had been filled with performative closeness, demanded by the book's inscrutable laws and the village's curious eyes. In public, they were a married couple, bound not just by necessity but by the social web that Agnes Pryce wove so deftly around the townsfolk, ensuring conformity through subtle threats and constant scrutiny. Yet in the sanctuary of night, when the world fell away to silence and shadow, the charade splintered into something far more raw and complex. Their shared bed was no longer merely a pragmatic solution for warmth and safety; it was a crucible where their defenses melted and reshaped, where their roles exchanged from masks to something perilously near truth.

Caroline often found herself staring into the darkness beside her, wrestling with a paradox that seemed to pull at every fiber of her being. The barrier she had built around herself meticulous, well-fortified, constructed from years of solitary study and self-reliance cracked under the persistent pressure of Thomas's unspoken need for connection and her own buried desire to be seen, understood beyond the boundaries of historical fact and cautious detachment. She was a woman of logic and certainty, grounded in the present despite the disorienting past, yet here she was, in a bed shared with a stranger thrust into this world beside her, the borders of her identity blurring with every passing night.

Thomas's own struggles were no less profound. His initial instinct to protect and to assert control had softened into something more tentative, more hesitant. Beneath the rugged exterior that had served him well in this unforgiving century was a man grappling with the bewildering intimacy thrust upon him. He was a stranger in Bramleigh, a variable out of place, yet he found himself anchored to Caroline in ways that defied logic. The simple act of sharing a bed a place traditionally sacred and private carried the weight of unvoiced promises and uncharted territories. Every subtle movement, every soft intake of breath, felt like a negotiation of uncharted emotional ground.

The vulnerability was mutual, though neither would admit it aloud. Thomas struggled against the urge to bridge the physical gap too soon, to reach out and dispel the tension with a touch, but restraint governed his actions, born not from coldness but respect for the tenuous trust they had begun to nurture. His fingers twitched at times, yearning to trace the contours of her face or to hold her hand in the dimness, yet he remained still, aware that the slow dance toward intimacy required careful steps, not sudden leaps. In his silence, there was a fierce protectiveness, a quiet promise that when the time was right, every boundary could be crossed, but not before.

Caroline, on the other hand, responded to this approach with a mixture of frustration and reluctant hope. Her rational mind clung to the rules of their survival avoid suspicion, maintain appearances, do not complicate matters with passion but her heart, unaccustomed and resistant to such rawness, throbbed with an ache neither of them dared voice. She found herself listening to the rhythm of his breath, feeling the faint brush of his thigh against hers, caught in the fragile tension between the public pretense they maintained and the private truths blossoming in the emptiness of their shared space.

The shared bed, therefore, became a paradoxical arena of contrasts: moments of unexpected tenderness shattered by currents of doubt and restraint. Sometimes, as sleep eluded them, Caroline caught Thomas's hand briefly under the throw, a fleeting touch charged with unspoken affection, only to be withdrawn seconds later as both recoiled from the implications. Other times, she felt the gentle pressure of his body shift nearer, a silent invitation that summoned her own response, yet the chasm of uncertainty held her back, a barrier of old fears and new realities. In these moments, the heat of the fire their bodies' warmth seemed to stand in stark opposition to the cold distance they still maintained between hearts and souls.

Beneath the surface of these struggles lay a deeper transformation, an alchemy of emotion and desire that neither could fully grasp but that both were irrevocably shaped by. Caroline's need for control, long her armor against vulnerability, encountered Thomas's quiet insistence on presence and connection. The bed, narrow and unyielding as it was, became a crucible where her defenses were tested, where the fortress of solitude she had built began to show cracks through which love and trust could seep. Meanwhile, Thomas, whose life had been shaped by survival instincts and a guarded heart, discovered a reservoir of patience and tenderness he had long hidden beneath layers of practical stoicism.

As the nights wore on, the space between them seemed to shift imperceptibly, a hair's breadth at a time, toward something more profound. They began to anticipate the brush of a hand, the shared whisper of breath, the vulnerability in a glance exchanged in the darkness. Their physical closeness became a language of its own a silent code of tenderness and restraint, fraught with the tension of unspoken promises. The bed was no longer merely a space of survival but a place where their identities faded into one another, where the boundaries between Caroline and Thomas dissolved into the simple human need for touch and reassurance.

Yet this intimacy was shadowed by the ever-present awareness of Agnes Pryce's watchful gaze and the village's unforgiving judgment. The stakes were impossibly high; their survival depended on concealment and conformity. Every tenderness shared in the quiet darkness risked exposure in the harsh light of dawn. Caroline's analytical mind churned incessantly, mapping out risks and consequences, while Thomas's instincts remained taut, ready to shield them both from any threat. Their shared bed was both sanctuary and battleground, a place where desire warred with fear, and where the promise of love glimmered despite the dangers.

In moments of rare candor, when exhaustion claimed them beyond resistance, their arms would involuntarily reach across the boundary they maintained. The heat of their skin against skin was a revelation a reminder that beneath the veneer of survival and the artifice of their assumed roles were two souls yearning for connection and acceptance. Caroline would feel the steady beat of Thomas's heart beneath her ear, a soothing pulse that rooted her in the present, while Thomas found comfort in the solidity of her presence, a silent affirmation that he was no longer alone in this unforgiving past.

But these instances of closeness were always tempered by the complex web of emotions that tangled them. Caroline's mind rebelled against the softness blooming inside her, wrestling the warmth of Thomas's touch into a tight coil of refusal. Her past modern, independent, self-sufficient whispered of boundaries and protocols, cautioning against the surrender of control that love demanded. Thomas, too, carried his own scars, a past marked by survival rather than surrender, teaching him to expect loss and betrayal rather than the quiet fortitude that intimacy required.

Still, each shared night drew them closer not just physically but emotionally. Caroline's habitual coolness thawed in the face of Thomas's gentle persistence, and the sharp edges of distrust softened in the glow of his careful hands and steady gaze. Their bedroom the tiny space beneath the sloping roof became a crucible where their relationship was forged anew, not by the demands of the book or the rigid social mores of Bramleigh, but by the slow, exquisite growth of genuine affection.

Every whispered confession in the dim hours, every tentative brush of fingers beneath the blanket, built a fragile trust that neither had dared to hope for days before. When finally Caroline caught herself leaning into Thomas's embrace, her breath catching on the cusp of surrender, she realized that the bed they shared was far more than mere furniture. It was the silent witness to their evolving bond, the place where the past and the present collided to create the possibility of a future shaped not by fear or obligation but by the dangerous, exhilarating promise of love.

Yet even as they edged toward tenderness, the struggle between control and surrender remained palpable. Caroline's fingers twitched with the impulse to pull away at the first spark of heat, reasons flooding her mind to justify distance even as her heart yearned to bridge the gap. Thomas understood this dance well; he held back his own desires, feeling the delicate balance required to nurture trust without overwhelming fragile boundaries. Their nights became a silent negotiation, an intricate choreography of restraint and longing, where every movement mattered and every glance carried weight.

The shared bed was a crucible of contradictions cold and warm, distance and closeness, fear and trust. Here, in this small space carved out against the vast backdrop of an unforgiving century, two souls coexisted in a delicate tension between need and hesitation, a tension that promised transformation if only they could find the courage to embrace vulnerability without fear. The struggle was far from over, but in the quiet glow of twilight, with Thomas's steady breath warming her cheek and the softness of fabric against skin, Caroline allowed herself for a brief moment to imagine a future where love, not fear, dictated the boundaries of their shared life. And in that fragile hope, the shared bed ceased to be a mere necessity and became the hearth where the slow-burning fire of their connection kindled into something lasting and true.

The heavy oak door of their modest cottage closed with a soft thud behind them, shutting out the fading light of a bleak winter afternoon and the murmuring voices of the village beyond. Through the narrow leaded windows, the last slanting rays of sun filtered weakly, casting long shadows across worn wooden floorboards that creaked with the chill. Caroline Moore paused just inside, the weight of their precarious situation settling anew on her shoulders as her eyes flickered over the sparse furnishings a coarse linen bed with a rough woolen coverlet, a small table cluttered with unwashed cups, and a cracked hearth stone that had long since lost its warmth. This cramped space was to be their sanctuary, their stage, and the crucible wherein their contrived marriage would either be woven into fragile authenticity or unravel into dangerous fiction. Her carefully constructed world of empirical history and neat certainties fractured beneath the inexorable demands of this place and time.

Thomas Reed stepped beside her, the breadth of his body filling the threshold like a sentinel guarding a fragile secret. His dark eyes held a trace of the day's fatigue, yet beneath it glimmered a cautious softening that no longer sought to dominate or retreat but rather to bridge the growing chasm between them. The forced proximity of their bed a shared bed, as dictated by the book's merciless law and the staunchly unforgiving mores of Bramleigh loomed as both a symbol of their public façade and an arena of private tension. Each night, the bed was both respite and battleground, where public displays of marital tenderness were prescribed and scrutinized by the ever-watchful eyes of their neighbors, while behind the closed door, restraint was an unspoken rule, born of fear and unfamiliarity.

Earlier that day they had barely escaped the sharp, suspicious gaze of Agnes Pryce, the village widow whose inscrutable countenance bore the weight of silent judgment. Agnes's subtle power lay not in loud condemnation but in the quiet orchestration of village gossip and legal threads that ensnared outsiders with ruthless precision. Caroline knew that any misstep, any hint of discord, could unravel their tenuous acceptance and invite swift expulsion or worse. The social laws of the 18th century were not merely rules but living currents through which the village's order surged unceasingly; to stand outside that flow was to risk being swept away.

Yet beneath the necessity of performance, a fragile ember kindled a tenderness that neither dared fully recognize in the daylight but that warmed the dark corners of their shared nights. Tonight, as the cold crept around the cottage and the wind whispered secrets through age-worn shutters, Caroline found herself sitting on the edge of their bed, fingers tracing the delicate embroidery of a pillowcase by candlelight, her mind spinning with contradictions. The book's stern instructions had shifted hours before, no longer dictating only practical survival but weaving in a more insistent call for emotional openness. It commanded honesty an honesty that threatened the carefully erected walls of her heart, constructed through years of scholarly obsession with control and detachment.

Thomas moved quietly, shedding his coat and sitting beside her with a gentleness that seemed almost reverent in this intimate space. He was close enough that she felt the warmth radiate from his skin, mingling with the faint, dusty scent of woodsmoke and earth. His eyes held an uncertainty, but also a growing resolve a need to reach beyond the awkwardness to something authentic, perhaps even redemptive. Caroline's breath hitched as the ache of their predicament settled deeper: two souls tethered by necessity but yearning for something more profound, yet caught in the delicate dance of public perception and private vulnerability.

Their marriage, a construct imposed by fear and law, demanded not only appearances but the weaving of believable intimacies. In the village square, they were a unit husband and wife who held hands with subtle ease, exchanged whispered courtesies, and shared stolen glances beneath the stern arch of the church tower. Among curious, wide-eyed neighbors, their closeness needed to border on the natural, the effortless, lest the shadow of suspicion darken their fragile refuge. Caroline had observed the couples of Bramleigh their gentle touches, the quick, knowing smiles shared beneath veils of quiet acceptance. Public tenderness was not mere display but a language of survival, a dance between connection and decorum.

Yet when the doors of their cottage clicked shut behind the village's watchful gaze, the language shifted. Words fell away, unrehearsed gestures replaced rehearsed ones, and the boundaries of their forced partnership bent under the weight of genuine sentiment. Caroline, so often the architect of control and certainty, felt the tremors of something irrational and disarming. To reach out, to let herself lean into Thomas's strength rather than pushing him away, required a surrender she had never before allowed. It was in these small moments the brush of fingers, a shared breath, a whisper that the veneer of the book's mandate began to peel away, revealing the fragile, pulsing core of trust beneath.

Tonight, as they settled beneath the rough quilt, Thomas's hand found hers with a tentative certainty. His thumb traced the back of her hand, slow and deliberate, igniting sparks of warmth that seeped through layers of guardedness. Caroline's pulse quickened, a mingling of fear and longing swirling in her chest. The shadows danced on the walls, caught between the flickering candlelight and the encroaching night, mirroring the fluid tension between them at once charged with promise and laced with caution.

Despite the closeness, restraint clung to their interactions like morning mist, dense with unspoken fears and the fragility of their constructed reality. To leap too far into intimacy too quickly risked not only their social standing but the very survival that the book's strange magic demanded. Yet to deny the growing bond that unmistakable physical and emotional magnetism was equally perilous, threatening to fracture the precarious balance of their fragile union.

Thomas's voice, low and measured, broke the silence: "Caroline, I " He faltered, the vulnerability behind his usual composure stark in the quiet room. "I know this is strange. All of it. But I want you to know... that I don't want this to merely be an act anymore."

She turned to him, searching his eyes for sincerity, finding there the flicker of a man who, like her, stood at the crossroads of fear and hope. It was a confession wrapped in shadows, delicate yet fierce. Caroline's lips parted but no words came; instead, she allowed her hand to tighten around his, a silent admission of the tumult inside her.

Their first kiss that night was hesitant a brush of warmth against cold lips that spoke of tentative trust rather than passion's blaze. The kiss deepened with careful slowness, a mutual exploration fraught with the residue of their mutual unfamiliarity, the stolen softness a balm against the hardness of their reality. It was both a promise and a question, a tentative bridge between two worlds, two centuries, two souls adrift in converging tides.

Yet even as desire flickered, restraint remained their sentinel. The world outside the walls demanded order and propriety, and inside, the residual wariness shaped their closeness like a chisel. They were strangers learning to inhabit a shared skin, feeling the contours and edges with cautious hands. Every touch was layered with history both personal and communal imprinted by rules and roles far older and harsher than any contemporary romance. Caroline's yearning to understand and to map this new intimacy was balanced by the urgent necessity to survive the brutal, unforgiving gaze of Bramleigh society.

In the days that followed, their public performances became more nuanced, their interactions honed by necessity and a growing, if reluctant, fondness. They walked through the village as a married pair should her hand lightly resting on his arm, their silences filled with the comfortable cadence of shared burdens. At the market, the women of Bramleigh cast appraising glances, some cold, some curious, but all weighed with the expectations of the tight-knit community whose lifeblood was conformity and continuity.

Behind closed doors, Caroline found herself rehearsing words she dared not speak aloud, contemplating the thin line between survival and surrender. Thomas's presence became a paradoxical comfort and challenge, his steadfastness both shelter and mirror, reflecting her deepest vulnerabilities. The bed where they slept was no longer just a prop but a terrain of shifting desires, fraught with the tension of unspoken feelings and the slow, inexorable beat of hearts edging toward a truth neither was yet ready to fully claim.

One evening, long after the village settled into its slumber, Caroline awoke to the faint sound of Thomas's breathing, steady and close. The candle had guttered low, casting the room in a soft, wavering glow. She reached out, resting her hand lightly against his chest, feeling the gradual rise and fall of muscle and breath beneath her palm. The moment stretched, fragile and exquisite, a silent conversation between two souls navigating the uncertain landscape of newfound affection. Thomas shifted, turning toward her with an expression that was at once tentative and tender, his fingers seeking hers in the darkness as though anchoring himself to a fragile lifeline.

"You don't have to pretend with me," he whispered, voice rough with earnestness. "Not here, not now."

Caroline offered the faintest smile, eyes glistening with unshed tears that were neither of sorrow nor joy but of release. "Neither do you," she replied, her voice barely audible in the stillness. The barriers that had once defined her sense of self control, detachment, distance crumbled in that quiet intimacy, replaced by a trembling vulnerability she had fought to suppress. In that vulnerable surrender, there bloomed something new: a tentative hope that amidst the turmoil of their forced journey, something genuine might take root.

Days blended into nights with a pulse that quickened and slowed in tandem with their growing connection. Each touch, each glance, each shared silence was a thread woven into the complex tapestry of their marriage. The public eye demanded a spectacle of normalcy, but within the private sanctum of their shared bedchamber, the performance dissolved in the warmth of honest presence. Their bodies and hearts learned the rhythms of consent and desire, threading together sensuality and emotion in a delicate balance that both comforted and challenged them.

Caroline, once resolute in her control, found herself yielding to moments of surrender, surprised by the sweetness of vulnerability and the strength it required. Thomas, who had begun as a stranger cloaked in mystery, revealed himself in tender openness, a man shaped by past wounds yet reaching toward new belonging. Each night, they peeled back the layers of their façade, their fingers tracing not only skin but the contours of trust and affection. It was a slow, intricate dance, choreographed by necessity but guided by growing love.

In the unspoken hush of dawn, as mist curled beyond the windowpane and birds heralded a new day, they lay entwined, the hard lines of their former lives softened by the promise of this shared existence. The book's arcane commands had brought them together, but it was the quiet tenderness between them the stolen touches in the dark, the exchanged smiles beneath vigilant scrutiny that began to rewrite the narrative of their fate.

Outside, the village kept its watchful vigil, the murmur of the past pressing firmly against their fragile present. But within this small chamber, amid the flickering candlelight and whispered confessions, Caroline and Thomas discovered a space where love could grow, unfettered by time, unbound by fear a testament to the enduring power of connection forged in the crucible of survival and shaped by the slow, steady flame of trust.

The bed was cramped, a narrow, creaking mattress stuffed with straw and old feathers that had seen better days a far cry from the plush comfort Caroline had once known in her own century. Yet, in this austere simplicity, the weight of their current reality pressed down on them far heavier than the lumpy bedding. The candlelight flickered timidly against the roughly plastered wall, casting long shadows that danced and shifted like restless spirits. Caroline lay rigid beneath the thin blanket, her fingers clenched at her sides as her mind spun in a whirl of thoughts she dared not voice. Despite the closeness forced upon them by necessity, a chasm of restraint yawned wide between them, filled with unspoken desire and the brittle crackle of tension.

Thomas, already clad in a threadbare linen shirt, lay beside her, his body a measured heat against the chill night air that slipped through the slight gap beneath the door. His eyes, dark and haunted by the day's perils, flicked toward Caroline often, tracing the sharp lines of her profile, the way her hair caught the flame's glow like spun gold, the subtle rise and fall of her breathing. Each glance was a tentative promise, a question unformed but urgent beneath the surface of propriety and fear. The physical proximity was both an invitation and a battleground. Neither dared the first step into the territory of vulnerability, where walls might crumble and truths spill forth.

There were moments earlier that evening when, in the common room of the cottage, they had pretended ease, laughing quietly over a shared cup of watered ale, their hands brushing accidentally or perhaps not so accidentally over the rough-hewn table. In the soft crackle of the hearth, Thomas had reached out to steady Caroline as she nearly toppled forward in the flicker of a sudden shudder. The brief, warm contact had lingered longer than necessary, a silent conversation of need and hesitation, desire restrained by the clattering chains of circumstance.

Yet, as they settled into the forced intimacy of shared quarters, a different rhythm took hold one woven with tension, unease, and the fragile beginnings of something heavier than mere obligation. The coldness between the sheets was symbolic of the distance they maintained, even in their proximity. Caroline's mind resisted the tide of warmth Thomas's presence evoked, clawing back to fragments of control anchored in facts and reason. But deep inside, beneath layers guarded by years of academic discipline and personal prudence, a quivering yearning stirred a pulsing ache she had long suppressed, now kindled by the steady strength of the man beside her.

Thomas was no less conflicted. His gaze often warmed with something more profound than mere camaraderie, a tenderness entwined with protectiveness that seemed to grow heavier each day. Yet he was acutely aware of the fragile line he tread the whispers of suspicion in the village, the ever-watchful eyes of Agnes Pryce, the looming threat of exile if their façade failed. Every touch had to be measured, every moment of closeness calculated to avoid igniting scandal or worse.

The silence between them was dense with unspoken words. Caroline's usual eloquence failed her, replaced by the tremulous flutter in her chest that spoke of hidden fears and secret hopes. She felt the pulse of his breath, steady yet uneven in the darkness, and wondered if he battled the same tumultuous tides that roiled within her. Their forced pairing had become more than a matter of survival; the walls they had constructed around their hearts began to crumble, crumbling fragment by fragment in the quiet rebellion of their private yearnings.

When Thomas finally reached out again, this time brushing a stray lock of hair from Caroline's forehead, the touch was featherlight a tentative caress that neither rushed nor demanded. It was a confession of sorts, a whispered admission that beneath the façades of duty and caution, there thrummed a beat of raw, aching desire. Caroline closed her eyes, leaning into the warmth, the solidity of him a tether that grounded her in a storm of emotions she scarcely understood. Her hand inched toward his, hesitating an inch away before brushing lightly against his knuckles, the electric current of their contact igniting sparks long denied.

This quiet communion became their secret language, a soft covenant that existed solely in these stolen moments when the world beyond the thin walls of their refuge dissolved into insignificance. The flickering candle's glow bore witness to hands tentatively exploring contours not yet mapped, hearts daring to beat in tandem under the muted safety of night. Their breaths mingled in the small space between them, a symphony of unvoiced hopes and mutual longing.

Yet, with every inch of proximity gained, an invisible barrier seemed to ascend, born from the shadows of their pasts and the uncertain futures that awaited them. Caroline's fear of dependence, nurtured through years of self-reliance and intellectual armor, warred with the dangerous allure of surrender. Thomas grappled with his own demons the lingering doubt that he belonged neither wholly in this past nor in the time from which they were torn. Each moment of closeness carried the weight of these inner battles, the tenderness underscored by the raw ache of vulnerability.

The night deepened, wrapped in the cold hush of winter's breath, and as the few embers in the hearth settled into ash, so too did a fragile peace settle between them a truce forged in shared solitude and whispered promises. Caroline felt her defenses soften just enough to allow a tentative warmth to spread from the tip of her fingers through her chest, blooming quietly in the sacred silence of their shared bed.

Their bodies remained pressed side by side yet careful, the space between them a testament to restraint and the slow build of trust. In these stolen moments, words were unnecessary. The language of their hearts spoke louder through the subtle brush of fingers, the gentle rise and fall of chests in synchronized rhythm, the way their eyes sought each other out in the gilded flicker of fading candlelight. It was in these fragile exchanges that the deepest yearnings found their voice a whispered promise that perhaps, despite the odds, this fragile bond could bloom into something real, something unbreakable.

As sleep finally claimed them, their limbs intertwined in a half-seeking, half-guarded embrace, the quiet murmur of breathing was laced with a new, tentative hope. Beneath the weight of history, danger, and the relentless passage of time, two souls, so recently strangers but now inextricably bound, dared to dream of a future where the heart might triumph over fear, and love might be their ultimate passage.

First Kiss

The small chamber was cloaked in shadows, the only light spilling from the flickering candle nestled in a rough iron sconce fixed to the wooden beam above their shared bed. The night outside was still but biting cold, seeping through cracks in the walls and chilling the modest blanket beneath which they huddled. Caroline's heart beat unevenly, its tempo shifting wildly between anticipation and anxiety, each pulse echoing the dissonance of her thoughts. Here, in the most vulnerable of settings, the narrow bed they were forced to share felt less like a refuge and more like a crucible, distilling every suppressed emotion until it was raw and undeniable. The silence between them was thick, heavier than the simplicity of the moment warranted, but born of a weighty understanding. They existed there suspended between the past and the present, two strangers compelled by a strange fate to inhabit roles they did not choose husband and wife yet thrust into an intimacy that defied any cold assumption of mere survival.

Caroline's gaze fell away from the dancing candlelight to Thomas, whose profile was softened by the shadows, the lines of his face sharpened by a faint lucidity born of the dim glow. His eyes, luminous pools in the low light, held a tentative hopefulness, mixed with doubt, uncertainty, and something deeper—something undeniably tender. His presence was a warm contrast to the chill that permeated the cabin, a steady anchor against the storm of thoughts that threatened to undo her carefully constructed composure. She had spent weeks weaving facts and histories into a protective armor, trusting only in knowledge, distancing herself from the reckless currents of human emotion. Yet here, beneath that low ceiling and between these thin walls, the rules shifted imperceptibly. It was as though the very air they breathed conspired to unravel their distance, to midwife a closeness both electric and terrifying.

Their bodies, pressed beneath the rough

linen sheets, followed the unconscious choreography of proximity slight brushes of skin, tentative shifts of weight each contact a spark with the potential to ignite or consume. Caroline felt the warmth of Thomas's breath as he exhaled slowly, his chest rising and falling with a quiet steadiness that spoke of restraint as much as desire. She was meticulous by nature, trained to analyze, to disassemble and understand the logic of human behavior through historical contexts, yet her own reactions defied simple explanation; a fierce protectiveness mixed with a longing that unsettled her more than she admitted. The lies of their charade posing as a married couple had slowly, resistibly morphed into something more authentic and complicated. The delicate balance between roleplay and reality blurred with every stolen glance and small gesture, their pretense becoming a fragile truth neither fully brave enough to voice.

Thomas shifted, a subtle movement that closed the infinitesimal gap between them. His fingers, calloused from unseen hardships, brushed back a stray lock of hair from Caroline's temple. The gesture was tentative, reverent, as though he feared the fragility of the moment might shatter in an instant. Caroline's breath caught, her control slipping as the warmth of his touch blossomed against her skin. There was an unspoken apology in his eyes a recognition of their shared vulnerability amidst a world that tolerated no weakness. The weight of their circumstances pressed on her relentlessly, yet now there was also an intense, unspoken yearning that both terrified and exhilarated her. It was as though the night itself held its breath, the silence charged with a kind of electric suspense that only those standing on the edge of surrender truly understand.

She turned to face him, their eyes locking in a gaze that seemed to bridge centuries, to reach into the secret chambers of each other's hearts. Caroline's hands trembled, a reflection of the tempest within. This was a battlefield where defenses crumbled, and she found herself disarmed, captivated by the worn sincerity that etched lines of experience and kindness into

Thomas's features. He inched closer, a question lingering in the tilt of his head, in the slow, deliberate way he sought permission through the depths of her stare. With no need for words, she granted it, the smallest nod sealing a pact forged in the quiet desperation of two souls finding solace in each other.

The first kiss was unhurried, tentative, a fragile weaving of lips that spoke of doubt and hope intertwined. It was a contact that brushed against nerves, igniting fires both startling and gentle. For Caroline, it was a revelation, a delicate fracture in the facade of control she had long wielded like a shield. It held a promise of surrender, of trust born not from reason alone but from the simmering heat of shared humanity. Thomas responded with an earnestness that was at once tender and commanding, his hand cupping her cheek with reverent care, as if afraid to mar the fragile newly formed connection. The taste of the past mingled with the present the faint musk of worn linen and the warmth of breath mingled with unspoken promises and the gravity of lives forever changed.

As they pulled back slowly, lingering in the softness of the moment, the weight of the cottage's silence returned, but it was no longer oppressive. Instead, it felt like a veil lifted, a boundary crossed that had once seemed insurmountable. There was electricity in the space between them, a powerful undercurrent that promised more, more understanding, more passion, more the kind of vulnerability that could heal or break. Caroline's hands found their way to Thomas's chest, her fingers tracing the steady beat of his heart beneath the worn fabric of his shirt. For a fleeting moment, the temporal boundaries that dictated their existence faded, leaving only the intimate truth of two imperfect people bound together by necessity and now by choice. The room, their shared bed, once a stage for pretense and survival, had transformed into a sanctuary where love began its slow, glowing ascent.

In that fragile space, hope blossomed alongside fear, the promise of a future unwritten and uncertain. The kiss was a beginning, a crack in the ice that covered the deep waters of their guarded hearts. It was an offering of warmth against the cold world outside, a silent vow that in this strange and unforgiving past, they had found something worth daring for each other.

Winter's Grip

The bitter breath of winter crept relentlessly into the cramped cottage that Caroline and Thomas now called home, each day a slow, grinding battle against the relentless cold that gnawed at their bones and frayed their spirits. The thick, tattered curtains that hung in heavy folds over the single mullioned window did little to keep out the sharp edge of the biting wind that swept in from the barren, snow-laden fields beyond Bramleigh. The hearth, their sole source of warmth, burned low and sputtered as they scavenged for every last bit of firewood, their meager supply dwindling swiftly with no honest prospects of replenishment until the thaw of spring. It was an unforgiving season, one that stripped away all illusions of comfort and forced every pretense into submission beneath the stark reality of survival.

Caroline, ever meticulous and composed in

her careful arrangement of historical facts and rigid plans, found herself crumbling under the oppressive weight of discomfort. The chill seemed to seep through her skin, a hostile invasion that no amount of wool or layered garments could fully repel. The exhaustion that clung to her was relentless, as if the very air had thickened into a suffocating fog, heavy with sickness and despair. One morning, she awoke shivering violently beneath her threadbare blankets, a fever burning beneath her pale skin, her breath ragged and shallow. The very control she clung to the knowledge and precision that had once been her fortress now slipped through her fingers like dry sand, powerless against the frailty that illness imposed. She was forced to surrender, for the first time without fight, to a vulnerability so absolute it terrified her.

Thomas was not blind to her suffering. The steady flame of his concern, kindled long before this winter's grip had tightened, roared into life with an intensity that surprised even him. There was something in watching Caroline   bright, exacting Caroline, whose every gesture had once been measured and deliberate   now diminished and fragile, that stirred a protective fervor unlike any he had ever known. His hands, calloused from the physical labors that sustained their survival, moved with gentleness as he arranged the straw mattress near the fire and tended the small pot of herbal tea he had managed to brew from dried leaves he'd scavenged. Each day, he remained by her side, his presence a quiet defiance against the harshness without and the sickness within.

Their roles, once defined by the necessity of charade   husband and wife only in appearance, surviving by the narrowest of social margins began to blur beneath the weight of these intimate trials. Thomas's usual rough-hewn composure softened whenever he looked at Caroline lying so vulnerable. His touch became more tentative, more tender, as though afraid to break the fragile vessel of her settling fever. Words of comfort, simple and sincere, cascaded from him with a warmth that melted the façade Caroline had so carefully maintained. In these stolen moments, the pretense of their marriage dissolved, revealing something far more complicated and true: a bond forged not merely from necessity but from a shared humanity pushed to its limits.

Caroline, in her fevered delirium, sensed the shifting nature of their connection as keenly as she felt the chill that wracked her body. The walls she had built around her heart, around her fears of dependence crumbled imperceptibly with each act of gentleness Thomas bestowed. There was a reckoning in her soul, a quiet admission that trust was not weakness but the very essence of survival. She could feel Thomas's breath against her hair, steady and grounding, a tether to the present when the fevered shadows threatened to pull her under. His steadfast devotion offered a new kind of knowledge, one no book could teach: the language of vulnerability spoken through touch and silent presence.

Outside, the wind howled as though echoing their internal turmoil, the world reduced to bleak hues of gray and white beneath a sky heavy with snow. The mere act of tending to firewood, hauling it through drifted paths, and securing enough food to stave off starvation became Herculean tasks. Thomas shouldered the burden of these daily trials with a grim resolve, unwilling to let despair invade the precious sanctuary he and Caroline created in their small refuge. Each time he returned with scant provisions or a few more sticks for the fire, Caroline felt a swell of gratitude mingling with a burgeoning affection that demanded recognition beyond coercion or practical necessity.

Their cottage, simple and near damp with age, seemed to shrink under the relentless cold, as if winter itself sought to suffocate whatever fragile hope lingered within its walls. Water froze thick in their limited buckets, forcing Thomas to risk venturing farther afield to the half-frozen stream, teeth clenched against the bitter air. Food stores, already sparse due to their outsider status and limited means, dwindled faster as hunger gnawed relentlessly at their resilience. Caroline's appetite was nonexistent, dulled by illness and underlying fear, but Thomas insisted she eat small morsels, coaxing with hushed words and firm insistence that carried the authority of a man no longer willing to tolerate fragility but one who revered her life above all else.

It was during one especially brutal night, when the snowstorm raged outside in unrelenting fury, that Caroline's fever reached its zenith. She was delirious, speaking in a half-forgotten accent and voices from dreams she did not understand. Thomas, sitting vigil by the sputtering hearth, refused to leave her side, his fingers tracing gentle patterns against the back of her hand, grounding her in moments when her tether to reality thinned dangerously. Each crackle of the fire was a kind of prayer, a whispered plea for endurance, and in the flickering light, he glimpsed not just the woman she was but the soul she was becoming one capable of surrendering control, embracing imperfection, and loving without reservation.

In these dark hours, Caroline's defenses not only fell away but revealed the aching loneliness that had been hidden beneath her disciplined exterior. Thomas felt it with a piercing clarity: the years of self-imposed isolation, the walls of history and logic that had kept her apart from others, were now cracked and vulnerable. His own heart, once guarded and uncertain, opened wider in response, carved by the suffering and the unexpected tenderness they shared. The performance of husband and wife morphed into a lived reality, fragile but undeniable, forged in the crucible of their shared hardships.

Dawn broke pale and weak through the frosted panes, casting jagged shadows across the room where Caroline lay resting, her fever finally breaking with a slow, faint sigh of relief. Her eyes fluttered open to meet Thomas's steady gaze no longer that of a stranger, but of a man who had become a sanctuary. There was an unspoken understanding in the way they looked at each other; in this small corner of a merciless time, they were no longer actors clinging to a script but companions, equal parts healed and hurting, drawn irrevocably together by forces beyond their control.

The snow still piled high outside, an

unyielding blanket that muted the world into silence, yet within their cottage, warmth stirred not just from the fire but from something tender and fierce, flickering alive in the space between their entwined hands. Thomas's voice, low and steady, broke through the quiet with promises not of survival alone but of care, commitment, and the slow blossoming of a love neither had dared to name until now. Caroline felt the resistances within her soften, the iron grip of rationality eased by the gentle gravity pulling her toward surrender. Trust was no longer a requirement imposed by the arcane book that bound them, but a choice they made of their own volition, fragile but fortifying against the relentless winter outside.

As days lengthened with the faint promise of spring, the hardships continued, but the fear that once shadowed their every glance gave way to a profound resilience anchored in connection. Thomas, once a stranger, was now the keeper of Caroline's whispered concerns and fragile hopes, his strength measured not just in muscle but in patience and unwavering presence. Caroline, in turn, found solace in the uncharted territory of emotional trust, learning that love's true power was not in control or knowledge but in the brave surrender to another's care.

Winter had stripped them bare, exposing weaknesses and fears too long buried beneath surface calm. Yet beneath that bareness, it had also forged a bond unbreakable by frost or time. In the hush between snowfalls, amid cracked hearths and shared breaths, Caroline and Thomas had discovered something far more enduring than the mere survival of body   a love tempered by hardship, vulnerable yet steadfast, and born not from destiny but from the courage to stand together when the cold was at its cruelest.

The biting cold of the Bramleigh winter had transformed the village into a landscape of frost-hardened earth and skeletal trees, their bare branches scraping a gray sky like tremulous fingers. Inside the modest cottage that Caroline Moore and Thomas Reed now called home, a dim fire struggled against the chill that seeped into the worn wooden beams. Caroline lay curled beneath a patchwork quilt, her breath shallow and uneven, a sheen of sweat glistening on her pale brow. The sickness had come swiftly, as if the damp, unyielding air had conspired with the cruel season to break her indefatigable spirit. She, who had prided herself on vigilance, on control over every circumstance, was now laid low, vulnerable and fragile in a way she had never allowed herself to be.

Thomas sat vigil beside her, the hard lines of his usually assured face softened with concern. The roles they had played their carefully rehearsed masquerade of matrimony were strips of a simpler facade now discarded in the face of real, unfiltered human need. No longer was it a performance of social compliance to avoid the prying eyes of Bramleigh; here and now, his care was an echo of something genuine, something deeper stirring within him. He murmured her name softly, brushing damp strands of chestnut hair from her pale face, his fingers lingering as though reluctant to let go. The heat of his hand was a tether, a quiet promise sent through the cold, reminding her she was not alone.

Caroline's eyes fluttered open momentarily, a flicker of recognition and discomfort crossing her gaze. She tried to speak, to articulate the inward storm roiling beneath her ribs, yet her voice was a frail whisper barely carrying the weight of her fears. The sickness was merciless, draining not only her strength but her well-honed reserve of composure. She had entered this forced arrangement with the confidence of a historian well-versed in the era's brutal realities, but now, confronted with her own frailty, even her knowledge seemed inadequate. The past was unforgiving, its winters harsher than the hearth's feeble flame, and Caroline was beginning to understand painters only capture the shadow of suffering, never the full descent into it.

Thomas moved closer, his touch deft and gentle as he dampened a cloth with warm broth, pressing it to her clammy forehead. His eyes, dark and searching, held an unspoken question, a yearning for a reciprocity beyond mere survival. Those moments silent, attentive, filled with a tender urgency wove a new kind of intimacy between them. The cold had stripped away the layers of pretense, exposing raw truths neither had dared admit. Caroline, so accustomed to holding others at arm's length with precise words and guarded emotions, found a strange solace in this unguarded care. The heat of the fever was not merely in her body but in the awakening of trust, a surrender to vulnerability she had long resisted.

As twilight deepened outside, casting long shadows through the narrow windowpanes, the cottage became a sanctuary of hushed dreads and tentative hope. Thomas tended to her needs without demand or expectation, his every action a quiet defiance of the harsh world beyond their walls. He bathed her aching limbs with water warmed over embers, his touch both practical and reverent, as though preserving a fragile bloom against the encroaching frost. When Caroline's trembling convulsions convulsed anew, he caught her in a steady embrace, his arms a bulwark against the storm that raged within her. In those moments, the artifice of their imposed marriage dissolved, replaced by a nascent devotion that no book or law could command.

Caroline's mind, usually so sharp and controlled, vacillated between fevered delirium and shards of lucidity. She recalled the weight of the unmarked book, the mysterious compulsion that had thrust her and Thomas across centuries, binding them in a pact of survival. Yet now, faced with the tangible reality of pain and dependence, such abstract bindings seemed distant, almost irrelevant. Her thoughts softened, not just from physical weakness but from an emotional thawing. The walls she had erected around her heart meticulously built through years of scholarship and solitude began to crumble under the relentless tenderness of Thomas's care.

The fire sputtered low as Thomas lit another candle, its flickering flame casting dancing shadows that painted the room in hues of amber and gold. He spoke little, his language one of steadfastness and presence rather than words, understanding that sometimes silence was the grandest comfort of all. His gaze never wavered from her face, cataloging every rise and fall of her chest, every subtle change in expression, as if memorizing her very existence. The unspoken admission of his growing love was palpable in the way his fingers traced idle patterns along her arm, the hesitance and hope mingling in his touch like uncharted territory.

Caroline, in this weakened state, found herself allowing moments of quiet reflection on the improbable path that had led her here. Once a woman defined by rationality, now she was tethered to a man by suffering and compassion, by the fragile, beautiful thread of mutual reliance.

She could no longer convince herself that this was all a calculated act. The lines between pretense and reality blurred with every stolen glance, every sigh caught in the smoky air. The ghost of their faux marriage gave way to something real, a foundation built from the shared crucible of hardship.

As the night deepened, the winter winds rattling the cottage's thin shutters, Caroline drifted in and out of sleep, her breathing gradually stabilizing beneath Thomas's unwavering watch. He remained at her side, resolute in his unyielding care, his very being a shield against the cold, both outside and within. The steady pulse of his presence was a balm, a quiet testament to an affection that transcended circumstance. It was the purest form of love forged not in grand declarations, but in the patient labor of tending, watching, and waiting.

With dawn's fragile light seeping through the frost, Caroline stirred once more, her eyelids fluttering open to find Thomas's face close, lined with exhaustion but radiant in its devotion. The decline in her fever was slow but undeniable, an echo of the strength their shared bond had already kindled. She reached out, her trembling fingers intertwining with his, a silent confession that needed no words. In that moment, the barriers of time, the doubts of identity, and the harshness of their situation fell away like snow melting under the spring sun. What remained was the undeniable truth: they were no longer merely strangers cast together by fate's whim, but two souls irrevocably bound by care, love, and the promise of a future forged in the crucible of the past.

The relentless winter wind howled outside, rattling the worn shutters of the little cottage they had come to call home, as though the very elements conspired to remind Caroline Moore of the precariousness of their existence in this unforgiving century. Inside, the dim glow of a single candle cast flickering shadows on the roughly plastered walls, revealing the particulate dust suspended in the cold air. Caroline lay huddled beneath a threadbare quilt on the narrow bed, her cheek flushed with fever. The ache in her bones was unrelenting, and her usual bastion of control the sharpness of her mind felt dulled and distant, submerged beneath waves of weakness and discomfort. The historian, who had prided herself for years on stoicism and self-sufficiency, found herself stripped bare of pretenses, vulnerable in ways she had never tolerated before.

Thomas Reed sat beside her, hands busy stroking a damp cloth against her clammy forehead, eyes shadowed with concern but steady with determination. He moved with a quiet confidence born not just of physical capability but of genuine care, an attentiveness that went beyond mere duty or performance. For days now, he had tended to her, fetching water from the well despite the biting cold, coaxing her to eat spoonfuls of broth when her appetite wavered, and sitting vigilant through restless nights when fever dreams claimed her. It was a tenderness she had not anticipated, one that unsettled her pride yet offered an unfamiliar comfort. Every small action threaded by his presence was imbued with a sincerity that belied the charade of their fabricated marriage a gesture that was no longer performance but something deeply real.

Caroline's insistence on control, her iron grip on fact and evidence, had been both shield and weapon ever since they arrived in Bramleigh. The past was, after all, the domain she understood best; through it, she had carved an identity rooted in certainty rather than caprice. Yet here, in the grip of sickness and far from her modern world's resurgence of antiseptic care and medicine, her knowledge could only provide cold comfort. She realized now how dependent she had become on Thomas, and that realization pried open the walls around her heart with painful but necessary force. Her body, betrayed by frailty, demanded surrender, and though resistance lingered in her mind, it began to ebb under the slow, steady tide of his persistence and kindness.

The night had grown colder, and the mist outside had thickened into a swirling curtain that obscured the world beyond their fragile sanctuary. Thomas adjusted the fire, then returned to her side, lowering his voice to a soft murmur as he wiped her damp hair from her forehead. "You need rest, Caroline. Your body is fighting for you, but it cannot do it alone." His words, simple in their truth, reverberated in the silent spaces of the room. For the first time, she let herself lean into that admission not the illness itself but the reality of needing another, of allowing herself to be cradled rather than bolstering alone against adversity.

There was no embarrassment in her eyes when she met his gaze, only a tentative acceptance. The firewall of her independence was breached, layer by layer, by a presence that did not seek to dominate or diminish but to uphold and steady. In his touch, she found the echo of a promise, unspoken but potent the pledge not merely to endure beside her but to intertwine their fates beyond necessity, beyond pretense. It was an intricate dance of trust, woven in the quiet moments when words faltered, but meaning deepened.

Caroline's mind wandered to the twisted nature of their predicament strangers woven into a social tapestry that demanded they pose as husband and wife or face exile, persecution. Yet now, the lines between performance and reality blurred so finely that it was impossible to disentangle one from the other. The initial spark of irritation she had felt toward Thomas for complicating her controlled existence softened into a warmth that seeped into neglected crevices of her heart. Each day spent in his care eroded the armor she had so rigorously constructed over decades a fortress erected to keep vulnerability at bay but now revealing its cracks under the pressure of shared hardship.

She remembered how, in the library mere weeks ago, she had confronted the curious book with detachment, armed only by intellect. The discovery had seemed an academic puzzle, a relic's mystery to solve. But here, in the strain of tangible reality, the abstraction of history became an embodied, living experience marked by pain and compassion, transformation and surrender. She felt the weight of centuries pressing down, not as a scholar distant from her subject, but as a participant forced to reckon with the rawness of human need.

Thomas's presence was both balm and catalyst; his strength gave her permission to be weak, his steadfastness a safe harbor from the storm raging both outside and within. She faltered and fell into sleep, unrested yet relieved, and when she awoke, the morning light filtered pale through frost-laced windowpanes, catching in the tendrils of her disheveled hair. Thomas was still there, seated silently, as if his vigil bridged days and nights without notice. The enormity of it struck Caroline anew the depth of his commitment was no act of convenience but a thread binding them irrevocably to one another.

The vulnerability she had long equated with failure now shimmered with possibility, a kind of fragile strength discovered in the act of yielding. She reached out, her hand seeking his, fingers curling timidly around his strong palm. His smile was a beacon, soft and sure, answering the quiet inquiry in her eyes with a promise of companionship not born from circumstance alone but chosen in the crucible of shared trial.

As the days wore on, the cottage, once a mere stage for deception, transformed beneath the alchemy of their growing affection into something that felt like home a sanctuary forged not from bricks and mortar but from the invisible architecture of trust and tenderness. The harshness of the season remained unforgiving, but within those walls, the cold receded, replaced by a heat spun from glances laden with unspoken longing, touches lingering past propriety, and conversations that stripped away layers of guardedness.

Caroline pondered the incongruity of her transformation the woman who had valued control over every facet of her life now found herself willingly dependent on another, her vulnerability a doorway to a kind of freedom she had never imagined. The fear of losing herself, of being consumed by necessity, ebbed into an understanding that true strength lay not in solitary endurance but in the courage to trust, to lean fully into the warmth of human connection.

In those moments, watching Thomas move with care and calm efficiency, her heart whispered truths her rational mind had long denied. This was no longer the mimicry of marriage for survival's sake; it was the blossoming of something genuine, tender, and fiercely real. Their intertwined fingers, the shared breath of a quiet room, the steady beat of two hearts learning to synchronize all these were testimonies to a love emerging from the ashes of circumstance, unbidden yet undeniable.

The winter's grip slowed the world, but within the small, dim-lit cottage, a different season bloomed a season of revelation, of yielding, of a woman learning that dependence was not a chain but a bridge. Caroline Moore, the historian who once measured life in facts and evidence, now found herself shaped by the living narrative unfolding between them. It was, perhaps, the most profound story she had ever known.

Emotional Truths

Facing Fear of Dependence

Caroline sat by the dim glow of the hearth, the flickering flames casting long shadows against the rough-hewn walls of their modest Bramleigh cottage. The warmth was barely enough to stave off the penetrating chill of the encroaching winter, yet it was the coldness within her cold, stubborn, and unyielding that she wrestled against most fiercely of all. Her fingers curled tightly around the woolen shawl draped across her lap, knuckles white with the effort of grasping something beyond her reach: a fragile sense of surrender. Even here, miles and centuries away from the life she had known, the visceral edge of her fear remained steadfast. It gnawed at her, whispering old truths she thought she had buried the sharp ache of dependence, the dread of losing herself to another. It was not just survival that tethered her to Thomas Reed; it was something far more dangerous and intimate, a perilous crossing into the unknown terrain of trust.

The past hours had shaken her more than she would admit aloud, even to herself. Their forced proximity in this relentlessly foreign world had drawn them into a binding masquerade poised delicately between necessity and something that teetered, trembling, on the cusp of authenticity. Each shared glance, every hesitant touch, was a challenge to the walls she had built around her heart walls sturdy enough to weather years of solitary scholarship and the kind of cautious distance learned from knowing too well how easily people could disappear or betray. Caroline's life before steeped in analysis, in facts and timelines had always been hers alone to command. To yield even a fragment of control was an anathema, a concession that felt dangerously like weakness. Yet the book with its mysterious power, the merciless rules it imposed, and the relentless scrutiny of Agnes Pryce had slowly eroded those certainties. It had forced a reckoning she had no choice but to face: what did it mean to depend on another in this unyielding world, especially someone whose own vulnerabilities and fears were stitched together so closely with her own?

She traced the rim of her cup absently, eyes drifting to the window where skeletal branches scraped the night sky like fevered fingers, the biting wind whispering secrets she dared not fully hear. Her thoughts spiralled inward, circling memories of a past life where autonomy was her shield and knowledge her sword, wielded to fend off the unpredictable chaos of human connection. But here, stripped of the comforts of modernity, of certainties and clear boundaries, those strategies felt fragile and inadequate. Thomas stoic, patient Thomas had become more than just a partner in survival; he was a mirror reflecting the very parts of herself she least wanted to acknowledge. His quiet strength and the steady rhythm of his presence unsettled her more than the bitter cold or Agnes's watchful menace. There was something profoundly intimate in their shared vulnerability in a place that offered no refuge for weakness, and it scared her as much as the palpable threat of expulsion from this community.

For so long, Caroline had convinced herself that dependence was a chain, a loss of autonomy that suffocated the soul. She measured her worth in how self-sufficient she could remain, how fiercely she could control the tangles of her emotions and the unpredictable tides of human need. But the past weeks had upended that logic challenging her premade notions with every stolen smile, every whispered conversation in the low light where pretense faltered and stark truths loomed. To depend was not simply to be weak; it was a risk, a willingness to expose the rawness beneath the polished façade. And within that exposure, there was also the glimmer of something fiercely, stunningly alive a connection that demanded honesty, vulnerability, and ultimately, love.

The warmth from the fire crept slowly to her chilled fingers, coaxing a sensation that mingled uneasily with the restless flutter in her chest. She had imagined herself as the one holding tight to reason, the guardian of their plan, but in the unguarded moments after darkness fell, when Thomas's tired eyes softened with unsaid understanding, she found her resolve loosening. It terrified her. How could she reconcile her need for control with the instinct to lean into his steady presence? Could she embrace the truth that she was no longer just Caroline Moore, the historian who clung to facts and timelines, but someone irrevocably changed by this strange, unbidden bond? The question echoed relentlessly in the silence of the night, an incessant refrain that demanded more than intellectual assent but a surrender of spirit she was reluctant to grant.

A soft creak from the door drew her gaze, and Thomas stepped into the room with quiet steps, his face etched with lines of fatigue yet alight with a gentleness reserved only for her. Without words, he crossed the small space to sit beside her, the warmth radiating from his body a balm against the creeping dread. He reached out, his hand finding hers in the dimness, their fingers entwining with a familiarity that belied the briefness of their acquaintance in this era. In that touch, a universe of unspoken promises shimmered between them the promise of protection, but also of acceptance and mutual reliance. Caroline's breath caught as warmth bled through her veins, loosening the knots of resistance that had long been her armor. Yet even as comfort welled within her, the old fears clawed upward the fear that dependence might strip away her identity, that her spirit would drown in the tides of need.

Thomas's voice broke the silence, low and steady, threading through the chill. "You don't have to carry everything alone," he said gently, his eyes searching hers for permission to bridge the gap that years of guarded solitude had built. "We're in this together. Not because the book demands it, but because I want to be."

Caroline's heart thrummed painfully, the cold walls of self-imposed isolation beginning to crumble under the weight of his words. It was not just about survival anymore; it was about something impossible to quantify or control. It was about trust trust she had never fully allowed herself to give, and the terrifying freedom that came with it. She swallowed hard, willing herself to be honest, even when honesty felt like stepping off a precipice. "I'm scared," she admitted, voice barely above a whisper. "Not of the past or this life, but of what it means to need you. To let someone be that close."

His smile was soft, understanding, as if he, too, had wrestled with his own ghosts. "I think we're stronger because of it," he murmured. "Because in trusting someone else, we find strength we never knew we had."

The embers glowed more fiercely, casting a delicate halo around them as Caroline studied the man beside her his steady gaze, the quiet reassurance of his presence. It was not a weakness they shared but a profound humanity. In this world where every moment was a battle to belong, to survive, dependence was no longer a chain but a bridge. And as she let herself lean into that fragile bridge, she glimpsed the possibility of a life not dictated by fear but shaped by love. It was terrifying and exquisite all at once a surrender not to circumstance but to the raw, unfiltered truth of their connection.

As night deepened and the village outside hushed into a brittle silence, Caroline bowed her head to the embered hearth, feeling for the first time the tentative stirrings of peace. The boundaries she had erected with such care were beginning to blur, swept away by currents she could no longer resist. And in the uncharted darkness, she found the fragile light of hope a hope born not from control, but from the courage to face fear, to trust, and to love.

In the dim glow of the hearth, the crackling fire casting quivering shadows across the rough wooden beams of their modest Bramleigh cottage, Thomas Reed sat with his hands clasped tightly before him, his gaze fixed upon the flickering flames as if they contained some elusive answer. The weight of the room felt heavier tonight, pressed down not by the chill of the crisp winter air that seeped through the gaps in the aged walls, but by the gnawing ache that had long nested within the chambers of his heart a fear no heat, no company, could easily thaw. He had carried it quietly, a cloak of invisible threads woven from his own whispered uncertainties. The fear of being as transient as the very smoke curling from the fire; of being doomed to exist in the lives of others as merely a passing shadow, never more than a fleeting presence destined to vanish just as suddenly as he had emerged within this foreign past.

His thoughts meandered back to the initial shock of the book's unyielding magic, that strange instant when time had fractured, and he found himself yanked away from the familiar contours of the modern world into this austere 1770s village. The sensation of being uprooted without soil to cling to had left him brittle, unsettled. Amid the bustle of Bramleigh's rustic life so alien yet so insistently real he had been plagued by the overarching question: Was any of this real for him? Could this place, this time, ever be more than an interlude, a detour before he was yanked back to his true existence? Or was he, without his consent, condemned to flit through moments not meant for him, never claiming space in the lives around him, never truly belonging?

He glanced sideways toward Caroline, whose eyes were cast partly in shadow but illuminated enough to reveal the subtle lines of tension drawn across her forehead, the faint quiver of vulnerability she rarely exposed. She who sought control above all else, who meticulously cataloged history yet was now thrust into living it, had found, somewhat paradoxically, moments of surrender. Thomas admired her resilience but tonight, she seemed a mirror of his own trembling soul, the fortress around her walls seeming breached. He wanted to reach across the modest hearth and close the chasm that yawned between them, but the barriers came not only from circumstance but from the walls built within themselves, walls he yearned to topple.

"Do you think," he began slowly, his voice low and hesitant, "that it's possible to… stay? To choose where and when to belong?" The question hung in the air, tentative and fragile. A fragile invitation to lay bare his own concealed dread.

Caroline's gaze shifted fully now, meeting his with a rare softness that betrayed her own internal war. "I don't know," she admitted, carefully choosing her words, her usual certainty melting into something more fragile yet deeply authentic. "I've spent my life trying to understand history from a safe distance, but living it feeling it changes everything. It's not just facts and dates anymore. It's us, tangled up in the moment, in each other. But the question, Thomas… what if the moment isn't permanent? What if it's only a breath, just enough to pull us apart again?"

He swallowed, the echo of those words striking a chord too true. The idea of returning to their original lives, or being torn apart by invisible currents of time and fate, was an ever-present shadow hovering close to his heart. His mind raced back to a life before the book's enchantments, one marked by places that never quite stuck, by relationships that frayed as swiftly as they began. A revolving door of faces and fleeting attachments, all leaving behind a residue of loneliness he could neither dispel nor escape. To know that even here, in this strange and raw existence, he might be destined to dribble back into irrelevance unsettled him to the core.

"But if we don't try if we accept that all this is temporary then what are we?" he asked, his voice straining under the weight of fear and hope intertwined. "Merely players in a story that doesn't want us as permanent characters? I've lived so long in the shadows of what might be, chasing permanence but never catching it, that the thought of building something lasting, real, feels foreign."

Caroline rose quietly, the soft rustle of her dress stirring the still air. With deliberate slowness, she closed the gap between them. Her hand brushed against his, tentative at first, then anchoring with a firm resolve that spoke of a willingness to confront, to share the depths that lay beneath brittle surfaces. "Maybe it's not about time," she murmured, "or even place. Perhaps it's about what we choose to hold onto, what we claim for ourselves despite the chaos. You've talked of belonging like it's been lost to you. But maybe it's here, in this imperfect, uncertain moment, that we can find something… real."

He looked down at their joined hands, the warmth of her touch igniting a light within his chest. The very act of touching, of feeling her skin against his, was a quiet defiance against his internal narrative of impermanence. It whispered of potential, of a shared defiance against fate's relentless ebb and flow. There was rawness in their connection, a truth forged in vulnerability and proximity rather than the trappings of time or circumstance.

"Sometimes," Thomas confessed, "I think my fear isn't just about the time we're thrust into. It's about never being more than a shadow, a visitor who never settles. I've buried that fear beneath layers of detachment for so long I forgot what it means to be... needed, or to need someone." His confession was a fragile bridge spanning the gulf he'd kept hidden. The weight of solitude he had borne was immense, but in this moment, it felt a little lighter, shared between the two of them like a secret traded in the dark.

Caroline's eyes glistened with unshed emotion, the brittleness in her usual composure revealing itself as her walls crumbled. "And yet you are here," she whispered, "with me. Not by accident, but because something in you wants to stay, to be real, to be more than just a fleeting shadow. We don't have to be prisoners of time or our fears."

A silence followed, not heavy or awkward, but quiet and charged, a breathing space between two souls daring to imagine something beyond survival and pretense. Thomas studied Caroline's face her fierce intelligence softened by a dawning tenderness and felt a flicker of courageous hope ignite. He wanted to believe her, to believe that what they were building, carefully and sometimes painfully, was more than forced circumstance. That it could transform into an anchor, a home etched not in stone or paper, but in mutual trust and affection.

The idea of permanence, once a distant, unattainable dream, began to shimmer with possibility. It was fragile like the delicate pages of the mysterious book that had relocated their lives but with each shared glance and each tentative touch, it grew stronger. To be permanent was to be vulnerable, and vulnerability was the uncharted territory they were navigating together. It was terrifying and exhilarating all at once.

Thomas's fingers tightened gently around Caroline's hand, a silent vow passing between them. His gaze lifted to her eyes, steady and searching. "If permanence is a choice, then I choose us. Here, now not as intruders in a history not our own, but as two people carving out a place to belong," he said, voice infused with newfound certainty.

She nodded, a soft smile curving her lips, a promise unspoken but deeply felt. The future, uncertain and fraught with peril, no longer seemed an unscalable abyss but a canvas waiting for the brushstrokes of their emerging story. Two souls entwined not by chance or survival, but by an intentional, tender weaving of trust and hope.

Outside, the village settled beneath a star-studded sky, ancient and unchanging. Inside, in the fragile sanctuary of their shared space, Thomas's fear of being temporary began to dissolve, replaced by the burgeoning realization that permanence was not the passage of years or the tactics of time travel, but the courage to be truly seen and to see in return the other who chose to stay.

The chill of the night seemed to seep through the thin, uneven walls of the cottage, wrapping the cramped space in a silent, icy embrace that even the humble hearth struggled to repel. Caroline sat close to the flickering fire, the flames casting wavering shadows that danced erratically upon the rough-hewn beams above. The scent of burning pine mingled with the dampness of unwashed wool and earth, grounding her in a reality she was still struggling to accept. Her fingers, once so adept at turning the sterile pages of ancient manuscripts and typing out precise notes in her journal, trembled slightly as she clasped the worn mug of ale warming in her hands. She was not accustomed to discomfort not just the physical variety, but the gnawing unease that stirred within her a vulnerability that had nothing to do with cold or hunger, and everything to do with exposure, both external and internal.

Across from her, Thomas rubbed his arms as if to coax warmth back into his skin, his gaze cast downward, shadows softening the rugged planes of his face. His usually confident posture had softened; the lines that mapped years of instinct and hard-earned caution bent slightly under the weight of unspoken uncertainties. In this rare moment away from the ever-present watchfulness of Bramleigh's tight-knit villagers and the electric tension of their forced performance, the fragile walls they'd each maintained seemed to falter, exposing fissures neither dared acknowledge before. The silence between them was heavy but not unkind more a shared breath suspended, waiting for one to daringly break the quiet and invite the other into a deeper space beyond mere survival.

Caroline's voice was tentative at first, a soft contrast to the crackling fire, "Do you ever…" She paused, fingers tightening around her drink, "Do you ever wonder if we can ever stop pretending? Not just with the villagers, but with each other? I mean what we're doing here. Is it all just a charade to get by?"

Thomas looked up then, eyes meeting hers with a complexity that softened the lingering distance. "Every day," he admitted, leaning forward, elbows resting heavily on his knees. "I tell myself it's just a role, a mask to wear until we find some way back to our own time. But sometimes, late at night, the mask feels... too heavy. I don't even recognize the man I'm pretending to be, Caroline."

Her breath hitched, not from the cold but from the admitting of truths she'd buried beneath layers of control and rationality. She had spent her whole life seeking mastery over the uncontrollable: history, emotions, circumstances anything that threatened to undo the fragile order she'd crafted around herself. Yet here, in this humble, functional scrawl of a cottage lost from her own era by centuries, she was stripped bare by necessity and proximity, forced into carrying not just physical burdens but emotional ones she barely knew how to unpack.

"Control was always my refuge," she confessed, voice lowering, almost a whisper now, "I thought if I understood enough, if I had the facts, if I kept my distance from… feelings, then nothing could hurt me. But here, I'm not even sure I know who I am anymore. And I'm terrified that when the book commands came to pretend intimacy, that was the limit that I'd never actually feel… anything real."

Thomas shifted, his eyes searching hers with a softness that stirred something deep within her an aching promise of tenderness that contrasted starkly with the harsh backdrop of their reality. "I'm not who I thought I was either," he said quietly. "I arrived here a stranger even to myself. But it's funny, in a way, how something as desperate as survival forces the truth into the open. I realized I'm more afraid of being alone, of having no one to trust, than I am of whatever else this place throws our way."

The weight of his words settled between them like a fragile truce, an acknowledgment that beneath their stoic exteriors, beneath the facades crafted to navigate centuries-old social dangers, lay the same basic aching need for connection and belonging. For the first time, Caroline felt the stiff walls around her heart tremble, and not in resistance but in cautious curiosity.

"I'm scared," she admitted, the admission no longer suffocating but strangely liberating. "Scared that if I let myself be vulnerable even with you I might lose the last hold I have on who I am. But also scared that without reaching out, I might lose something deeper. Something… essential."

Thomas's gaze softened, and he moved closer, the space between them narrowing with the tenderness of shared fragility. "Maybe losing control isn't losing yourself. Maybe it's finding who you were always meant to be, beneath the armor."

Her breath slowed, chest rising and falling in the quiet heat of the moment, and she found herself reaching out not with calculation or hesitation, but with an instinct as raw as courage. Her hand hovered for a heartbeat before settling lightly over his, warmth mingling with the cold that had lived between them. It was a small contact but immense in significance, a bridge built not of necessity or survival but trust.

The moment stretched, charged with a quiet electricity that neither had dared hope to feel in the midst of such turmoil. Caroline's heart, usually a conductor of cold reason, beat fiercely in her chest, not from fear but from the tremulous stirrings of hope. She met Thomas's eyes, reading the vulnerability mirrored there, and in that exchange found the beginnings of something far more enduring than the harsh mandates of the book or the perilous constraints of 18th-century village life.

"I don't know the future," she whispered, voice thick with emotion. "But here right now I want to try… to be more than the roles we were forced into. To be honest with each other, even when it's hard."

Thomas nodded slowly, thumb brushing over her knuckles, a gentle rhythm that spoke of burgeoning connection. "Then let's start there. No more pretending, no more hiding behind what we think we should be. We're flawed. Fragile. But maybe, together, that means we're strong."

The fire crackled, the room alive with shifting light and warmth as something new kindled between them. It was not passion yet not the blazing, physical kind that had simmered beneath cautious glances or stolen touches but the softer, steadier glow of understanding and acceptance. It was the kind of intimacy born not from convenience or obligation but from unguarded truth, the kind that demanded bravery and promised transformation.

As the night deepened and the village outside settled into its own rhythms of quiet suspicion and watchful eyes, Caroline and Thomas remained seated near the hearth, two solitary souls slowly unraveling the threads woven tight by fear and circumstance. Bound by the mysterious book and the unyielding rules it imposed, they nevertheless found in their shared vulnerability a freedom neither had anticipated: the liberation of authentic connection amidst chaos.

The hours passed softly, their conversation flowing from confessions to reflections, and even to tentative hopes for what might come beyond the grim realities pressing down upon them. Caroline spoke of her yearning not just for knowledge but for meaning and belonging, while Thomas revealed fissures beneath his stoic exterior, the scars of a life marked by uncertainty and displacement. Neither glossed over pain nor wore masks; instead, they faced each other through the smoky tendrils of the fire's breath, raw and real.

In this sacred space of mutual vulnerability, the barriers that had separated them between past and present, between stranger and confidant crumbled piece by piece. The cottage, with its humble furnishings and utilitarian simplicity, transformed from a mere shelter into a sanctuary where two fractured souls began stitching themselves whole again.

When the first light of dawn filtered hesitantly through the dusty panes, signaling the reluctant return of the outside world's harsh scrutiny, Caroline and Thomas remained entwined in a quiet synergy of mutual understanding. The journey ahead was still uncertain, fraught with danger both visible and hidden, yet now they faced it not as two isolated survivors but as partners woven together by empathy and trust a bond forged not merely by circumstance but by choice.

As Caroline gathered her shawl and rose, feeling the residual warmth of his hand in hers, a tentative smile touched her lips, no longer guarded but open. It was a promise to herself and to Thomas: to surrender her fear of loss, to embrace the messy, beautiful complexities of connection, and to step into whatever future this strange, fractured world offered undaunted and united.

And as Thomas met her gaze, steady and unwavering, the faintest flicker of hope kindled bright within them both, lighting a path forward across the uncertain, shadowed terrain of their shared passage through time and through the heart.

Love's Choice

The fire sputtered low in the hearth, its embers glowing with a gentle warmth that contrasted sharply with the biting chill of the winter night outside. Caroline sat by the flickering light, the heavy velvet curtains drawn tight against the wind's relentless howl. She watched the flames dance, almost hypnotically, their warm hues a stark contrast to the turmoil that churned within her. In the days that had passed since their arrival in Bramleigh, so much had shifted not just her surroundings, but the very essence of her being. The rigid walls of certainty and control that had once framed her world had begun to crumble, replaced by a softness she barely recognized in herself. The book, the forced proximity, the daily performance of a marriage she had always regarded as a social formality all had conspired to strip away her defenses, revealing vulnerabilities she had long buried beneath layers of discipline and intellectual detachment.

Thomas sat opposite her on the narrow cot they now shared, his features softened by the firelight. His eyes held a depth of understanding that defied the harshness of their circumstances. He had become more than a mere companion forced upon her by an extraordinary circumstance; slowly, inexorably, he had become the anchor that held her in place amid the overwhelming storm of uncertainty. She found herself watching him now, tracing the line of his jaw, the way his brow furrowed with unspoken thought, the subtle shifts as he grappled with his own unspoken fears and hopes. There was no pretense between them here, in these shared quiet moments. No need for the charade that the outside world demanded. Here, they were simply two souls adrift, seeking solace in the fragile, flickering certainty of one another's presence.

The decision had not come abruptly but unfolded over countless small moments glances exchanged in the dim light of their cramped cottage, the brush of a hand as they passed a shared cup of warming cider, the silent promises conveyed in whispered confessions through restless nights. Caroline had always believed choice was the bedrock of freedom, yet here she faced a paradox: surrendering control did not mean surrendering herself. Rather, it was embracing the possibility that love, in its most profound form, flourished not from rigid boundaries but from the raw, unguarded truths we dare to reveal.

She remembered the hesitation in Thomas's eyes the first time their hands had intertwined, tentative and uncertain, mirroring her own apprehension. Each step had been tentative, a delicate dance of testing limits and seeking permission. Theirs was a slow-burning fire, stoked not by reckless abandon but by deliberate, mutual respect a knowing that the deepest bonds were forged not in conquest but in consent. Caroline had learned, painfully and tenderly, that vulnerability was not weakness but a courageous act of faith. In yielding, she did not lose herself; she found a new strength in the fragile intimacy that grew between them.

That night, as the wind howled beyond the walls and the shadows played their silent games across the wooden beams, Caroline felt the full weight of her choice settle within her. To truly live, to truly love, she must let go not of her identity, but of the illusion that she could control every facet of her existence. In the fire's glow, she reached out, her hand brushing against Thomas's, a silent invitation laden with meaning. His fingers closed around hers, warm and steady, a grounding force in the midst of uncertainty.

Their breathing deepened in unison, a rhythm established not by obligation but by desire and trust. Words became unnecessary; the space between them was charged with an electric tenderness that transcended spoken language.

Caroline leaned into Thomas's presence, surrendering the last fragments of doubt that had clung to her like shadows. His lips met hers with a gentle assertion, a promise rather than a demand, igniting a crescendo of sensation that was as much emotional as physical.

In the intimacy that followed, every touch was a dialogue, every sigh an expression of burgeoning love. Caroline's mind, usually so attuned to factual certainty, surrendered to the ebb and flow of sensation and emotion, discovering in her own skin a new lexicon of feeling. Thomas's hands were reverent and sure, tracing the delicate contours of her body with an artistry born of genuine care. There was no haste, no pressure only the profound union of two incomplete souls seeking completion in authentic connection.

Her walls, painstakingly erected over years of scholarship and self-reliance, fell away beneath the tender insistence of his care. In this act of surrender, Caroline discovered freedom not from control itself but from the need to wield it as a shield against the unpredictable tides of human intimacy. Thomas watched her with an unwavering devotion that mirrored her own awakening, the firelight reflecting in his eyes a tenderness that spoke of promises yet to be fulfilled but already held sacred.

The hours slipped away unnoticed as they moved together through that sacred space a realm where time lost its rigid structure and the boundary between past and present blurred into irrelevance. Each kiss, each caress, wove them closer into a tapestry of trust and desire, transforming the artifice of their forced marriage into a living testament to love's transformative power.

When dawn's pale light finally crept through the shuttered windows, Caroline lay nestled against Thomas's chest, her heartbeat a steady pulse beneath his steadying hand. The world beyond their small refuge remained fraught with dangers both social and legal, with the ever-watchful eyes of Agnes Pryce lurking like a shadow waiting to pounce. Yet in this fragile cocoon of vulnerability and consent, they had found a reprieve a sanctuary where love could grow unburdened by fear or pretense.

Caroline's thoughts turned inward, reflecting on the journey that had led her here. The Book of Passage, that mysterious tome found in the hallowed halls of Arkwell Library, had brought them to this unlikely chapter of their lives. What had begun as a bewildering, often terrifying ordeal of survival and deception had blossomed into something profoundly real a love forged not in the convenience of circumstance but in the crucible of shared hardship and earned trust.

Her mind lingered on the paradox of control and surrender, the delicate balance that now defined their relationship. She understood, at last, that control was not an end unto itself but a means to create safety a safety that enabled true intimacy to emerge. And in surrendering her need to dominate the narrative, she had invited Thomas not only into her world but into the very fabric of her being.

His steady breath against her skin was a

reassuring cadence, a rhythm that promised continuity amid the shifting uncertainties of their existence in 1770 Bramleigh. They had laid down the burdens of performance and embraced an authentic connection, allowing love's transformative embrace to heal wounds both visible and unseen.

As the morning light grew stronger and the reality of their situation pressed once again upon them, Caroline felt a quiet resolve settle within her. They would face Agnes's threats, the village's suspicion, and the harshness of a world not made for outsiders not as strangers banded in desperation but as partners bound by choice and genuine affection.

Her hand found Thomas's, fingers entwining, a silent vow passing between them. This time, the bond was unbreakable not an imposed fiction dictated by a mysterious book but a living, breathing truth authored by their mutual courage and undeniable love.

In that surrender of control, Caroline discovered the deepest freedom of all: the freedom to love without reserve, to trust without fear, and to embrace a future forged by their own hands, on their own terms.

The fire within the hearth cast elongated shadows across the timbered walls of the cramped cottage, its flickering light dancing on the worn tapestries that Caroline and Thomas had managed to procure since their arrival in Bramleigh. The chill of the encroaching winter seeped through the cracks in the walls, pressing the cold against their skin, a constant reminder of their vulnerability. Yet amid this frigid isolation, a different warmth had blossomed between them an ember growing steadily into an unquenchable flame, fueled by countless shared trials and whispered confessions. The performance they had maintained for weeks husband, wife, strangers bound by necessity was dissolving under the weight of something far tenderer and infinitely more dangerous: genuine desire and burgeoning love.

Caroline's initial resistance, born of a lifetime structured around control and reason, now wavered under Thomas's steadfast patience and unassuming strength. Her hands, once clenched against the uncertainty of emotional dependence, trembled slightly as they brushed against his roughened palm. Each touch was a revelation, a tentative exploration of territory previously forbidden by doubt and self-imposed boundaries. She had spent years buried in archives, cataloging the lives of people long passed, studying social rituals designed to shield the heart from chaos, yet now she found herself entangled in the raw, dizzying vulnerability of physical connection, where words often faltered and the heart spoke in a language both primal and profound.

Their nightly conversations had softened into silken threads of warmth, weaving a tapestry of intimacy that festered with longing beneath the surface. Thomas's gaze, once sharp with the vigilance necessary for survival in this alien era, now carried a gentleness that stirred a yearning within Caroline she could not quell. The playful teasing smiles exchanged over shared meals had given way to lingering glances heavy with unspoken promises, the spaces between them charged with a magnetic tension fragile yet insistent. Each breath drawn together was a silent confession, every accidental touch a declaration of vulnerability and longing.

That evening found them drawn closer than ever, seated side by side upon the narrow settee, the scant distance between them both a barrier and an invitation. The book that had brought them together lay forgotten on the rough-hewn table, its spell weakening as their connection deepened beyond the pages. The fire sputtered but refused to die, as if reflecting the glowing embers of their shared desire. Thomas's calloused fingers brushed a silken strand of Caroline's hair behind her ear, the simple gesture reverberating through her senses like an electric current. His eyes searched hers, seeking permission, a silent covenant forged not from obligation but from mutual yearning.

Caroline's breath hitched; the carefully constructed walls she had built around her heart began to crumble with every heartbeat. She was no longer merely surviving the performance demanded by the book and taboos of Bramleigh but surrendering to a daring unknown whose promises shimmered in the shadows. As his hand caressed the side of her neck, tracing the delicate curve with reverence, she felt her own hands tremble with an unfamiliar fire, a surrender that was both terrifying and exhilarating. The moment hung suspended, heavy with anticipation, as if the world itself held its breath in reverence to the fragile dance unfolding between them.

When their lips finally met, it was with the softness of a whispered confession, a tender exploration that deepened into a heated, urgent dialogue. The kiss grew bolder, lips parting to invite, hands reaching and tracing the planes of familiar yet newly discovered flesh. Each touch was a promise and a plea, a negotiation of desire and consent written in the language of skin and breath. Caroline's fingers tangled in Thomas's hair, anchoring herself in the fever of the moment, while his arms encircled her with protective strength, conveying a silent vow: in this impossible world, they found in each other their sanctuary.

Physically, they moved with the delicate caution of lovers navigating uncharted waters, yet beneath their tentative caresses surged an undercurrent of fierce urgency. The cramped room seemed to pulse with their mounting heat, every breath and heartbeat synchronized in a rhythm as old and instinctual as time itself. Their bodies pressed against one another, barriers dissolving as clothing was shed with a reverent trembling, revealing the stories etched in scars and smooth skin alike a testament to survival, to the pasts that had shaped them into the people who now stood naked not only in body but in spirit.

Caroline marveled at the paradox of this union: the very physicality she had once dismissed as distraction now opened gates within her she had kept locked, chambers housing long-buried yearnings for touch, for acceptance, for the seamless melding of two souls. Thomas, whose strength had always been his shield, now wielded it to nurture, to cherish, administering ministrations that were as gentle as they were fervent. In his gaze, she found no conquest but a reverence for the person she was beneath layers of armor, a commitment to honoring her vulnerability rather than exploiting it.

Their union was not a frantic surrender but a carefully choreographed dance between hesitation and desire, control and abandon. Every murmur, every gasp, every shivered sigh was an essay in trust, proof that the performance enforced by the mysterious book had given way to authentic connection, a form of love that neither had anticipated yet neither could deny. As they moved together through the night, the world beyond the cottage faded into insignificance the oppressive social laws, the prying eyes of Agnes Pryce, even the temporal dislocation that had thrust them into this perilous past all suspended by the fragile intimacy between them.

With each crescendo, Caroline shed more than her clothes; she cast off layers of fear and self-doubt. Thomas's touch was a balm against years of loneliness and the relentless discipline of her scholarly detachment. She found herself responding with an abandon that frightened yet exhilarated her, surrendering to sensations that swelled not only in her body but in her soul. It was as if the very act of loving him transformed her understanding of herself, reshaping identity from a rigid history bound by facts into a living, breathing narrative crafted through trust and shared vulnerability.

The morning came not with dawn but with the gentle fading of their breathless reverie a soft lingering in the warm embrace they had forged against the winter's chill. Light spilled golden through the small window, illuminating the quiet aftermath of their union. Caroline rested her head against Thomas's chest, listening to the steady beat of his heart, a rhythm that now echoed with the promise of belonging and hope. In that silence, so full of unspoken words, they discovered the most profound passage of all: the passage from performance to truth, from survival to love.

Though the book's mysterious directives had commanded their proximity, it was their own courage to surrender that had truly bound them.

No longer were they captives of circumstance but architects of their shared destiny. The tentative steps toward passion had blossomed into a fierce, unshakable bond a love that not only defied the suffocating constraints of 18th-century Bramleigh but transcended time itself. Their bodies, once occupied solely with survival and pretense, now moved in harmony with newly awakened hearts, weaving a tapestry of intimacy that promised to endure through the tempests yet to come.

Emotional Grounding

The evening air in the small cottage hung heavy with a warmth that was neither wholly physical nor entirely imagined. It was a tension that had been building, simmering beneath layers of circumstance and necessity, a thread of connection woven through each shared glance, each tentative touch that had slowly pulled Caroline and Thomas from the safety of performance into the fragile, tremulous territory of genuine intimacy. In the flickering candlelight, shadows played across the worn wooden walls, casting their features in a softer, more vulnerable light. The space between them was charged neither rushed nor hesitant but perfectly balanced on the slender edge where desire meets trust. The very air seemed to pulse with the unspoken hopes and fears of two people caught in a new world not of their choosing, yet slowly, inexorably, of their own making.

Caroline's heart beat with an erratic rhythm that was at once thrilling and frightening. For so long, her life had been one of precise order, scholar's control, and measured detachment facts and dates as firm anchors in a sea of uncertainties. But now, as Thomas's steady gaze held hers, she felt the fracturing of those anchors, the beginning of a surrender to something no classification or historical account had ever prepared her for. It was not just lust, although the fire that burned low and steady between them was undeniable, awakening every nerve ending with its promise of discovery. What unsettled and fascinated her was the burgeoning trust the awareness that beneath the surface of their forced proximity lay something genuine, something they both fiercely guarded yet desperately needed to nurture. Thomas was no longer simply a companion in this strange new reality; he was becoming the center of her world, a refuge from the relentless demands of survival.

Thomas, too, felt the tremor of newfound emotion. His initial instinct had been straightforward: protect, survive, endure. But

Caroline's intellect, her fierce independence, and the subtle vulnerability she gradually allowed him to glimpse stirred something deeper inside him a longing not only to safeguard but to truly know and cherish. The touch of her hand against his felt less like a necessity of circumstance and more like a promise, fragile and trembling but undeniably real. In this quiet room, with the steady crackle of the fire punctuating their muted breaths, the walls that had once surrounded him the barriers of suspicion, caution, and a guarded past began to crumble. The slow unfolding of their connection was as much about emotional revelation as any glance or gesture; it was an affirmation that love, forged amid adversity and social peril, could transcend the roles they had unwillingly adopted.

Their journey to this moment had been marked by careful steps a dance of glances and gestures measured against the unforgiving scrutiny of the village and, more perilously, Agnes Pryce's watchful eyes. Every shy smile, every reluctant touch, had been a brick laid in the foundation of a relationship that first existed in necessity and had evolved, imperceptibly yet inexorably, into something far more profound. Now, stripped of pretense, the walls between them began to fall, leaving raw, unguarded souls exposed to one another's truths. Caroline's breath caught as Thomas's hand brushed a loose strand of hair from her temple, his fingers gentle as they traced the delicate line of her cheek. In that moment, time slowed, and the cacophony of their previous lives the noise of threats, the pressures of survival, the weight of the mysterious book's commands vanished into the ether.

Yet, the power of this intimacy came not only from the physical but from the mutual understanding that underpinned every movement. Consent, respect, and emotional vulnerability were the steadfast pillars upon which this fledgling love was built. Neither rushed nor forced, their closeness was a negotiation of boundaries and desires, an ongoing conversation expressed through touch, glance, and softened words. Caroline, who had thrived on control, found herself relinquishing it cautiously, trusting Thomas to guide her gently into realms she had never dared traverse before. Thomas, who had initially been the protector, discovered an equal partner in Caroline someone whose strength and intellect enriched him and whose willingness to embrace vulnerability enriched their connection.

As Thomas leaned closer, the warmth of his breath mingled with hers, a silent question hanging between them, an invitation to cross the final threshold from performance to authentic union. Caroline's fingers trembled as they found their way to his shirt, the fabric rough yet grounding beneath her touch. Their lips met slowly, with an exquisite tenderness that spoke of longing and hesitation, of promises whispered in the language of quiet surrender. The kiss deepened, a flame kindled from years of latent desire, a flame that refused to be extinguished even by the coldest social expectations or the harshest judgment. It was here, in the softness of their embrace, that the vast differences of time, place, and circumstance seemed to blur and dissolve, leaving only the raw, elemental ache of two souls yearning to be whole.

Yet, the richness of their connection was not without its complexities. Caroline's mind raced with the practicalities she had always prized questions of safety, social consequence, and the implications of their union in a time where appearances were everything. Would this love survive the harsh judgment of Bramleigh's rigid social order? Could she allow herself to be vulnerable without losing the self-possession she had always relied upon? Thomas's own insecurities whispered doubts the fear that his past, unmoored and unknown, might never truly find belonging, no matter how fiercely he loved. And yet, every challenge, every hesitation, was met with a quiet, mutual understanding that love was not a destination but a journey fraught with uncertainty, yes, but illuminated by the courage to trust and to surrender.

Their bodies spoke truths their words could not yet fully capture. Skin against skin, the mingling of warmth and breath, became a sacred dialect of intimacy a translation of desire, need, and respect so profound it transcended the constraints of their circumstance. The cottage, small and humble, transformed into a sanctuary where time itself seemed to slow, giving space for the tender weaving of two lives into one. Here, in the soft rustle of linen sheets and the whispered cadence of confessions, Caroline and Thomas found a rare and precious thing: a connection rooted not in necessity, but in choice. Each touch was a silent vow, each caress a binding promise that they were no longer merely surviving together but living, fully and unabashedly.

Throughout that night, voices quiet and pulses steady, they navigated the delicate balance between passion and respect. There was no room for haste or pressure only the unfolding of trust in its most beautiful form. Caroline, who once viewed emotions through the lens of academic detachment, discovered the profound liberation that comes from surrendering to feeling without fear. Thomas, roughened by life's hardships yet tender at his core, embraced the truth that strength does not diminish in vulnerability but is often born from it. Together, they mapped new territories of love territories where consent was celebrated, where desire and respect intermingled in an exquisite dance, and where true connection could flourish despite the odds.

In the morning light, as dawn crept softly through the narrow window, Caroline awoke with a clarity that had eluded her in the years past. Love, she understood, was not a surrender of self but an expansion an invitation to share fears and joys, to build a life sustained by mutual respect and unwavering trust. The memory of the night's fragile, passionate exchange settled within her like a promise, an affirmation that no matter what shadows awaited outside the cottage's walls, they had forged an unbreakable bond. Thomas lay beside her, peaceful and real, no longer a stranger or mere protector, but a partner bound by shared vulnerability and profound affection.

Their journey from perfunctory roles to authentic love was not marked by a single grand gesture but by countless small moments gentle touches, whispered assurances, and quiet glances that conveyed volumes. It was a testament to the power of emotional grounding in the face of uncertainty, a reminder that passion, when accompanied by genuine trust and respect, could be transformative. The Book of Passage had brought them together, forcing their fates to intertwine, but it was their own will, their choice to embrace each other fully and without reservation, that truly shaped their future. In the delicate interplay of desire and devotion, Caroline and Thomas discovered not only the depths of their longing but the courage to build a love that would withstand the trials of both past and present.

The cottage, with its humble hearth and simple furnishings, had become a crucible for their transformation a place where necessity gave way to tenderness, where the line between pretense and reality blurred into oblivion. Outside, the village of Bramleigh continued its watchful existence, its social strictures and silent judgments looming. But within these four walls, Caroline and Thomas carved out their own reality, one where they could be honest, vulnerable, and utterly themselves. Theirs was a love not born of convenience or obligation, but of profound respect and the shared willingness to risk everything for a glimpse of true connection.

And so, as the morning sun painted the worn wooden floorboards with a soft golden light, they faced the day not as strangers thrown together by fate, but as partners united in heart and soul. Their love was no longer a secret performance but a living, breathing entity strong, tender, and infinitely precious. It was a love that had weathered fear and uncertainty, that had embraced both passion and restraint, and that stood resilient against the tides of time and circumstance. In the quiet intimacy of their shared space, Caroline and Thomas found their emotional grounding a foundation upon which they could build a future, together, with trust, respect, and unshakable devotion.

Agnes's Escalation

The sharp autumn winds rattled through the rafters of Bramleigh's thatched cottages, carrying with them whispers and suspicions that had begun to solidify into something palpably hostile. In the narrow lanes where Caroline and Thomas had once found a tenuous refuge, the scent of burning leaves mingled with sharper currents of unease. It was not lost on the villagers that the strangers' presence, initially dismissed as an odd curiosity, had grown into a persistent irritation. Agnes Pryce, with her keen eyes and unyielding demeanor, had transformed what was once mere gossip into a concerted campaign of surveillance and accusation, deftly wielding the intricate social web of the village to her advantage.

From the moment Caroline and Thomas arrived, Agnes had cast a long shadow over their lives, her thin-lipped smile and polite inquiries masking the cold calculation beneath. She had circulated whispers of impropriety and idleness, painting the pair as idle vagabonds who had no rightful claim to stay in Bramleigh. This was no idle scapegoating born of petty jealousy; Agnes's concern was rooted in the rigid laws that governed property and parish relief, laws that, in her mind, existed to preserve order and tradition. Through her network of informants bustling midwives, wary merchants, and sharp-tongued seamstresses she had led the villagers' speculation into concrete allegations, framing Caroline and Thomas as a danger not merely to societal norms but to the very safety of Bramleigh.

The parish authorities, previously indifferent, now found themselves drawn into the escalating tensions. Agnes had penned carefully worded complaints to the parish constable and the overseers of the poor, emphasizing the couple's suspicious behavior, their lack of clear employment, and their refusal to submit to the customary registration required of newcomers. She spoke with the quiet authority of a woman well-versed in local governance, wielding scripture and statute with equal ease. Her documents detailed the strictures imposed by the Poor Laws, underscoring how Bramleigh must not become a refuge for those who would leech upon the community's resources. Agnes's tone was grave, bordering on pious; her concern seemed to stem from a genuine desire to protect the village, yet beneath it lay an unmistakable personal vendetta, a need to demonstrate control amid the upheaval the strangers had introduced.

For Caroline and Thomas, the mounting threat was almost invisible at first, creeping upon them like a winter fog. They had felt the village's suspicion furtive looks over teacups, cold silences exchanged across opposite ends of the market square but the official summons jolted them into stark reality. A summons that demanded their presence at the parish hall, a drab, sandstone building whose heavy wooden doors seemed to close a noose around their chances for survival in this alien world. Upon their arrival, the atmosphere was thick with claustrophobic tension, a chamber filled with grim-faced men familiar with the power held by written word and recorded testimony. The parish constable, a stout man named Wilkins whose expression bore the weary lines of too many long winters, read aloud the accusations: vagrancy, failure to register, suspicion of immoral conduct under the guise of a sham marriage.

Caroline's pulse quickened as their fate hung suspended in the heavy silence of the room. Her mind raced, scouring every fragment of knowledge stored in her historian's memory, every legal nuance gleaned from dusty tomes on 18th-century British law. She attempted to marshal reason and fact as weapons, but the room was not a place for academic debate it was a crucible of entrenched social hierarchy, where power rested as much on perception as on proof. Thomas stood rigid beside her, his physical presence a silent assertion against the tide of hostility. But even his confidence, so vital in their everyday survival, could only shield them to a precarious extent.

Agnes sat at the center of this gathering, her lips pressed into a thin line, eyes gleaming with quiet triumph. Her campaign had begun as a ripple of discontent but had cascaded into a wave that threatened to engulf them utterly. She spoke with dispassionate clarity, outlining the illegalities of their stay and the potential costs to the village, framing her vigilance as the only means to preserve the community's moral and economic fabric. Her speech was laced with veiled warnings and subtle reproaches toward those in the room who might sympathize, a reminder that dissent carried consequences. Caroline sensed the room was not just judging them but being subtly coerced into complicity, the fear of social outsiderdom directing even the most indifferent toward allegiance with Agnes's cause.

Out in the gray light of the approaching evening, as they left the parish hall, Caroline and Thomas felt the weight of the village's gaze transform from passive suspicion to threatening expectation. The notion of expulsion, once an abstract fear, now gleamed sharp and imminent.

Their once-shared haven a cramped, creaking cottage that smelled of peat smoke and worn wood seemed suddenly fragile, as though the walls themselves might crumble beneath the pressure of Agnes's relentless scrutiny. The book's earlier commands to maintain their facade of marriage felt heavier with every passing day, the performance no longer a mere survival tactic but a precarious act under the spotlight of communal judgment.

Thomas, ever attuned to the shifting moods of Bramleigh, tightened his jaw as he spoke in low tones about the village's unofficial power hierarchies. He understood that Agnes was tapping into more than laws; she appealed to traditional fears fear of outsiders, of destabilized order, of the unknown. Trust was scarce in Bramleigh's close quarters, and Agnes exploited this scarcity with clinical precision. Caroline, for all her scholarly detachment, could not deny the creeping coherence of Agnes's influence, nor the chilling suggestion that their survival hinged not solely on adherence to social roles but on an acceptance they were still far from obtaining.

Despite the mounting peril, Caroline found an ember of resolve glowing within her a determination not only to endure but to unravel the mechanisms that kept Agnes's grip so firm. She began to observe the subtle codices of village interaction; how Agnes's smile softened just enough in public to mask her sharp edges, how alliances were brokered not in grand declarations but in whispered agreements by firesides and markets. Caroline recognized that to counteract Agnes's campaign they would need more than mere denial or withdrawal; they had to claim a place, to insert themselves into the village's social fabric despite the woven web of suspicion.

Yet the path was fraught and tangled. Agnes's arsenal extended beyond legal accusations; it was an intricate dance of moral censure and social ostracism. The widow's power lay in her reputation as a paragon of propriety, a mantle she defended fiercely through meticulous compliance with every village ordinance and through the vigilant policing of others' conduct.

She was the embodiment of Bramleigh's rigid expectations, a living testament to the cost of deviation. Caroline, with all her modern sensibilities, felt the isolating pressure of the past's unforgiving gaze, the way survival demanded not only knowledge but a surrender to performances and pretenses that gnawed at the edges of identity.

Their conversations at night became charged with an urgency that neither could ignore. In the flickering candlelight of their shared parlour, Thomas's voice took on a protective edge as he articulated plans to counter Agnes's moves. He spoke of forging bonds with those villagers less inclined to malice, seeking allies in the tradesmen whose livelihood depended more on cooperation than on gossip. Caroline, meanwhile, wrestled with acknowledging her own vulnerabilities the need to trust others, to expose the cracks in her carefully constructed armor. The book's commands, once rigid and prescriptive, now seemed less a guide and more a reminder of the fragile tightrope they walked between survival and revelation.

Amidst this mounting tension, the village itself seemed to lean into the rift Agnes had cultivated. In the market square, once lively and indifferent, the whispers matured into pointed questions. Children, previously instructed to shun the strangers, now openly stared with a mixture of curiosity and judgment.

Even the clergy, whose sermons were meant to inspire charity and kindness, preached caution when encountering those who bore no clear station or heritage in Bramleigh. The community's collective eye, sharpened by Agnes's campaign, scrutinized Caroline and Thomas with relentless precision.

The couple's every action became a performance laden with consequence: the way they moved through the village, the subtle shifts in posture that betrayed discomfort, the careful exchanges of glances that tried to convey understanding without admission. Caroline found herself increasingly reliant on Thomas's instinctual knowledge of demeanor and social cues, his protective presence a bulwark against the tidal wave of suspicion. Yet, even this built-in alliance felt precarious as Agnes's shadow continued to lengthen, darkening their days and infiltrating their moments of fragile solace. The book's impersonal commands now seemed less like a safeguard and more like a set of shackles binding them to a fate dictated not by their own choices but by the relentless machinery of a small, watchful society.

Despite the oppressive weight of Agnes's threat, the flickering spark of hope stirred quietly within them. Caroline understood that the story was still being written, that Bramleigh's social tapestry was not yet fully woven around their exclusion. There were fractures and unanswered questions among the villagers those uncertain of Agnes's harsh judgments, those still willing to see beyond the surface. The challenge lay in finding and nurturing those silent points of resistance, to navigate the treacherous currents of social power with care and determination.

As the days bled into the low light of early winter, the campaign against them reached a fever pitch. Agnes organized meetings with village elders beneath heavy shawls and thick skirts, letters exchanged in careful script between houses. No corners of Bramleigh remained untouched by her influence.

The couple found themselves privy to the same dark, murmuring gossips that once flitted at a distance, now sharpened into direct accusations and veiled threats. Agnes's ultimate aim was unambiguous: to sever them from the village before the encroaching cold rendered their position untenable.

It was a siege of societal will, an intricate assault that tested every strand of Caroline and Thomas's newfound bond. Yet beneath the pressure, their alliance solidified in unexpected ways. They found strength not only in resistance but in the shared vulnerability Agnes sought to exploit. Each whispered conversation, each guarded smile, each furtive reassurance became a subtle act of defiance, a reaffirmation that their existence however transitory or constructed was no mere illusion to be dismissed.

At twilight one evening, as snowflakes began to drift onto the cracked panes of their cottage window, Caroline sat cradling a steaming cup, staring into the depths of a world that seemed both alien and inexorably hers. The edges of control she prized so fiercely blurred beneath the weight of communal judgment, leaving her exposed but more attuned to the fragile threads tethering her to this past. Thomas's quiet presence beside her was both comfort and challenge, an unspoken promise that the path forward demanded surrender but also courage.

In that moment, they understood that Agnes's campaign was not simply a battle over land or legal status; it was a crucible that would forge or fracture the identity they were painstakingly weaving together. Their survival hinged on navigating the shifting tides of power, trust, and performance on choosing not only what roles to play but who they dared to become amid the echoes of a society both unforgiving and mesmerizing. The story of their passage was far from over, and as the cold deepened outside, inside the small cottage a new, fierce determination took root the choice to face down the threat not merely with resistance, but with a fierce, unyielding claim to belonging.

Parish Questioning

The cold breath of dawn had barely lifted when the raucous murmur outside the modest dwelling disturbed Caroline's restless sleep. She lay rigid beneath the threadbare quilt, ears straining to catch the edge of voices that, despite their muffled tone, carried unmistakable sharpness. Thomas, still half-dressed and sharp-eyed from long night watches, silently rose and pressed his ear against the weathered wooden door. The sound that reached him was no ordinary village whisper something heavier, more official, threading its way like an invasive vine into their fragile sanctuary. It was the parish officials come at last, summoned by the steely, unyielding will of Agnes Pryce.

Caroline bristled against the chill gripping her skin, more from unease than cold. The whispered rumors that had once lingered like shadows now openly solidified into an inescapable reality: the village authorities had come to scrutinize their existence. Their sudden arrival in Bramleigh, unaccompanied, unintroduced, posed a thorny question to the local parish, guardian of order and custom in equal measure. Agnes, with her hawkish gaze and relentless persistence, had long cultivated this moment, weaving doubt and dread with ease and cruelty. The parish's intervention was no mere social curiosity it was a legal inquest that prickled with latent menace, threatening expulsion and ruin.

Thomas opened the door with a measured breath, revealing the trio of parish constables who craned their necks around to survey the interior and then fixated on the two intruders who had dared take residence under Bramleigh's strict codes. Their leader, a gaunt man with a weatherworn face and an authority he wielded like a weapon, stepped forward, glancing at a document as if its printed words carried divine power. His voice was thin but forceful. "By order of the parish court, we are here to question your right to assume residence in Bramleigh," he said, punctuating the statement with a cold stare that unsettled Caroline far more than she cared to admit. "You have been reported as vagrants, without lawful means or standing. It falls upon us to ascertain your identities and purpose."

The room seemed suddenly too narrow, suffocating. Caroline's heart hammered in defiance as she rose, the historian's practiced composure cloaking her turmoil in disciplined restraint. "We mean no disturbance. We have secured lodging, and I assure you, our presence is neither idle nor unlawful." Her voice, steady but courteous, drew a scrutinizing glance from the officials, their skepticism palpable. Still, it was no moment for false defenses; under such scrutiny, every word could become a weapon or a saving grace.

Agnes Pryce, who had remained hidden like a vulture surveying her prey, now stepped into the doorway, her expression carved from stone. She had dressed with careful intention, her widow's black softened only by the glint of her silver-edged spectacles that magnified the unforgiving sharpness of her eyes. "I trust, gentlemen," she began, her voice silk laced with steel, "that your inquiry addresses the considerable disruption these two have caused. We have records of a stranger arriving without introduction, without sponsor, and without the community's consent." She paused, letting the weight of her accusation settle like a drawn blade. "Bramleigh, as you know, cannot suffer the wandering or vagrant, whose presence invites misfortune. They have been masquerading as husband and wife an assumption both suspicious and improper, given the lack of formal proceeding or records to attest their bond."

Caroline felt an incendiary twist in her gut, the old historian's disbelief clashing against the urgent necessity to survive this threat. "We were forced into presenting ourselves thus out of necessity," she said, catching Thomas's supportive gaze. "Our knowledge of the past, our intention to blend, was never an attempt to deceive maliciously but to protect ourselves from the harsh judgment of outsiders."

The parish constable's ink-stained fingers tightened on the parchment as he consulted his notes again, voice colder still. "Custom requires all newcomers to undergo examination of character and standing, particularly when lodging within the confines of the parish. Your failure to report and legitimize your stay is cause for concern. The parish shall conduct a formal hearing, and until such time, you are to remain within this dwelling, neither to engage in labor nor social affairs." His authoritative command hit like a stone wall, sealing them into their fragile cocoon, fenced in by suspicion and legal constraint.

Thomas stepped forward, his posture protective and resolute. "We understand the customs and do not seek conflict. Yet these accusations, amplified by gossip, threaten our very survival. We request your leniency and an opportunity to prove our worth to this village."

Agnes inclined her head, a subtle, chilling smile playing upon her lips. "Prove it, then, lest the parish court find your presence detrimental to the good order of Bramleigh," she intoned, her warning both veiled and direct.

As the parish officials withdrew, their steps hollow and echoing, Caroline closed the door with a trembling hand and sank into the nearest chair. The weight of the parish's scrutiny, of Agnes's relentless machinations, bore down upon them like a palpable storm. What had begun as whispered suspicions was now a formal trial of their very existence a trial that demanded more than mere knowledge of history or feigned social grace. It demanded navigation of a complex and unforgiving system of laws and customs, a system eager to cast out those who deviated from its rigid boundaries.

The next days unfolded in a blur of whispered preparations and anxious strategy. Caroline, ever the scholar, poured over fragmented parish records Thomas had rescued from a treacherous foray into the village archives while she rehearsed carefully crafted but honest responses to expected inquiries. Thomas, his broad shoulders carrying the palpable burden of their precarious position, patrolled the perimeter with the quiet vigilance born of both instinct and affection. Their shared ordeal, though fraught with tension, began to kindle a burgeoning closeness a tether forged in shared adversity that neither could yet fully admit.

When the appointed hour arrived, the hum of gathering voices echoed through Bramleigh's modest meeting hall, a place where village elders and parish officers convened to arbitrate disputes, dispense justice, and preserve community harmony. Caroline's gown, modest but carefully arranged to blend with local customs, felt heavy upon her skin not just in fabric, but in the significance it bore. Thomas stood beside her, the façade of a distant country gentleman now utterly transformed into the sturdy husband she was expected to embody. The hard eyes of the assembled audience bore into them with the weight of centuries-old precedent, machinery of order ready to crush divergence.

The questioning was relentless. Agnes Pryce presided with an icy precision, recounting the "facts" she had meticulously gathered late-night meetings, unexplained arrivals, absence from church registers, and the suspicious ease with which they had integrated themselves despite their ambiguous origins. Caroline responded with candid explanations tempered by historical insight, emphasizing the genuine affection that had begun to root between them and the practical necessity behind their assumed marriage. Yet every word was met with murmurs, skeptical glances, and the grim nods of those who upheld the old ways without mercy.

When the final probing silence settled, a verdict hung heavy in the air. The parish court conceded that the couple's living arrangement and the honesty they now displayed mitigated some fears, but the absence of formal documentation and sponsorship was irrefutable. The order was clear: they must prove their merit through service to the community and strict adherence to social norms, or face expulsion upon the next session. Agnes's triumphant smile was barely concealed as she concluded with a pointed reminder that the parish's goodwill was no guarantee and that any further deviation could spell their removal.

Back in the narrow confines of their cottage, Caroline allowed herself a moment of vulnerability, fingers trembling as she sank against the wooden wall. The legal gauntlet had been thrown, harsh and unyielding, but the faint flicker of hope in Thomas's steady gaze emboldened her. Survival in Bramleigh demanded more than conquered history; it demanded the surrender of control, the trust in each other, and the willingness to forge a real bond where once only pretense existed. The parish questioning was not merely a trial of their presence, but a crucible in which their true union and their future must be forged.

The days following the unsettling accusations seemed to shrink Caroline and Thomas into a ever-tightening coil of anxiety and caution. The once faint murmurs among Bramleigh's villagers had blossomed into a venomous chorus of suspicion, carrying with them not only the sting of social ostracism but the tangible, looming threat of official intervention. Each glance from a neighbor felt laden with consequences; the once welcoming, if reserved, eyes now sharpened into instruments of judgement. It was as though the village had coalesced into a restless tribunal, the weight of every whispered word pressing down upon them. The fragile semblance of safety they had carved out within the cramped walls of the cottage began to feel like a cage, its bars forged by suspicion and the cold steel of the law that Agnes Pryce wielded with merciless precision.

Agnes, resolute and cunning, had quickly transformed from a mere figure of local authority into an omnipresent specter shadowing their every move. Her influence extended well beyond the reach of polite society; she embodied the strict enforcement of Bramleigh's social codes, a guardian of order whose methods were as subtle as they were unforgiving. Where once Caroline and Thomas had hoped to remain unnoticed, they found themselves under Agnes's vigilant gaze, each action scrutinized and cataloged. It was no longer adequate to simply exist in this community; they had to convincingly blend into a world that seemed determined to peel away their layers of pretense. The pressures of performance posing as husband and wife, adopting the roles demanded by eighteenth-century decorum now twisted into a desperate struggle to outmaneuver not just gossip but the impending machinery of parish law.

The parish authorities, alerted by Agnes's calculated insinuations, wasted no time in casting a shadow of official suspicion. The village constable, a stoic man with little room for leniency, arrived at their door with a dossier of complaints and a stare that carved away complacency. Caroline's pulse quickened as she recognized the stark reality of their predicament: they were no longer mere outsiders subject to idle chatter but alleged vagrants, accused of trespassing upon social order and threatening the stability of the community. The notion was both surreal and devastating, a cruel inversion of their desperate need to find sanctuary. Thomas's presence beside her was a steadfast anchor as the constable's voice bore down with a gravity that brooked no argument. They were summoned to prove their legitimacy, under threat of swift expulsion a fate that in this unforgiving time could mean ruin, or worse.

Within the charged silence of their meeting with the parish overseers, Caroline's mind raced, dissecting every piece of historical knowledge she had ever gathered, only to find their usefulness limited by the relentless immediacy of their situation. The 1770s laws regarding vagrancy were merciless, designed to root out and cast aside those deemed undesirable, outcasts who disrupted the fragile balance of rural life. Agnes's accusations, though veiled in propriety, carried the brutal weight of these laws; to be branded vagrants was to be condemned not merely socially but legally, with consequences cascading far beyond mere whispers and glares. Caroline fought against the instinct to freeze, to retreat behind cold logic, realizing that twisting facts into rare comfort was insufficient against the raw force of prejudice and suspicion.

Thomas, who initially had seemed the less encumbered by knowledge, revealed a keen instinct for survival. His presence, a protective shield against the encroaching threat, grounded Caroline's resolve. He navigated their conversations with a wary composure, balancing deference with assertive defense when challenged by the parish officers or confronted by villagers emboldened by Agnes's proximity. Yet beneath his calm exterior flickered the undercurrent of tension the shared unspoken fear that their tenuous grasp on their assumed identities might unravel under the strain of inquisitions and insinuations.

Even as the formal interactions wore on, Agnes's influence seeped into the undercurrents of village life, galvanizing a growing alignment against them. The quiet parlor gatherings turned into pointed discussions, eyes darting to the disguised couple as if awaiting the moment their deception would be uncovered. The cottage, once a sanctuary carved from desperation, began to feel less like a refuge and more like a stage set for exposure and humiliation. Caroline sensed the fragile truce between appearances and reality fraying at the edges; every day required a new layer of vigilance, a deeper submersion into roles that barely masked their true selves. Each time they spoke in the presence of others, carved out spaces to pretend familiarity, their breaths quickened under the oppressive weight of potential discovery.

Amid the mounting pressure, the stark contrast between their own values and the rigid expectations of Bramleigh's society became painfully clear. Caroline, trained to dissect history as a detached observer, grappled with the visceral immediacy of living under the social codes she once studied from a distance. Her instinct to rely on facts and measured control clashed violently with the unpredictable cruelty of a community mobilizing to evict what it labeled as a threat. The lessons of the past, once contained within the neat margins of books, now writhed tangibly before her eyes. To survive, she would have to surrender the illusion of control, embracing a vulnerability that racked her with doubt. Thomas, too, wrestled with the constraints, embodying the protective strength necessary to navigate these treacherous waters but grappling inwardly with his own sense of alienation and the fear of losing the fragile identity they had painstakingly constructed.

Their nights grew restless, shadows of paranoia creeping with the dwindling light. The threat of expulsion hung like a guillotine, its blade poised to sever them from the only foothold they had managed to secure. Protected moments of respite were fleeting, constantly interrupted by the harsh realities beyond their doorstep. Caroline's thoughts spiraled into what-ifs: what if Agnes's influence succeeded beyond mere social exile what if the parish authorities condemned them to deeper punishment, branding them as vagabonds to be driven from not only Bramleigh but from any semblance of a home? Each imagined scenario intensified the cold knot of dread anchoring her stomach, pulling tight with the knowledge that their survival depended on balance so fine it seemed impossible to maintain.

In the rare instances when the cottage lay quiet and the village's scrutiny temporarily faded, Caroline and Thomas found themselves confronting the raw, unvarnished truths beneath their forced masquerade. The intimate spaces between them, once filled with tentative politeness and cautious observation, began to thrum with a deeper urgency born from shared peril. Caroline's carefully constructed defenses softened in the warmth of Thomas's steadfast presence, his touch a reminder that beneath the facade of survival was the undeniable pulse of human connection. Their conversations, once strictly practical, laced with a blend of disbelief and exhaustion, began to touch on the unspoken fears and hopes that tethered them together. In those moments, the cold calculus of history gave way to the fierce warmth of trust and longing, a fragile flame flickering against the encroaching darkness.

Yet even as their bond strengthened, the ever-watchful eyes of Agnes refused to relent. She intensified her efforts, weaving a tapestry of subtle threats and public insinuations, her words hotly barbed with the sharp edge of social condemnation. Her actions were not mere cruelty but a calculated assertion of power, a demonstration that control within Bramleigh was absolute and that any challenge even one as desperate as Caroline and Thomas would be met with ruthless opposition. The village's social order was her domain, and she wielded it with an unwavering grip, unsparing in her enforcement of conformity.

The crossroads at which Caroline and Thomas found themselves was fraught with peril and possibility. The choice to flee remained tantalizingly close, but the thought of abandoning the fragile life they had begun to build instilled its own brand of terror. To leave was to return to uncertainty, to a past and future neither fully understood; to stay was to risk total ruin at the hands of an unyielding enemy. Within this crucible of doubt and defiance, their connection, forged in necessity and tempered by adversity, became their greatest weapon and their most profound vulnerability. The village of Bramleigh, with its rolling hills and narrow lanes, had become not only their prison but the unlikely crucible of their transformation for in the rising danger, amidst threats and whispered condemnations, love took root, defiant and fiercely alive.

As the first snows threatened to blanket the village in cold silence, the pressure compounded, sharpening the stakes and drawing every moment taut with the urgency of survival. Caroline and Thomas remained bound together not merely by circumstance but by a burgeoning resolve that transcended fear. They would not be erased, not by gossip nor by the iron hand of parish law. Whatever tempests Agnes Pryce sought to unleash, the couple resolved to meet them head-on, their tenuous alliance blossoming into a formidable force of shared courage. The book that had brought them here may have bound them with its inscrutable commands, but it was their will, their growing love, and their refusal to surrender that would ultimately define their passage through this perilous chapter of time.

The Door Appears

The Final Directive

The air in their cramped cottage felt heavier than ever, the weight of the final directive pressing down on them as tangibly as the thick winter fog clinging to the windows. Caroline sat curled on the edge of the threadbare mattress, the ancient book resting on her lap but unopened; she barely had the strength to meet Thomas's gaze as he paced in slow, measured steps, his brows drawn tight in the kind of thoughtfulness that made the room seem smaller. The flicker of the lone candle cast shifting shadows across the walls, echoing the turmoil that churned relentlessly in both their hearts. It was more than a choice; it was a crossroad dividing the lives they had known from the fragile, uncertain existence they had begun to forge here a life painstakingly built on half-truths that had gradually blossomed into something raw and unguarded, something infinitely more dangerous than any law or social order. The book, once a cold, inscrutable artifact dictating their survival with mechanical impartiality, now pulsed with an urgency that spoke not just in commands but in unspoken promises and possibilities a final, haunting challenge wrapped in layers of fear, hope, and the profound unknown.

Caroline's mind raced as she thought back to the earliest moments in the Arkwell Library, when the mysterious tome had first called to her and Thomas in tandem, bridging centuries with an unbreakable link neither of them had wished for yet couldn't deny. The stark contrast between her measured, studied existence as a social historian and the brutal immediacy of life in Bramleigh had shattered every illusion she held about control. She recalled the cold grip of fear the first night, when the village's unforgiving gaze threatened to unravel her very being, and how Thomas's steady presence became a balm both reassuring and maddening, pulling her back from the edge of desperate despair. Now, with this final command, the book's message was no longer about mere survival but about transformation, about surrendering to life's unpredictable currents and accepting that the path forward could not be dictated by history's cold facts alone.

Thomas's voice broke the silence, low and rough, charged with a vulnerability that had become as much a part of their shared story as the whispered exchanges in the dark. "We can't go back, Caroline. Not really. If we do, we lose this us. Whatever this is we've found in each other. The book... it's giving us a choice, but I don't think it's just about time or place. It's about who we are, what we're willing to risk." His eyes searched hers, fierce and pleading. "Do you feel it too? The way it's changed us? We can't unmake those feelings."

Caroline swallowed hard, the knowledge far more painful than the unknown. Every scholarly muscle within her revolted against the irrationality of emotions that refused neat categories or logical patterns. And yet, staring into Thomas's face, marked by equal parts strength and uncertainty, she felt the undeniable truth this forced companionship had grown into a bond that transcended the artificial boundaries of centuries. The book's relentless ticking, much like a heartbeat, urged her to confront the truths she had so carefully barricaded behind layers of research and reason. The love that had bloomed from necessity was no longer a fragile pretense but a fiercely guarded flame demanding recognition.

The choice offered was stark: return to the safety and familiarity of their own time, disjointed perhaps but sovereign and intact, or remain in Bramleigh, embracing the uncertainty of a past defined by its rigid social strictures yet enlivened by genuine affection and a daring hope for belonging. The implications rolled over Caroline like a tidal wave were they to resign themselves to relinquishing all they knew for a life forged alongside each other in a world both foreign and unforgiving? Or was the pull of modernity, with its freedoms and complexities, irresistible enough to sever the bond forged in adversity? She wrestled with the bitter taste of knowing that either path would fracture something essential, that the option to blend past and present did not exist, that their love had been the price of admission into one world or the other.

Thomas, sensing her hesitation, moved closer and reached for her hand, anchoring her trembling fingers in his own. His touch was both an affirmation and a question, a silent vow woven through the flickering candlelight. "I don't want to be a stranger to you. Not now. Not ever. If this book's final demand is about surrender, then I'm ready to surrender to you, to us. But I can't do this alone."

The earnestness in his words softened the iron knot of Caroline's heart. She realized that the essence of the book's mysterious mandate was not mere obedience to time's cruel dictates, but an invitation to break free from the tyranny of isolation an urging to find courage in vulnerability, to choose love in defiance of fear. For Caroline, who had always prized autonomy and control above all else, the prospect was both exhilarating and terrifying. The possibility of committing herself fully, not just to the illusion of protection but to the messy, tender reality of mutual dependency, demanded a kind of trust she had never before granted another soul.

As the night deepened, their conversation meandered through the memories of shared moments quiet evenings huddled over modest meals, the stolen glances that had crystallized into longing, the whispered confessions wrapped in the safety of shadows. Each memory was a brick in the fragile edifice of their new life, a testament to how much they had endured and how much they had dared to hope. The village's omnipresent threat had softened in the face of their growing intimacy; Agnes Pryce's cold, calculating menace now seemed almost distant, a reminder of the past's unforgiving embrace rather than an immediate danger. Caroline understood, with a sharp clarity, that choosing to remain meant confronting not only external threats but also the deep-seated fears that had defined her entire existence the fear of losing control, the fear of being unmoored from the identity she had meticulously constructed.

Yet, the alternative was equally daunting. Returning to their own century meant stepping back into lives marked by fractured relationships and unanswered questions, lives where the warmth and fervor they had kindled risked fading into the oblivion of what might have been. The very notion of their connection surviving the temporal rift seemed fraught with doubt, the ache of parting almost worse than the fear of exposure in 1770. Caroline found herself imagining the sterile, impersonal spaces of libraries and lecture halls, the silent company of dusty volumes and lifeless facts, contrasted against the vivid, breathless reality of their days together in Bramleigh the snow-dusted woods, the coarse blankets in their cottage, the tender brush of a hand in the dark. Which world held more truth? Which offered a life worth living?

They spoke long into the night, unraveling threads of hope, fear, and desire with a raw honesty born of necessity. The book lay between them, a silent witness to their agony and resolve, its final words a painful beacon lighting the narrow path ahead. The message was clear but merciless: this was not merely a crossroads of time but a crossroads of the heart. To choose one meant irrevocably leaving the other behind. There was no middle ground, no safe retreat into the certainty of the past or present; only the galvanizing, unsettling power of a love that demanded risk and sacrifice.

Caroline's thoughts drifted to Agnes Pryce once more, the embodiment of the harsh social order waiting to punish any misstep. Agnes was more than a widow wielding influence she was a living symbol of the constraints they sought to escape, a reminder that the world of Bramleigh was a labyrinth of peril beneath its quaint exterior. To stay was to defy the very forces Agnes represented, to claim a place among those who had no right to belong. But it was also to claim each other, to assert the authenticity of a bond that had transcended survival tactics and morphed into genuine partnership. For every cautious instinct that whispered of danger, another flame inside Caroline's heart flared with the fierce determination to seize this rare, exquisite chance at happiness one born not of circumstance but of choice.

Thomas squeezed her hand gently, anchoring her spiraling thoughts with the quiet certainty of his presence. "Whatever happens," he said softly, "I want to face it with you. Not as strangers bound by fate, but as partners who've chosen each other, against all odds. The book's final directive it's asking us to stop pretending, to embrace what's real between us. It's terrifying, but it's also the only way forward."

Caroline's breath caught, a mixture of fear and exhilaration flooding her senses. The final directive was not just an end; it was a beginning. It demanded that they relinquish the safety of detachment, confront their deepest vulnerabilities, and courageously step into the unknown together. It was a message that dispelled the illusion of control she so desperately clung to and illuminated the path towards a love unbounded by time, bound instead by trust and choice.

In the cold stillness before dawn, they made their unspoken pact. They would embrace the uncertainty, defy the rigid strictures of the past, and honor the fragile, fierce love that had blossomed amidst hardship. The book's last words were no longer a command but a declaration of the power of human connection the power to transcend fear, to find belonging in another's arms, and to choose love as an act of radical courage.

Caroline closed her eyes, feeling the steady beat of Thomas's heart against her palm and the quiet strength of a promise that could outlast centuries. The final directive had revealed its true message: that beyond the boundaries of time and history, the greatest passage they could make was the passage into vulnerability, trust, and the profound, transformative power of love.

The dim glow of the hearth cast flickering shadows over the worn wooden beams above, lending the small room an intimacy that felt both comforting and suffocating. Caroline sat beside Thomas, her fingers entwined in her lap, trembling ever so slightly as if betraying the storm of thoughts swirling inside her. The book the cursed, mysterious artifact that had brought them to this strange new past lay closed on the rough-hewn table, its presence both a tether and a torment. It had promised a passage, a journey through time, but now offered them an agonizing choice a return to the future they belonged to or a reluctant surrender to the time into which they had been thrust. Neither option felt safe, neither path certain. Caroline's heartbeat thudded erratically, each pulse echoing the fear that had rooted itself deep within her, a lurking dread that gripped her with tendrils of cold anxiety. The very idea of leaving this place, of stepping through the veiled threshold back to the life she knew, filled her with a paralytic terror. It wasn't simply the fear of the unknown future awaiting her; it was the devastating uncertainty of what leaving might unravel between them.

Thomas shifted beside her, his broad frame curved protectively, yet his own turmoil writhed visibly beneath the surface. His usual steady composure was fractured as he grappled with the magnitude of what this moment demanded more than survival, more than adaptation, this was the crucible where their hearts, forged in the harsh fires of necessity, now faced the ultimate trial. He reached out, brushing a stray lock of hair from Caroline's brow, the gesture quiet but laden with unspoken questions. Could he imagine returning alone? Could she? The thought of parting, after months of forced closeness betraying a kind of reluctant affection, ripped at him with merciless intensity. They had not merely learned to coexist; through the veils of danger, suspicion, and the daily struggle to navigate Bramleigh's rigid social labyrinth, they had built something fragile yet undeniable. The weight of that growing bond met him in every gaze, every shared breath, and now this precipitous choice threatened to shatter it all, casting them back into a world where their connection might dissolve like mist at dawn.

Caroline's mind raced, grasping at memories moments that had surprised her with their warmth and sharpness. The way Thomas had steadied her when the biting wind of winter cut through their tattered clothing, the quiet evenings where conversation dwindled into comfortable silence, the tentative touches that had blossomed from mere necessity into something more urgent and tender. How could she undo those moments, those feelings, and reinsert herself into a future where such intimacy had never existed? Her usual fortress of knowledge and control crumbled under the weight of vulnerability, forcing her to confront a frightening question: was this 18th-century village, with all its crude hardships and looming threats, now the only place where she truly belonged? The concept unsettled her deeply. Returning meant reclaiming her identity as a historian, a modern woman armed with facts and reason; yet staying threatened to erode those very foundations, to cast her as a provincial wife bound by conventions she had always observed with critical detachment. The paradox clawed at her: to leave was to preserve her sense of self, but to remain was to embrace the intoxicating, terrifying reality of love and belonging.

Thomas's gaze bore into hers then, steady and unwavering, a beacon amidst the chaos of her doubts. "Caroline," he breathed softly, his voice threaded with both resolve and an aching vulnerability, "we can't pretend this is just survival anymore. Whatever we choose, it changes everything. I " He stopped, swallowing thickly, wrestling with the emotions that threatened to spill. "Leaving means losing what we might have found here together." The admission hung between them like a fragile crystal, gleaming with hope yet dangerously fragile. Caroline's throat tightened as she wrestled with the truth in his words. The book's earlier demands, that they pose as husband and wife to survive, had been a forced deception. But now, beneath the veil of necessity, a profound reality had taken root. To pretend no longer felt possible, nor desirable. Yet, the magnitude of becoming something permanent, something real in a different time, was both exhilarating and terrifying. Their future, once so assured in its predictability, now fluttered like a leaf in a storm unsettled, unpredictable, and infinitely fraught with peril.

The room seemed smaller, the air thicker, as Caroline struggled to breathe past the swell of emotion. She thought of the cold roads lined with gnarled trees, the village's watchful eyes, Agnes Pryce's calculating presence sharpening the edges of their peril. Yet here, in this cramped space filled with only the quiet crackle of fire, those dangers felt distant shadows compared to the tempest raging within her. What was survival if it meant sacrificing the very core of one's being? Could she surrender her modern independence, her resolute self-reliance, for a chance at a love that defied logic and time? The thought unsettled her, yet at its core, also sparked an ember of fierce hope. To love was to risk everything to submit to uncertainty, to trust in the unseen. Caroline had spent a lifetime building walls, convincing herself control was safety. Now those walls threatened to crumble, revealing a raw, unguarded truth that terrified even as it beckoned.

Thomas shifted again, closing the slight distance between them until their hands brushed tentatively. The simple contact ignited an ember of courage within Caroline, a tacit reassurance that, whatever the path, they would face it together. Yet, even as warmth bloomed between them, anxiety tightened its grip the agonizing weight of what "together" truly meant. In their modern lives, bonds were straightforward, unburdened by the suffocating strictures of an 18th-century village. Here, every glance, every whispered rumor carried the potential for ruin. Their love, slow and trembling, was vulnerable to a society that demanded conformity and punished deviation with ruthless precision. Could passion born in forced proximity withstand such scrutiny?

Could trust, seeded amid suspicion and fear, flourish into something unbreakable? Caroline doubted, yet could not deny the fierce need to try.

The past whispered through the room like a lingering breath, its unyielding traditions pressing down with the weight of centuries. Outside, the world pressed on, indifferent to their dilemma. The fire sputtered low, drawing shadows into painful starkness, mirroring the stark choices that lay before them. To leave was to return to order and familiarity, a world where survival would mean rebuilding everything from scratch, without the shared history now etched in their souls. To stay was to embrace chaos and uncertainty, but with a promise fragile, perhaps foolhardy that love could carve out a sanctuary amidst the brutality of time. Caroline's thoughts swirled relentlessly. Was she ready to abandon her past, to erase the certainty of her own identity for an uncertain future steeped in hardship and yearning? Was Thomas?

He caught her gaze, the flicker of determination steadying in his eyes. "I don't want to lose you," he said quietly, the depth of his feeling unvarnished and raw. "Whatever happens, we'll face it as more than just strangers thrown together by a strange fate. We're more than that now." He paused, searching for the right words to bridge the chasm of fear between them. "If we go back, will all this" he gestured between them, encompassing the unspoken connection "mean nothing? Or is it what changes everything?"

Caroline swallowed hard, the question reverberating through her like a bell tolling in a quiet cathedral. The thought that everything they had endured, every stolen moment of tenderness and defiance, might vanish if they separated was almost unbearable. Yet, the doubt gnawed at her: could love even survive in a world that had not prepared either of them for such an existence? Was the promise of passion enough to anchor them against the tides of time's cruelty?

The shadows deepened as the night crept forward, drawing the room into cold silence. Caroline rose suddenly, her movement abrupt, searching for footing in the maelstrom of emotion.

She paced the length of the tiny cottage, her palms pressed to the rough wall, seeking grounding in its stubborn solidity. The past was real, cruel, and unyielding. The future was unknown, vast, and full of possibility yet bound with chains of isolation and loss. And between them stood this fragile man, Thomas Reed her partner, her adversary in fate's cruel game, her companion in this bewildering journey his presence a beacon in the void. The fear of leaving was not just about stepping back into the future; it was about the deep-seated terror of losing what had blossomed between them under impossible conditions. It was about facing the unknown not as individuals, but with the aching knowledge that what their hearts demanded might defy reason, time, and chance alike.

Returning meant relinquishing the extraordinary intimacy born in hardship, sacrificing the life that had grown out of necessity into something genuine and fiercely protective. Staying meant dragging remnants of a modern existence into a world that demanded total surrender. The stakes felt unbearably high, the equation impossible to solve without loss. Caroline's breath caught as she looked at Thomas. Her voice trembled but held steady. "I don't know if I'm brave enough to choose," she confessed, the raw truth breaking free amid the flickering shadows. "But I do know that I don't want to choose alone. Whatever comes, I want you with me."

For the first time, a faint, hopeful smile curved Thomas's lips. The fear of leaving did not vanish it could not but it was tempered now by the promise of shared courage. They were bound, not merely by circumstance or a strange, enchanted book, but by the tender, resilient threads of something profoundly human: love, fierce enough to face the shadows, whatever time it might inhabit.

The cold candlelight flickered across the worn wooden table where Caroline and Thomas sat facing one another, the weight of their decision pressing heavily between them as if the very air had thickened with the gravity of what lay ahead. Shadows danced on her face, casting her pale features into stark relief, the worry etched deep in her brow making her look at once fragile and fierce a paradox as complicated as the choice before them. She clasped her hands tightly, struggling to steady the tremor she did not dare admit to, the treacherous flutter in her chest that only grew with each silent beat. Before her, Thomas's eyes searched hers desperately, no longer the stranger she had met in a modern library but a man carved by chapters of hardship, intimacy, and shared secrets. The man she had come to depend on in ways that transcended mere survival. Between them lay the revealed truth: the book that had bound their fate now demanded their final verdict, a cruel ultimatum that would carry them either back to a world governed by modern certainty or deeper into the unforgiving yet strangely alluring past.

Neither spoke at first, each lost to the visions that stirred in their minds fleeting images of the lives they could reclaim or the life they might build anew. Caroline's thoughts tugged her violently to the familiar places she knew: the hum of the city, the sanctuary of the Arkwell Library with its quiet reassurance, the casual freedoms of a time where women like her could choose her own path without fear of immediate social exile or the chilling threat of legal retribution. She longed for the comfort of logic, the simple clarity that facts and research had always offered her. Yet beneath the surface of that intellectual refuge was the raw ache of loss so profound it threatened to shatter the very foundation of her reason.

The world she had stumbled away from was no longer sufficient, having been forever altered by her journey through time, by the intimacy she had found in a place where every unguarded moment carried peril.

Thomas's gaze was unwavering but shadowed with its own turmoil. The past was his home now, more so than any memory of his life before the book's merciless twist. The sunlit fields of Bramleigh, the cramped cottage they shared, even the watching eyes of Agnes Pryce it was all painfully real. He knew the risks that came with staying, of the social traps and whispered accusations that could ruin them, but here, in the heart of 1770, he had become something more than a nameless interloper. He was Caroline's protector, her partner in a dangerous dance, and, now, something far deeper. Yet the idea of uprooting everything just to slip back into a shadowed past, a life they had left as strangers, frightened him more than the uncertainty of remaining. Would the modern world welcome them back as the same people who had so suddenly vanished? Or would they be ghosts cast aside by time itself?

Their shared silence stretched on, a fragile thread connecting two hearts teetering on the brink of a decision that would shatter their existence or forge it anew. Caroline broke the stillness first, her voice a brittle whisper laced with vulnerability she rarely allowed herself to reveal. "I don't know if I can go back, Thomas. Not like this. After everything... after us." Her fingers trembled as she reached across the table, searching for his hand, grounding herself in the warmth of his touch. Their palms met, a simple gesture loaded with unspoken promises and the tender revelation of feelings that had grown from desperation into love. "Back in the library, it was all order rules, facts, control. But here, with you, it's chaos and fear. And yet... I feel more alive than I ever have."

Thomas exhaled slowly, his jaw tightening as he fought against the swell of emotions threatening to overwhelm his steadfast exterior. "When we first found ourselves trapped in

Bramleigh, I thought survival would be all that mattered. I told myself just hold on to the day, get through the dangers, fake whatever roles we must. But the truth is..." He paused, eyes gleaming with quiet depth. "This isn't just about enduring anymore. You've given me reasons to want more. To hope. You've been my anchor in the storm, Caroline. If we go back, I'll lose that. I don't know if I can."

Her breath caught, the rawness of his admission opening a chasm in her carefully constructed defenses. The unyielding historian who had sought refuge in facts had been undone by a man whose strength was less about brute force and more about the courage to feel deeply against all odds. The vulnerability in his voice mirrored her own, revealing layers of desperation beneath the guise of calm resolve. Despite the danger, the cold scrutiny of Agnes's gaze that still lingered in the corners of her mind, despite the ever-present threat of exposure and expulsion from the only time they truly belonged to now, Caroline's heart whispered truths louder than fear.

"I'm scared," she confessed, voice barely above a breath. "Scared of losing everything I've worked for. But I'm more scared of losing you." The admission felt like a release, a small victory carved from her exhausting battle to maintain control. "Is our love worth the risk? Worth the sacrifice of two entire lifetimes? Could we survive in the uncertainty of the future or the relentless strictures of the past?"

The flicker in Thomas's eyes softened as he leaned forward, his other hand joining hers, their fingers entwined as though pledging fidelity not just to each other, but to the impossible path they faced. "Love isn't about certainty, Caroline. It's about choice. About standing with someone when there's nothing else to hold on to but trust. We've already made this choice, haven't we? Every day we've stayed united, protecting each other against a world that refuses to accept us, we've declared that together, we are stronger than any fear than any time."

The warmth of his affirmation spread through her, seeping into places she thought had been hardened past repair. She recalled the long nights spent by the hearth, the quiet moments before dawn when they shared stories of who they were and who they wanted to become. Each memory was a thread weaving them closer, crafting a tapestry of belonging born not from the era they had chosen or been thrust into but from the rare alchemy of love. There was no turning back to the isolation of her former life where knowledge reigned supreme and human connection was a distant second. If choosing meant leaving that world behind and embracing all the unknowns this one held, then that was a trade Caroline was willing to make.

Yet the tension between heart and mind persisted, a stubborn knot she could not fully unravel. "If we stay, if we truly claim this place as ours... How do we face the judgment of Bramleigh? Agnes Pryce will not relent. We have no standing here, no protection beyond each other. We can never forget the risks." Her gaze faltered, shadows of doubt pooling in her eyes. "And if we go back go home how do we rebuild what's broken between us? Can we truly return to the modern world as changed people? Will they understand what we've become?"

Thomas nodded solemnly. "No matter the choice, the cost is high. But I would rather face the scorn of a past that fears us with you by my side, than live a lifetime in the comfort of the future without you." His voice grew fierce, resolute with the depth of his devotion. "I want to be more than a footnote in some forgotten history. I want to be your husband in every sense this life offers us. And if that means defying time itself, then so be it."

The room seemed to hold its breath as Caroline absorbed the magnitude of what he said the weight of all their moments, the promises whispered in fragile intimacy, the laughter mingled with tears amid the crude reality of their days in Bramleigh. It was not just a declaration of love but a battle cry against a world intent on denying them existence. For the first time,

Caroline saw beyond the historian's lens of detachment; she saw a future sculpted by raw human truth and boundless possibility. The woman who had thrived on certainties found herself standing at the crossroads of her identity between the safety of a past she knew well and the perilous, unpredictable promise of a new life forged in love.

Tears pricked her eyes, not from sorrow but a profound release, a surrender that was as much strength as it was vulnerability. "Then let us choose to brave the unknown with hands clasped together," she whispered, voice trembling but fierce with conviction. "If we are to be cast as outsiders, let us be outsiders who belong to each other first. Let Bramleigh see the truth of us, no matter the cost."

Thomas reached across the table, his fingers tracing the gentle contours of her face, as if imprinting the moment into his very soul. "Together," he echoed, his voice thick with emotion. "Forever."

Outside, the wind carried the distant howls

of winter, cruel and unyielding, but inside that small room, Caroline and Thomas found a warmth beyond the reach of time or fear. Their choice had been made not between worlds, but for love, a love fierce enough to transcend the boundaries of eras, an identity forged not by circumstance, but by the indomitable strength of their bond. In the quiet aftermath of their decision, the book remained closed on the table, its power diminished now that the true passage had been crossed the one from mere survival to belonging, from strangers to soulmates, from captivity to freedom.

As dawn crept slowly over Bramleigh's rooftops, Caroline rested her head against Thomas's shoulder, the fragile hope of a shared life blooming in spite of uncertainty. Though the roads ahead were uncharted, thick with trials and threats, they had found their compass in each other a passage beyond the confines of time, tethered only by the steadfast heartbeat of love.

Confrontation and Claim

Public Declaration

The chill of the damp autumn air clung to Caroline's spine as the square filled with gathering villagers, their breath visible in soft clouds against the fading light. She stood at the center, her heart a steady drum within her chest, eyes locked on the stoic faces assembled before her. The time for evasion had passed; the moment demanded courage she had summoned from depths she scarcely knew she possessed. Around the edges of the square, the familiar rough-hewn buildings of Bramleigh watched silently, their thatched roofs shadowed under the darkening sky. It was here, amidst the very heart of the village that had shaped so much of their ordeal, that Caroline would sever the invisible chains that Agnes Pryce had relentlessly tightened upon them. She felt Thomas's strong hand brush against hers, a tangible anchor in the mounting tide of apprehension swelling within.

Agnes stood apart from the crowd, regal in her widow's black, her eyes cold embers of disapproval and authority. She had wielded her power like a blade, subtle but unyielding, cutting through any semblance of normalcy Caroline and Thomas had tried to nurture. Agnes's whispered denouncements had spread like wildfire, darkening their reputation until suspicion bloomed in every wary look cast their way. That woman's grip on the village was suffocating a web woven from social mores, legal threats, and an icy resolve to expel the outsiders who dared disrupt her order. Caroline knew that to defy Agnes outright was to invite ruin, yet to yield meant perpetual exile from both the village and the fragile new life they had dared to build. The stark clarity of choice set her feet ablaze with resolve: silence was complicity, and performing their faux marriage was no longer enough. The truth raw, unvarnished, irrevocable had to be spoken loud and clear, so that no whisper could twist it into doubt.

Clearing her throat, Caroline summoned a calm she did not fully feel, scanning the faces in the crowd. There was fear there, yes, but also curiosity, a hunger for the story that had become village legend. Whispers flickered at the edges like restless shadows, as if the very air anticipated her words. Thomas stepped beside her, a steady presence whose gaze lent her strength his expression serious, protective, and unyielding. Together, they formed a united front, a living testament against the tides of suspicion. "Hear me, good people of Bramleigh," Caroline began, her voice trembling only momentarily before settling with the weight of conviction. "For too long, deception has been our shield, forged of necessity and desperation. But that shield shall break today, for I stand before you not as a stranger playing a part, but as one who has come to belong." Her words carved through the murmurs around her, a spark igniting the stillness.

The crowd shifted, eyes narrowing, some open with disbelief, others glinting with hope. Agnes's lips curled in a disdainful sneer, but her eyes flickered with something closer to unease beneath the veneer of control. Caroline pressed on, diving into the heart of the confession that had thumped relentlessly in her mind since that fateful morning in the Arkwell Library. "Thomas Reed and I arrived here by chance or perhaps by fate," she said, a faint smile touching her lips despite the tension. "Thrown into your world with but a book as our guide and a fragile pact to protect one another. We played at marriage to survive your laws and your watchful laws, but the lines between pretense and truth have long since blurred." Her gaze found Thomas's, a shared flame kindling in the space between them that no outsider could deny. "He is my husband, not just in the eyes of the book, but in my heart and soul."

A gasp rippled through the onlookers, rippling as if a sudden gust disturbed the leaves on a sleeping forest floor. Caroline felt the weight of every eye skeptical, accusing, stunned upon her, yet a fierce clarity steadied her voice. "We ask for your acceptance, not as strangers to be cast away, but as members of this community, bound by love, trust, and the desire to build a life within these walls. We seek no favors, only fairness and the chance to prove our worth beyond the book's commands and the shadows of suspicion." Her words hung in the heavy air, echoing against the timber and stone as if the village itself listened. Thomas's fingers tightened around hers, a silent vow reaffirmed.

Agnes's voice cut through the whispers like a whip crack, sharp and commanding. "This is folly! A dangerous charade that undermines the order of Bramleigh. Their presence threatens the fabric that holds us together. They are not of this time, nor part of our kin." Her accusation was heavy, meant to crush what Caroline had just dared to build. But the villagers, long accustomed to Agnes's tyranny cloaked in civility, did not burst into the scornful chorus the widow expected. Instead, pockets of murmurs grew into steady conversation, uncertainty blossoming where once there was unquestioned deference.

Caroline seized the moment, her words now imbued with a fierce, almost desperate hope.

"Agnes Pryce, you speak of order and kin, but what kinship is there in fear? What order in exile and suspicion? Thomas and I have lived among you, have shared your hardships and joys. We have learned your customs and respected your ways. It is love not fear that binds us now." She stepped forward slightly, letting the glow of courage warm her cheeks. "If you have questions, ask us. If you seek proof, we shall not hide behind silence. But do not mistake our past silence for deceit. We claim our place here with you and among you because it is where our hearts have found home." Her declaration rang out with the undeniable power of truth spoken from the soul.

Slowly, faces softened; old Mrs. Wilkes, who ran the village bakery, nodded subtly, and a few younger villagers exchanged glances heavy with unspoken empathy. Even the once-guarded eyes of the blacksmith betrayed flickers of curiosity rather than suspicion. Caroline sensed the fragile thread of acceptance beginning to weave itself anew through the tapestry of their lives. Thomas stepped forward, voice low but resolute, "We cherish Bramleigh not as a place to hide, but as the soil in which we will plant our future. We do not seek to change your ways but to live honestly within them. We ask only for your trust, a trust we will earn in time."

Agnes's face contorted with a mixture of fury and fear, realizing that her grip on the narrative was slipping. She opened her mouth to strike back, but the murmurs of the crowd grew louder, an undercurrent of quiet rebellion swelling beneath the surface. The villagers, long oppressed by Agnes's unyielding dominance, responded in subtle ways a murmured agreement, a nod, even the tentative step of a child reaching toward Caroline's outstretched hand. The power in the square was shifting, the old order bending to a new reality forged by courage, truth, and love.

Caroline's pulse thundered in her ears as she absorbed the moment this convergence of fear and hope, dread and possibility. The words had been spoken. No longer could Agnes's whispered threats cling so tightly to their lives. The village had witnessed the truth laid bare, and in that public proclamation, Caroline and Thomas claimed not just acceptance, but a place within the heart of Bramleigh's story. Her gaze met Thomas's once more a shared smile, tentative but certain and in that look, a promise bloomed: whatever trials lay ahead, they would face them together, not as strangers bound by circumstance, but as husband and wife, woven irrevocably into the fabric of a new beginning.

Defying Agnes

The air in the village square was crisp and sharp with the first biting edge of winter, the sky a heavy gray blanket muffling the usual hum of daylight activity. Caroline stood alongside Thomas beneath the somber shadow cast by the ancient elm tree, its barren branches an intricate web silhouetted against the cold, sullen sky. They had been summoned or rather, compelled to present themselves here by Agnes Pryce, whose reputation for silent subjugation and veiled menace lingered like a noxious fog over Bramleigh. Today's gathering was no customary town meeting; it was a tribunal disguised as community concern, an unequivocal threat clothed in the thin veneer of social propriety. The small crowd that had assembled was an odd mixture of curious onlookers, wary villagers, and Agnes's loyal confidantes, all carefully arranged to project the illusion of consensus. But beneath the surface, Caroline and Thomas could feel the tangible weight of judgment pressing in on them, closing the narrowing circle with suffocating inevitability.

Caroline's heart pounded fiercely, each beat a reminder of how precariously their fate balanced. For months, they had endured Agnes's casual inspections, her pointed questions disguised as helpful advice, and the tacit threats embedded in her chilly glances. Yet this this formal challenge was unlike any prior confrontation. It was a call to account not just for their presence in Bramleigh but for their very identities, forged in the fire of necessity and sealed by a bond created under duress but growing ever more genuine. More than a performance, their marriage had become a refuge, a new reality they had painstakingly constructed amid the cruel rigidity of eighteenth-century orthodoxy. Agnes's relentless scrutiny threatened to unravel it, to pull them apart, and expose them to the unforgiving mechanisms of expulsion and worse.

As Agnes stepped forward, the crowd's indifferent murmuring quieted into an expectant hush. Her figure, wrapped in sober woolen garments and draped with the weight of unquestioned authority, exuded an austere power. There was no need for raised voice or dramatic gestures; her presence alone commanded obedience and fear. Her eyes met Caroline's with an icy sharpness, a challenge masked by faux civility. "Mrs. Reed," she began, her voice measured and deliberate, "it has come to our attention that certain irregularities persist in your comportment, in disregard of the laws and customs which bind this village together." The formal tone was a weapon, a calculated twist of words designed to alienate and intimidate. Caroline felt the unspoken accusations as palpable as daggers falsehood, deception, and nonconformity.

Holding Thomas's hand beneath her layered skirts, Caroline drew strength from the warmth and certainty of his grip. Thomas's expression was resolute, tempered by a quiet fury that escalated under Agnes's insinuations. Caroline returned Agnes's gaze with a steady calm she forced herself to summon, the flame of defiance kindling beneath layers of frost. "Madam Pryce," she replied, voice firm though laced with an undercurrent of controlled emotion, "we abide by the customs and laws insofar as they permit our continued residence among you. Our intentions have never been to sow discord but to live in harmony, as any members of this community might wish." The words felt both an olive branch and a gauntlet thrown down. There was no denying that their presence had stirred unease, but Caroline refused to bow to fear or silent exclusion.

Agnes smiled a thin, cruel curl that failed to reach her eyes. "Harmony requires truth, Mrs. Reed. Pretension and artifice can only breed unrest. Your claim, after all, is one of marriage, yet many here harbor doubts." The whisper that followed was almost tender compared to previous encounters, but Caroline perceived it as venomous. The insinuation echoed loudly in the square, reverberating through the expectant eyes that watched their every move. To question the authenticity of their union was to cast shadows over their honor and standing an accusation that, in ambient 1770 Bramleigh, could bring ruin.

Thomas's jaw clenched, and he stepped forward, his broad shoulders squared as if to shield Caroline from the rising tide of hostility. "We marry not by convenience or falsehood," he declared, voice carrying across the hushed crowd with an authority that brooked no dispute. "But by choice, born of necessity and conviction. Our bond is no mere charade, Agnes Pryce." His direct confrontation struck a chord disrupting the simmering tension with an undeniable assertion of their reality. The villagers shifted uneasily, the fragile social order trembled under the weight of such unequivocal declarations.

Caroline watched his courage with a rising tide of admiration mingled with hope. Despite decades of historical study and a lifetime of retreat into facts and data, it was moments like these charged with raw emotion that forged true transformation. Their forced proximity, the trials endured, the stolen glances and whispered confessions, all converged into this singular moment of revelation. The realization that control must sometimes surrender to vulnerability, that survival demanded more than feigned perfection, blossomed in her heart like a dormant seed breaking free of frozen soil.

Agnes's eyes narrowed, the smile retreating into a scowl. "Words are wind, Mr. Reed. What proof have you beyond declaration? Neither ring nor vows have been exchanged as per custom, making your claim questionable." She gestured sharply toward the modest cottage where they had taken sanctuary, the place Agnes had deemed unbecoming and inappropriate for any truly legitimate union. "And the law is firm without proper sanction, your presence here remains illegal." Her voice dropped, a dark promise in its cadence. "I shall be compelled to report this matter to the magistrate, to preserve the village's honor and safety."

The crowd murmured again, the earlier curiosity slipping into unease and apprehension. It was a moment pregnant with possibility an imminent threat looming like a gathering storm. Caroline glanced at Thomas, feeling the steadiness in his gaze, the fierce protectiveness that had grown into something far deeper than mere obligation. They had come too far to crumble now. They owed themselves and one another a defiant stand, a challenge that might yet carve a path toward acceptance and belonging.

Drawing a deep breath to steady an erratic heartbeat, Caroline stepped fully into the light of the square, the all-too-familiar sensation of vulnerability giving way to a newfound resolve. "You speak of proof, Agnes Pryce," she said, voice clear and unwavering, commanding attention and silence. "Then witness it now." Turning to Thomas, she reached for his hand and lifted it gently. "I claim Thomas Reed not as a stranger, nor as a charade, but as my husband. In front of God and our neighbors, I declare what my heart has come to know: this is no pretense. It is truth." Her words fell like a bell's chime, resonant and unyielding, cutting through the thick miasma of suspicion.

The crowd's breath caught collectively. There was a pause in the rigid rhythm of village life; the social machinery seemed suddenly unsure how to proceed. Some faces betrayed surprise, others admiration; a few displayed unmistakable discomfort. Agnes's mouth tightened, lips pressed thin as though struggling to find a retort, a counterstroke. For once, Caroline's directness forced the widow into silence a silence weighted with the recognition that her carefully spun web of control had been rent, likely irreparably.

Thomas lifted Caroline's hand, brushing a kiss across her knuckles with solemn tenderness, sealing their claim. His voice softened, speaking not to the crowd but to her alone, yet loud enough for all to hear. "I stand beside you, Caroline. Our bond is forged in both hardship and choice. No edict or custom can undo what we have become." The intensity of his gaze and the sincerity threading every word reinforced the potency of their union, echoing beyond the scrutiny of an unyielding world.

In the moments that followed, murmurs rippled through the assembly like stirred leaves. Whispers of approval mingled with hesitant condemnations, but the undeniable presence of unity between Caroline and Thomas had altered the atmosphere. They were no longer merely outsiders or pretenders; they had asserted their place, claimed their identity not granted by others but chosen by themselves. Agnes's grip on the village's social leash slackened, and with it, the immediate threat of expulsion diminished. The widow's façade cracked beneath the weight of authentic human connection, revealing the vulnerability lurking behind her iron will.

Caroline felt something shift inside her, a melting of old fears and rigid boundaries. The harsh landscape of Bramleigh, with all its dangers and restrictions, had become a place where love not merely survival could take root. Thomas's steady presence beside her was the affirmation she had long denied herself: that control was not the opposite of strength, but that true strength sometimes demanded surrender, trust, and embracing uncertainty.

As the villagers slowly dispersed, the chill in the air seemed less biting, the sky less oppressive. Agnes Pryce retreated with the dignity of a woman bested but not broken, already plotting her next maneuvers, perhaps, yet for now contained. Caroline and Thomas remained together under the skeletal elm, hands entwined, bonded by a declaration that transcended centuries and risk.

The Book of Passage had thrust them into a history fraught with peril, yet through defiance and love, they had carved a passage of their own one illuminated by truth, courage, and an unbreakable connection that no whisper nor threat could extinguish.

In this pivotal confrontation, the boundaries between past and present, obligation and desire, had blurred into irrelevance. What remained was the undeniable reality of two hearts bound against the odds, forging a future from the fragmented threads of history and choice. The village might cling to its customs, but Caroline and Thomas had, with their defiance, rewritten the narrative not as passive players but as authors of their shared destiny. And in the quiet strength of that moment, amid the cold and tentative acceptance, the promise of love's transformative power shone brighter than any edict penned by tradition or fear.

The village square was alive with the usual hum of midmorning bustle the clatter of wagon wheels against cobblestones, the murmur of exchanges between traders and townsfolk, the occasional bark of a dog weaving through legs and livestock. Yet beneath this familiar rhythm, Caroline and Thomas could sense a heavier pulse, an undercurrent of anticipation that set the day apart from any other. From the moment Caroline had, with trembling resolve and fierce clarity, stepped forth before the gathered populace to claim Thomas Reed as her lawful husband, the atmosphere had shifted. Eyes, wide with a mixture of disbelief and curiosity, turned toward them, probing the sincerity of this sudden assertion.

For Caroline, this moment stretched like an eternity, every heartbeat amplified as she met Agnes Pryce's steely gaze, the widow's expression unreadable yet undeniably formidable. Agnes had ruled Bramleigh's unspoken laws and frosty social pecking order with an iron hand swathed in silk, her whispered condemnations and subtle manipulations upheld as a customary morality. To upend that balance, to publicly cast doubt upon Agnes's authority by declaring something so personal and irrevocable this had been the crux of their fragile survival. But now that the deed was done, the village's reaction would seal their place in this world, whether as anomalies cast out or new threads woven into its tapestry.

Slowly, as if reluctant to break a spell, the villagers sensed the weight behind Caroline's words. They recognized the risk she had taken not merely for her own sake, but for both of them. The whispered gossip, once suspicious and sharp, softened cautiously into tentative acceptance. Mothers who had watched their children shy away from Caroline's foreign manners now exchanged nods, some with sympathy, others with reluctant approval. The local blacksmith, a grizzled man named Harold who rarely spoke unless provoked, glanced at Thomas with a measured respect, his eyes briefly acknowledging the strength it took to stand unflinching under such scrutiny. Even the market vendors, usually quick to mock outsiders, offered small, tentative smiles.

Yet acceptance was not immediate, nor was it wholesale. Among the crowd, certain hardened faces remained skeptical lined with years spent defending tradition and wary of disruption. Caroline could feel their eyes still cutting through her like cold blades, accusing her of deception, of overstepping the bounds of propriety. It was instinctive, a reflexive clinging to the familiar in the face of change. But against this, the undeniable truth of their unity, their shared vulnerability and courage, wove a firm undercurrent that no amount of whispered dissent could undo.

As the morning sun climbed higher, casting splintered light through the village's thatched eaves, small gestures began to ripple outward, marking the subtle but undeniable shift in communal attitude. An elderly widow approached Caroline hesitantly, her voice trembling yet warm as she offered parcels of cured meats and fresh bread, traditional tokens of friendship extended in cautious acceptance. Children from nearby cottages, previously shy and untrusting, lingered at a respectful distance, their curiosity piqued by the propriety and quiet command Caroline and Thomas now embodied as a couple. Even Agnes, though maintaining her composed exterior, betrayed the faintest flicker of uncertainty a recognition, perhaps begrudging, that her hold over the village's moral reins was slipping.

In the days that followed, Caroline and Thomas found their place within Bramleigh's daily rhythms solidifying in ways both subtle and profound. Invitations to gatherings, previously nonexistent or laced with polite exclusions, began arriving more frequently, tentative but genuine bridges toward belonging. The village inn welcomed them openly, its proprietor exchanging knowing glances and folded smiles that spoke of newfound respect. Tasks once intercepted or redirected by Agnes's informants now passed unchallenged, while neighbors offered baser assistance tending to the garden, sharing thrifty advice on heating their modest cottage through winter's chill acts that underscored the shift from suspicion toward community.

Internally, Caroline wrestled with the unaccustomed warmth of these exchanges. Her historian's mind cataloged each interaction, measuring the delicate balance of acceptance balanced against lingering fears. Her desire for control, once so tightly held, softened under the weight of belonging, revealing the invitation to vulnerability she had resisted since crossing through time. Thomas's steady presence beside her became a quiet anchor, his confidence and calm complementing her tentative steps into integration. Together, their union, once a construct born of necessity, blossomed into a genuine partnership acknowledged by those around them not merely tolerated, but embraced.

The turning tide of opinion did not come without challenges or moments of doubt. Agnes, ever watchful, maneuvered with subtlety, her influence less overt but no less potent. Rumors fluttered on the village breeze questions about pasts, origins, legitimacy but each murmured suspicion lost strength in the face of Caroline's candid steadiness and Thomas's emerging role as a respected figure within the local social fabric. When Agnes sought to convene a formal hearing under the pretense of community welfare, the tide of public sentiment had turned enough to render such actions hollow. Instead, Agnes's authority, once formidable, suffered an erosion that mirrored the deeper transformations in Bramleigh's heart.

Crucially, the act of Caroline claiming Thomas as her husband transcended legalistic formality; it was an emphatic declaration of identity forged against time's indifferent currents. Their bond, once an artifice imposed by a mysterious force, now embodied choice and sacrifice, intertwining past and present in a way neither had anticipated but both embraced. This fusion sparked a ripple effect through the village, challenging entrenched notions about outsiders and the nature of belonging itself. Bramleigh's inhabitants, moment by moment, began to look beyond the constraints of rigid social hierarchies, allowing themselves to imagine a community enriched by transformation and the unexpected strength found in unity.

Even beneath the surface of social acceptance, Caroline and Thomas nurtured a more intimate victory the forging of a shared life balanced between dependence and independence, between control and surrender. Their public defiance of Agnes's authority fed their private understanding that survival in this era demanded not just compliance but authenticity. In the quiet spaces of their cottage, away from prying eyes, they built trust inch by patient inch. Shared meals, whispered conversations by candlelight, and moments of tentative touch formed the foundation of a partnership both passionate and tender. Their love, ignited by necessity's flames, burned with increasing clarity and depth, a beacon of hope and belonging within a world that had once been foreign and forbidding.

This profound transformation was not lost on the community. Neighbors began to see Caroline and Thomas not as anomalies to be tolerated but as neighbors to be valued. The distinction between outsider and insider blurred, redefined by shared experiences of hardship and resilience. Traditions, too, adapted; festivals included gestures acknowledging their participation, local customs adjusted subtly to accommodate their presence. Agnes Pryce herself, constrained by the shifting tides, retreated into a more measured role, her grip loosened by the indomitable will embodied in Caroline and Thomas's union.

By embracing their ostensible fate and claiming their place in Bramleigh, Caroline and Thomas had woven themselves into the village's living fabric. What began with uncertainty, suspicion, and the weight of survival challenges transformed into acceptance, respect, and community. Theirs was a triumph not merely of love enacted in defiance, but of identity deliberately reclaimed amid the relentless passage of time a testament to the human heart's capacity to find home where least expected and to solidify bonds that outlast even the strictest of social laws.

The Final Choice
At the Threshold

The dawn broke softly over Bramleigh, its golden light streaming through the lattice windows of the little cottage where Caroline and Thomas stood side by side, fingers entwined, hearts pounding with an urgency that was impossible to silence. Outside, the village stirred to life: a low murmur of distant voices mingled with the sharp clatter of carts on cobblestones, the occasional neigh of horses, and the penetrating call of a rooster asserting the day's arrival. Within the cramped room, however, an expansive silence hung between them quiet yet electric, brimming with unspoken promises and the weight of decisions too monumental to be uttered into the morning air.

Caroline's gaze flickered to the battered volume lying on the rough-hewn table, its cover now unadorned and inert. For weeks, it had been the strange arbiter of their unnatural union an external force compelling them to navigate a perilous world with deception and courage, dictating terms in an inscrutable language laced with authority and menace. The book's commands had been their tether to survival, yet also their cage, shackling them to roles neither wished to embrace fully. But now, as the first rays of light stretched across the timber beams overhead, the book lay silent. Its once vibrant pulse of mysterious energy had diminished, buried beneath quiet pages that no longer whispered threats or instructions, signaling an end to its hold over their lives.

Thomas shifted closer, his hand tightening around hers, grounding her in the moment. His eyes, still shadowed from nights of restless uncertainty, now blazed with something untamed and steady a fierce determination that seemed to burn away the remaining fear clinging to the edges of her mind. "Are you ready?" His voice was low, thick with the weight of all they'd endured together. Caroline swallowed hard, feeling the familiar pulse of nerves tangled with a burgeoning hope. She had spent weeks resisting the inevitable embrace of this place, this time, and especially the man beside her. But all resistance had worn thin, like the delicate lace that frayed at the edges of her clandestine gowns. Now, standing on this precipice, the chasm between past and future yawned wide and daunting, yet remarkably inviting.

Her breath fluttered as if caught in a trance. "I don't think I'll ever be 'ready' in the traditional sense," she confessed with a tremulous smile that crept along her lips, "but I am certain that this us this is where I belong." The words fell between them, delicate yet irrevocable, more potent than any oath they had spoken under the shadowed gaze of Agnes Pryce or beneath the harsh glare of judgmental villagers. Theirs was no longer a performance of marriage for survival's sake; it had blossomed into a true bond forged in the crucible of hardship, trust, and unexpected tenderness. Thomas's smile was slow and genuine, breaking through the last walls she'd built around herself.

Their cottage door, a haphazard construction of aged oak and rusted iron hinges, beckoned them forward both a barrier from the past and a portal to what lay beyond. Caroline hesitated only for a fleeting instant, the memories of cramped quarters, biting cold winters, and Agnes's piercing gaze intertwining with the warmth of stolen moments and whispered confessions. Every ache, every stolen glance, every brush of flesh beneath coarse linens led here, to this threshold. Drawing in a steadying breath to calm the whirlwind in her chest, she tightened her grip on Thomas's hand, letting his steady assurance settle her and turn uncertainty into a quiet resolve.

As they moved forward, feet shuffling against the worn wooden floorboards, the air itself seemed to shift, thick with anticipation and the scent of aged parchment mingled with the faint musk of woodsmoke from the hearth that flickered in the corner. The book, once bedecked with arcane symbols and pulsing with unseen power, lay closed a silent sentinel that no longer wielded control. Caroline stole a glance at it, her eyes lingering on the smooth, unmarked cover as a wave of release washed over her. No longer would their actions be dictated by invisible commands or the looming threat of exposure. Theirs was a life reclaimed by their own hands and hearts.

Crossing the threshold, Caroline felt a curious mixture of fear and exhilaration surge through her. Outside, the village awaited with its familiar routines, its scrutiny, but also its potential for something they both yearned for: a place to belong, not just as pretenders or fugitives from time, but as true inhabitants of this rugged landscape. Thomas's presence beside her was an anchor and a promise. His steady gaze met hers, quiet and unyielding in its assurance. "Together," he said simply, as if that single word could suffice for every trial and triumph to come.

Together, they stepped into the morning light, the subtle crunch of gravel beneath their boots grounding them in reality yet blessed by that strange touch of transcendent magic that had brought them here in the first place. The village breathed around them rough-hewn faces breaking into cautious smiles as they passed by, curious eyes softened by recognition of the bond Caroline and Thomas embodied, genuine at last. Their days of masquerade were done. The village, with all its rigid expectations and dangers, would still challenge them, but now they faced it not as strangers tethered by an unyielding book, but as partners bound by choice and love.

Caroline's heart swelled with an unexpected warmth as Thomas guided her toward the village square, the bustle of market vendors and the distant tolling of the church bell filling the air with a comforting rhythm. For the first time since their arrival, the future stretched out before her not as a gauntlet of survival but as a canvas ripe with possibility.

She could almost hear the soft cadence of laughter mingling with whispered promises, feel the budding connection to this place no longer an exile but a home. And through it all, there was Thomas, his hand in hers, the lines of his face softened in this new dawn of belonging.

In that quiet moment, Caroline understood that the book's silence was not an end but a beginning. It was the relinquishment of external control and the emergence of their own agency, the blossoming of a love that had been seeded in adversity and nurtured in vulnerability. The delicate dance of trust and surrender had transformed something cold and mechanical into something fiercely alive, pulsating with the raw power of shared humanity. They had crossed a line not just in the doorway of a cottage, but in the woven tapestry of time and destiny itself.

The sky above Bramleigh was painted with hues of soft rose and timid blue, the promise of a new day unfolding like a whispered secret on the breeze. Caroline's pulse echoed in her ears, steady and sure as the first step in a journey chosen freely, not commanded. The road ahead was uncertain, lined with the familiar trials of any life threaded through time's indifferent loom, but no longer would the threat of the book shadow their every move. Instead, their love resilient, fragile, and glorious would be the beacon guiding them forward.

Behind them, the cottage stood humble but steadfast, a symbol of all they had endured and all they had become. The book, now silent, rested in the dust upon the shelf, its pages no longer a map or a chain. Caroline cast one last look before turning fully toward Thomas, her eyes bright with unshed tears of a new beginning. "Here," she breathed, "is where we choose to be."

Thomas's smile crinkled the corners of his eyes, mirroring the tenderness blooming deep within his soul. "Here, and always," he promised, drawing her close as the village welcomed them not as strangers bound by circumstance, but as a couple forged in defiance of time itself.

Together, they stepped out into the day, crossing the threshold far more profound than the physical into the infinite realm of love freely given and freely claimed, where past and future faded into insignificance beside the limitless power of the present.

The late afternoon sunlight had softened to a gentle, golden haze as Caroline and Thomas stood side by side on the narrow path leading to the little cottage that was now more than just a refuge it was their home. The scent of damp earth mingled with the faint fragrance of thyme and wildflowers growing untamed along the edges of the road. Around them, the world of Bramleigh stretched in quiet acknowledgment of their presence, the ancient trees whispering their approval and the distant bleating of sheep punctuating the peace. For the first time since the chaotic spell of arrival, cloaked in confusion and uncertainty, neither of them felt the pull of another time no frantic thoughts of the Arkwell Library or the life left behind pinned their hearts to a past impossible to reach. Instead, there was only this moment, this place, and the intertwined breath of two souls who had fought to find each other amidst the enigma of centuries.

The threshold to their humble cottage was no longer a boundary marking exile or imprisonment; it was a portal to a future etched with the promise of renewal. Caroline's fingers trembled slightly as she reached out, her hand brushing against the rough-hewn wood of the door, worn smooth with years of weather and faithful use. It was a tangible link to the world they had stepped into a world where knowledge alone could not shield them, where survival demanded courage, compromise, and a heart softened by vulnerability. Thomas glanced at her, his dark eyes reflecting a flicker of the warmth that had grown steadily from their forced alliance into something resembling hope, and then into undeniable love. That transformation, unexpected and profound, had unraveled the tight threads of guardedness both had woven around their spirits.

Now, the man who had seemed so invincible, so wrapped in instincts honed by necessity, stood as a testament to the power of surrender of trusting not only in another but in the unknown future they would face together.

Without a word, their hands found each other, fingers entwining with a quiet certainty that spoke volumes. Caroline, who had long believed control was the fortress safeguarding her against chaos, finally allowed herself the exquisite vulnerability of complete surrender. To Thomas, this was not weakness but a courageous relinquishment, a gesture revealing trust deeper than any scheme or survival tactic. Their joined grip was a silent vow as solid and unyielding as the timber framing the cottage entrance that whatever trials lay ahead, they would navigate them side by side. The sound of the book, the mysterious guide whose hold had both threatened and protected them throughout this odyssey, fell away into an almost reverent silence. The absence of its commands was not an ending marred by loss but a profound closure, a gift allowing Caroline and Thomas to reclaim agency over their lives, their selves, and their love.

Stepping through the doorway together, the interior welcomed them with a humble warmth. The small hearth, cold but intact, promised many fires yet to come fires they would kindle together, sharing stories, secrets, and dreams long deferred by circumstance and time. The hand-carved table, rough but sturdy, seemed to invite them to sit, to create rituals that would root them firmly in this century and in each other's hearts. Caroline's gaze swept over the simple furnishings the worn stools, the plain curtains filtering soft light through the windowpane and she felt, for the first time, a deep and steady contentment settle like a balm upon her restless soul. This was not a displacement but a homecoming, not a retreat but the beginning of a deliberate and passionate claim on life itself.

Thomas closed the door behind them with a softness that belied his strength. He pulled Caroline close, his warmth a fortress against the encroaching twilight and the chill of uncertainty. Their bodies pressed together, heartbeat catching and releasing in tandem, an unspoken affirmation blooming in the space between breaths. Time, no longer a rigid master dictating their fate, stretched elastic and inviting before them. Through the pane, the village of Bramleigh rested quietly rustic rooftops crowned with moss, winding paths where life unfolded in rhythms different yet no less profound than any modern city pulse. Here, history was not merely recorded in books but lived, breathed, and shaped by hands like theirs.

Caroline's fingers traced the line of Thomas's jaw, marveling at the solidity of this man who had emerged from shadows of incomprehension to become her steadfast partner. In the delicate interplay of light and shadow, she saw the reflection of their journey moments of fear and defiance, tenderness and fiery passion, laughter shared in stolen pockets of peace, and tears wiped away with gentle reassurance. The book, once a symbol of both fear and curiosity, rested silently on the narrow windowsill, its pages closed as if satisfied that the task had been fulfilled. It no longer dictated their actions or thoughts; it had done its work and released them, leaving an emptiness filled not with despair but with limitless possibility.

They moved deeper into the room, letting the quiet envelop them like a soft cloak, and as the shadows grew longer, Caroline felt the weight of her past reservations dissolve. The meticulous historian who once clung tightly to facts beyond feeling began to understand that some truths were forged not from documents or relics but from the heart's quiet surrender. Love, she realized, was an uncharted history a delicate manuscript inked in moments of trust, of passion, of courage in vulnerability. And in Thomas's steady presence, she discovered something precious: a partner who accepted her complexities and challenges without hesitation, whose strength was magnified not by dominance but by an authentic desire to protect and cherish.

Outside, Agnes Pryce's influence waned as the days turned, her shadow no longer casting doubt or fear upon their shared path. The village's once watchful gaze softened, the social web untangling to allow space for something new and unspoken. It was as if the world itself recognized the legitimacy of their bond, not as a contrivance enforced by an arcane book, but as a love chosen freely despite the odds. The cottage walls echoed with quiet laughter and whispered hopes, the hearth's first crackle promising warmth beyond the physical a warmth born from acceptance, belonging, and the shared promise of tomorrow.

In that stillness, Caroline and Thomas sealed their unspoken vow a commitment that transcended the confines of time and circumstance. The book's silence was no void but a sacred pause, inviting them to script their own narrative with fearless hearts. Hand in hand, they stood embraced in the quiet twilight, ready at last to live wholly and passionately in the place where past and present converged, where love was both refuge and revolution. The path back was no longer a burden, for they had chosen forward into a life rich with promise, where every breath was a passage toward new horizons, and every touch a testament to the transformative power of love embraced without hesitation, without regret.

The brittle crispness of the autumn morning stretched thinly across their shoulders like a whispered promise, a delicate thread tethering Caroline and Thomas to the present moment that swelled with the weight of eternity. They stood side by side, breath mingling in quiet plumes, the soft rustle of fallen leaves beneath their worn boots the only sound in the settled hush of Bramleigh village. The world around them felt slower now, quieter, as if holding its breath in reverence for what was to come. The small cottage, once a cramped refuge, now stood as a sanctuary saturated with memories etched deep in wood and hearth every creak, every faint scent of smoke and lavender weaving into the fabric of their shared existence. Caroline's hand tightened around Thomas's, fingers intertwining as naturally as if they had always belonged together, woven by the same loom of fate that had stitched their lives into this tapestry. Beneath their fingertips, the once palpable weight of the Book of Passage rested on the worn table, its pages, which had commanded their every step with an insidious will, now utterly blank. The thick paper, once adorned with indecipherable ink swirling with hidden meaning and cryptic phrases, lay barren, mute. It was as if the book itself had exhaled its final breath and succumbed to a silence more absolute than any darkness.

The transformation was profound. No longer a mystical arbiter of destiny, the book's surrender symbolized the closure of an arduous chapter, the relinquishment of its uncanny grip that had dictated their lives with merciless precision. At last, Caroline felt a lightness within her that she could only describe as freedom a lightness borne from stepping beyond the shackles of imposed fate and embracing the uncertain yet vibrant pulse of their existence together in Bramleigh. The book, which had loomed like some spectral warden over their hearts and minds, was now nothing more than a relic, a vessel emptied of its old power. She lifted her gaze to meet Thomas's eyes, those familiar orbs that had become her anchor through every peril and passion, and smiled a quiet, genuine curve of lips that shimmered with both resolve and tender affection. It was a smile grounded in the hard-won knowledge that their journey, once governed by a spectral text and the inscrutable rules within, was now theirs alone to script.

There had been a moment, late into many sleepless nights, when she feared this finality might never come. When every flicker of hope seemed swallowed by the dark suspicion that they were still pawns in an endless game with no resolution. Yet here, standing beneath the silver-streaked sky in a world stitched from centuries past but made vibrant by their presence, Caroline sensed the last tendrils of that spectral control dissolve into the early dawn. The book's emptiness was not a void to be feared but a space pregnant with possibility an uncharted horizon where the contours of their love, no longer bound by mystical coercion, could flourish in the stark light of truth.

Thomas's voice barely broke the stillness, soft and low, carrying the weight of every unspoken feeling that had gathered in the quiet spaces between them over countless trials. "It's over," he said, as if announcing the end of a storm long awaited. There was no triumph in his tone, no exultation only a profound relief, a tentative wonder that perhaps they had finally escaped the labyrinth. His fingers tightened around Caroline's, grounding her, steadying them both against the tremors of uncertainty. She nodded, feeling the resonance of his words deep in her chest, where love and fear and hope tangled in a complex symphony.

Her mind drifted back to the very first time they had touched that enigmatic volume in the Arkwell Library a moment charged with curiosity and disbelief, laced with the sharp sting of skepticism. Never had she imagined that a single, unmarked book could rip open the seams of time itself, thrusting her into an era both beautiful and brutal, where survival demanded masks and the stakes were measured in lives and hearts. How far they had traveled since then not merely in miles or seasons, but through revolutions of the soul. From defensive, cold distance to shared vulnerability; from mere strangers to lovers who had forged something real, something timeless amid the merciless strictures of the past.

Now, standing here in Bramleigh, the village waking slowly to the promise of new light, the echoes of their past selves lingered only faintly, like shadows retreating before dawn. The villagers, their faces etched with curious suspicion and growing acceptance, moved through the streets with the mundane grace of everyday life, unaware that two of their own had conquered the most extraordinary of bonds. The oppressive gaze of Agnes Pryce, once so felt and feared, had finally faltered, dissipating like mist under the dawn. That quiet, insidious control no longer loomed replaced instead by a fragile but genuine peace that pressed tenderly against the walls surrounding Caroline and Thomas's entwined lives.

Caroline dared to breathe deeply, savoring

the earthy perfume of the wet ground and smoldering hearths, letting the scent swirl within her lungs like a benediction. This was no longer a borrowed existence, no longer a forced pantomime of love and partnership. With the book's silencing, their personas had shed their last layers of artifice, revealing two souls irrevocably bound by choice, by sacrifice, and by the messy, exquisite thrum of human connection. The future before them stretched wide and uncharted, a landscape where trust had finally triumphed over control, and surrender had cultivated the most unexpected power of all the power to create and hold love without conditions.

Thomas's hand slid to her cheek, thumb tracing the soft curve with reverence, and in that gesture, Caroline felt the final confirmation of their bond. It was no longer written in ink or summoned by incantation, but forged in moments of shared laughter, whispered fears, and aching embraces. The heat of their closeness was no longer a secret to be guarded but a flame to be nurtured, wild and fierce and beautiful. Her heart swelled under the tender weight of belonging, swelling with gratitude for the strange and winding path that had brought them here not just to a time and place, but to each other.

There was a stillness to the room that settled like a gentle tide, comforting and complete. The book, once a formidable architect of fate and fear, now rested inert, its pages as blank as the sky beyond the window, stripped of their inscrutable commands. Caroline reached out, brushing her fingertips over the empty paper, feeling the cool, smooth surface beneath her touch. It was a quiet goodbye and an unspoken promise that this chapter was both ending and beginning, wrapped in the silent eloquence of empty pages waiting to be written anew by their own hands.

In this moment, time did not race or slow; it simply was. The past and future loosened their grip, yielding space for a present that shimmered with fragile hope and fierce determination. They did not speak the words aloud, but both understood the truth etched deep within: the book's power was gone, but the bond it had compelled into being was real. It pulsed between them, steady and unyielding, a testament to the human heart's capacity to bloom under pressure, to turn captivity into freedom, and to transform fear into a love that would endure beyond the boundaries of time itself.

The world outside beckoned softly, its familiar cadence of village life a lullaby that promised simplicity and hardship in equal measure. But inside their shared haven, beneath the gentle shadow of time's passing, Caroline and Thomas had found something extraordinary an irrevocable choice to live fully in the moment, to accept the unfurling chapters of life with open hearts. The Book of Passage had sealed their fate not by dictating it, but by delivering them into a love that neither time, nor trial, nor silent pages could ever erase.

As the morning light spilled into the cottage, gilding the worn wooden floorboards and illuminating the steady rhythm of two lives entwined, Caroline pressed her lips to Thomas's temple, a touch as tender as a whispered vow. With that simple act, they crossed the threshold wholly and irrevocably not just into the village, or into the past they had come to call home, but into a future sculpted by their own hands, guided no longer by the ghost of the book, but by the unyielding strength of the love they had chosen to claim.

Epilogue: A New Beginning

Morning sunlight filtered through the narrow panes of the cottage window, casting golden patterns onto the rough-hewn timber floors where Caroline and Thomas began their day. The rhythms of Bramleigh had quickly become the pulse to which their lives moved, a seamless cadence blending toil, quiet moments, and the subtle social dance woven tightly through the village's skein. Each dawn, as the mist curled low over the rolling fields, the couple rose with a shared sense of purpose born not just from necessity but from a slowly deepening affection that had, over months, grown in the fertile soil of hardship and endurance. Their mornings were modest rituals: Thomas stoking the hearth's fading embers while Caroline prepared a simple meal, their movements synchronizing with an ease that had eluded them in the uncertainty of their first bewildered days here. Though their home was small, the space bore marks of their attention the carefully swept hearth, a neatly stacked pile of kindling, and a collection of wildflowers pressed between the pages of a well-worn book, a silent testament to the life they were building, page by patient page.

Emerging from their doorway, the village unfolded like a living tapestry in soft, rich hues of thatched roofs and winding lanes bordered by hedgerows heavy with wild berries. Life in Bramleigh was governed less by the rush of hours than by the dictates of the land and the unspoken codes of community. Each day was framed by work tending to chickens that clucked and pecked in the yard, foraging for herbs along the hedgerows, and carting water from the well that nourished both garden and fire. The village mornings hummed with the sounds of labor; the rhythmic chopping of wood, the low murmur of gossip threading through small gatherings, and the distant ringing cry of children at play. Caroline, whose modern sensibilities had once prized precision and control, found solace in these tangible, grounded routines. Though her knowledge of history had offered her intellectual survival, it was the simplicity of daily tasks that began to root her firmly in this place, cultivating a new kind of confidence born of endurance rather than study.

Thomas, ever the protector and provider, moved with a deft familiarity around the village chores, blending instinct and adaptability. His lean hands were skilled in mending fences and forging tools among the village blacksmith's shop, discreetly earning the respect of locals who once eyed him with suspicion. The transformation from stranger to neighbor was subtle but undeniable. His broad shoulders bore the weight of physical labor that had neither city streets nor library stacks prepared him for, yet he found a quiet pride in the sweat that glistened on his brow and the strength resilience demanded. Each evening, as the sun dipped low, his hand would find Caroline's in the dimming light, a tacit wordless promise exchanged across the divide of their vastly different origins now fused into a shared narrative. Together, they were no longer mere visitors from another time but residents woven into Bramleigh's enduring fabric.

The community itself moved like an organism with hidden depths quiet gestures of kindness masked under wary glances, a delicate balance of social order maintained by unspoken customs and the ever-watchful eyes of Agnes Pryce. The widow's influence lingered in the village as silently as the earthy scent of smoke from the chimneys. At first, Caroline's sharp mind cataloged Agnes's interventions as mere inconveniences restrictions placed upon 'outsiders' in a world far less forgiving than the one she knew. But with time, the subtle manipulations and veiled threats became threads of tension woven into their daily interactions. There were occasions when Agnes's henchmen would cast elongated shadows near the edges of their property, or when whispered warnings came disguised as village gossip. These moments tested the resilience forged between Caroline and Thomas, drawing them ever closer as allies against an unseen threat that could rupture the fragile peace their new life depended upon.

Yet, despite Agnes's shadow, there were moments of unexpected warmth and inclusion. The village market, held on Saturdays beneath the sprawling arms of ancient oak trees, was both a public stage and a court of social negotiation. Here, Caroline and Thomas would mingle with farmers and tradesfolk, exchanging goods and pleasantries, silently selling the illusion of their conjugal bond beneath stoic gazes and whispered appraisals. Caroline, with her keen intellect and unassuming grace, found herself drawn into conversations about crop yields and weather patterns, her questions framed with enough local knowledge to both charm and deflect suspicion. Thomas, with his ready smile and quiet strength, lent an ear to the laborers' tales and guarded their place within this tight-knit enclave with a steadfast vigilance. Slowly, the village began to accept them not as anomalies but as threads woven into its complex social loom, a testament to the power of persistence and the human need for connection.

The seasons shifted with a steady surety, marking the passage of time more reliably than any clock or calendar Caroline had known. Spring brought the blush of blossoms and new hopes, their garden awakening under tentative touches and careful nurturing. Summer stretched languid and golden, filled with the buzzing of bees and long twilight walks through fields heavy with hay. Autumn's crisp winds swept in gold and crimson leaves, and with it, a time of harvest and reflection. Winter, austere and biting, tested their endurance in ways both cruel and intimate. It was during the cold months that their relationship deepened most profoundly, the forced closeness of their shared hearth giving way to moments of vulnerability carved from the long nights. Caroline, who had once guarded her heart behind walls of scholarly detachment, now found herself relinquishing fragments of control to the warmth of Thomas's whispered reassurances and the strength of his arms around her shivering form. Their physical intimacy was not merely the fulfillment of passion but a tender testimony to trust earned and fears faced together, a slow dance of discovery beneath blankets heavy with the scent of woodsmoke and earth.

Beyond their cottage, the village bore witness to stories as old as the land itself whispers of past loves and losses, secrets buried deep beneath cobblestones and wild hedgerows. Caroline often found herself wandering these quiet spaces, letting the past and present intertwine as she contemplated the strange, beautiful irony of a life forcibly rewound yet now so fiercely embraced. Each dawn found her inhaling the crisp air, feeling the solid pulse of Bramleigh beneath her feet, a grounding counterpoint to the fleeting, all-too-human emotions stirred within. Thomas, too, carried the weight of this dual existence battles fought in forgotten cities and dusty archives now replaced by the intimacy of shared meals and stolen glances. Their identity was no longer solely defined by the ghosts of future or past but by a present forged in fire and tenderness, a narrative they authored together amid the challenges of a world that demanded conformity yet at last yielded to their quiet rebellion the creation of a new family, born not of bloodlines but of choice and love.

In the village gatherings that lit up the rare festivals and communal prayers, Caroline and Thomas moved with an ease that surprised even themselves. The laughter that once felt foreign now flowed naturally, their voices blending in songs sung around flickering fires, the warmth of shared stories wrapping around them like a protective cloak. They exchanged knowing glances, each recognizing in the other the distance they had traveled from suspicion and fear to belonging and hope. Through whispered conversations beneath starlit skies, they planned futures unfurling beyond the constricting scripts imposed by the mysterious book and the cruel eyes of Agnes. The village that had once seemed a prison of roles and restrictions had slowly become a sanctuary where they could imagine a life lived on their own terms, where love was not merely an imposed necessity but a chosen foundation, strong enough to defy time itself.

The echoes of their earlier struggles

remained, etched faintly along the edges of their consciousness like the palimpsest of a forgotten chapter. Yet the victory lay in what they had built an unshakable partnership forged not in the flush of passion alone but through the shared burdens of survival and the gentle unraveling of defenses. Caroline's sharp mind no longer sought to dominate but to understand and adapt; Thomas's sturdy presence evolved beyond protector to equal, confidant, and beloved. Together, they navigated the complexities of a community wary of outsiders and suffocating in tradition, ever mindful of the boundaries they could not cross and the freedoms they had carved anew. Their daily routine was thus more than mere survival it was an ongoing act of rebellion, proof that even imposed identities could be transcended when love was allowed to blossom beneath the weight of expectation and history.

In the quiet hours before dawn, when the world lay hushed beneath a veil of mist, Caroline and Thomas would sit together on a weathered bench outside their cottage, hands entwined, breathing the scent of earth and rain-washed fields. Caroline, her gaze tracing the familiar contours of the village rooftops against the softening sky, often marveled at the journey they had undertaken. The uncertain strangers who landed in Bramleigh were gone, replaced by two souls intertwined by fate and choice, their love a beacon burning steady against the shadows of past and future alike. Thomas's hand in hers was no longer a shield against threat but a quiet promise of belonging and enduring partnership. They had endured suspicion, adversity, and the ruthless strictures of a society that demanded conformity, only to find freedom in the very place that once threatened to unmake them.

Life in Bramleigh was neither simple nor without struggle, but within its rolling hills and cobbled streets, Caroline and Thomas found a truth that transcended time. Their daily rituals, once rigid and dictated by need, now shimmered with the gentle glow of home in the shared smiles exchanged over morning bread, in the stillness of twilight strolls beneath ancient oaks, and in the tender touch that conveyed more than words ever could. They had navigated the chasm between past and present, fact and feeling, control and surrender, emerging not just as survivors but as architects of a shared future. In the steady cadence of their lives, woven tightly into the fabric of Bramleigh, they had discovered that love tested by time and trial was the truest passage of all.

The morning sun filtered softly through the heavy linen curtains, casting a warm, golden glow across the worn wooden floorboards of their modest cottage. The quiet hum of village life wafted through the open window distant chatter at the market, the clatter of a cart rumbling down the cobblestones, the faint bleat of sheep guarded beyond the fields all underscored by the gentle creak of the timber walls settling as though the house itself were breathing alongside them. In this tranquil moment, Caroline stirred slowly from sleep, the coolness of dawn brushing against her skin like a tender whisper. At first, the familiar weight beside her was a soothing presence a warmth that no longer felt imposed or forced, but rather a steady, anchoring pulse in her day-to-day existence. She opened her eyes to find Thomas, his chest rising and falling with measured ease, the first strands of daylight caressing the strong planes of his face, softening the outward hardness that had once been a shield against the unknown.

Gone were the days when their marriage was a delicate pretense, a role played out under the watchful eyes of a suspicious village and a condemning, unyielding book that had dictated their every interaction. That oppressive force had long since dissipated, leaving only the true partnership that they had painstakingly built from the fragile foundations of survival and necessity. Caroline had once prized control, the certainty of facts and the unyielding walls of history as her refuge, and Thomas had guarded his instincts like a blade, wary and reserved. But now, in this sunlit room filled with the quiet promise of ordinary moments shared, those walls had been dismantled, brick by brick some torn down with struggle and surrendered fears, others carefully constructed into lasting bonds that neither time nor circumstance could erode.

She slipped quietly from beneath the covers, the wooden floor cool beneath her bare feet, and moved toward the window. Beyond the garden gate, the first blossoms of early spring were beginning to unfold, swaying gently in the breeze like the whispered hopes of new beginnings. This small patch of earth once foreign, hostile, a cage of strict social laws and hidden dangers had transformed into a sanctuary, a place where they were no longer outsiders grasping desperately at disguises but belonged fully, unequivocally. Her fingers brushed the worn book that lay on the windowsill, its leather cover scuffed by countless hands, the faded pages now a relic of the past they had transcended. The tome that had once ruled their lives no longer held sway, for their bond was no longer something born of obligation or survival, but a testament to choice and resilience.

Thomas rose quietly behind her, his presence a comforting weight against her back as he draped an arm around her waist, drawing her gently into his side. "The garden's ready for planting soon," he murmured, voice low and rich with an affectionate warmth that made her smile. "The villagers will be glad for a taste of fresh herbs and vegetables after the long winter." His words, so simple and domestic, carried a deeper resonance for Caroline proof not only of their acceptance in Bramleigh but of their integration into the rhythms and hopes of life unfolding naturally, far from the constricting demands of the past and the book's cruel edicts.

She leaned back against him, allowing her head to rest lightly on his shoulder, feeling with a deep, almost overwhelming certainty the reality of what they had become: two people no longer pretending or bargaining with fate, but crafting a shared existence grounded in mutual respect, trust, and affection.

Their marriage was no longer a fragile performance to ward off suspicion; it was real. It was messy and imperfect, marked by the inevitable clashes of two strong-willed souls who had once been strangers but had grown irrevocably intertwined. It was laughter that echoed through this very room over minor disagreements; it was silent understanding during long, solitary afternoons spent in separate corners of the house; it was the raw vulnerability beneath the surface when fears and doubts crept unbidden yet were met not with judgment, but unwavering support.

Caroline recalled the countless moments they had weathered together the nights when the chill seeped through the cracks in the walls and they had huddled close by the hearth, sharing body heat and whispers until the cold felt less menacing. The times when the weight of Agnes Pryce's scrutiny had threatened to unravel them, each accusation and thinly veiled threat a test of their resolve. The slow, tentative steps toward intimacy, where longing and tenderness mingled with the aching knowledge that their feelings were once forbidden, complicated by histories neither could rewrite but both chose to transcend. These memories did not fade; they colored their present with depth and texture, serving as reminders of their journey not only through time but through the labyrinth of their own hearts.

Thomas tightened his embrace as Caroline turned in his arms to face him fully, the intensity in his eyes an ember born of steadfast love rather than passion's fleeting flame steady and grounding. His hand cupped her cheek with gentle reverence as his lips brushed against her forehead, a silent kiss filled with promise and gratitude for what they had salvaged from chaos. "I don't know where I would be without you," he confessed, his voice thick with emotion. "Not just here, in this place but in any life. You have made me more than I ever thought possible."

Her breath caught at the weight of his words, and she pressed her hand to his chest, feeling the steady beat of his heart beneath her fingertips. "And you have taught me what it means to surrender," she whispered, "to let go, even when it terrifies me. To trust that love… real love… can be our refuge." The words were no longer theoretical or academic; they were lived truth a truth that resonated deeply inside her, softening the edges of the woman who had once been so guarded and self-reliant. Here, with Thomas, she had discovered a different kind of strength, born from vulnerability and shared hope.

The door creaked softly open, and a small figure entered the room Thomas's apprentice, a curious boy hired to help with farm work and chores, eyes bright with the innocence of youth and the quiet admiration of a man who had found his place in the world. Caroline smiled, ruffling the boy's unruly hair as he settled by the hearth, casting a warm glow over the space that was undeniably home. It was a life crafted not from the pages of a dusty tome or dictated by the rigid expectations of society, but from the choices they had made choices to build, to nurture, to love fiercely despite all odds.

Outside, the village of Bramleigh bustled gently with its own rhythms, a community that had come to accept and embrace them not because of the façade of compliance but because of the kindness and integrity that they had demonstrated through quiet acts of daily courage. Agnes Pryce's shadow had long since dissolved into history, replaced by neighbors who greeted them with genuine smiles, and local farmers who sought their counsel on matters both practical and personal. The village was no longer a cage but a tapestry of connections woven carefully through trust and shared humanity.

Later, as twilight deepened into night, Caroline and Thomas sat by the fire, the flickering flames casting dancing shadows over the familiar contours of their faces. Their talk drifted from plans for the coming season to dreams once distant but now within reach the possibility of children, of raising a family bound not only by blood but by love; of expanding their garden and perhaps one day opening a small shop to share the fruits of their labor with the village. Each aspiration was a thread strengthening the fabric of their shared life, a testament to the transformation from enforced partnership to true marriage.

In the quiet intimacy of that evening, their hands intertwined, Caroline marveled at the journey they had undertaken not just through time or history, but through the complex and beautiful terrain of human connection. The book of passage that had brought them here was no longer a master but a bookmark, a reminder of where they had come from, while their hearts wrote new chapters chapters filled with laughter, longing, trials overcome, and, above all, love fiercely claimed and freely given.

There was no longer fear of loss or separation hanging over them like a dark cloud; instead, there was certainty in the life they had forged together. Each day was an embrace of the unknown, faced side by side, equipped with a trust that no external force could sever. For Caroline Moore and Thomas Reed, their genuine marriage was not a conclusion, but a beginning a promise lived out in every tender glance, every heated touch, every shared silence and laughter, all etched indelibly into the enduring story of two souls bound beyond time and circumstance.

As the flicker of the fire softened and sleep beckoned, they closed their eyes together, comforted by the profound peace that comes with knowing one's place in the world in each other's arms, in Bramleigh, and in the delicate yet resilient tapestry of chosen love. Here, at long last, was home.

Looking Forward

The morning light spilled gently through the aged panes of their modest yet warmly adorned cottage, casting a soft, golden glow upon the room that Caroline and Thomas now proudly called home. The air held a freshness that whispered promises, not just of the new day, but of all the tomorrows they had chosen to build together together, without the coercing hands of an ancient, enigmatic book or the suffocating weight of past fears. The subtle hum of village life drifted in faintly, blending with the crackling hearth that anchored them to this very space, a sanctuary shaped by love, resilience, and surrender. Caroline sat by the window, her fingers tracing idle patterns on the aged wood of the sill, eyes unbound by the scholarly distance that once defined her every gaze. Instead, they softened with a quiet warmth, reflecting the gentle intimacy of a life embraced rather than endured. Her heart, once guarded by walls built from precision and control, now blossomed with a steady bloom of trust and hope an echo of every stolen glance from

Thomas and every smile that broke through the fog of uncertainty. The years that had unfolded since their arrival in Bramleigh felt both infinite and achingly brief, stitched together by moments of struggle and tenderness, of fear relinquished and love reclaimed. The past with its constraints, the future once shrouded in inescapable fate, had been reshaped by choice a profound, sacred act that had transformed two strangers into partners, and that partnership into something enduring and fiercely alive.

Thomas moved quietly behind her, the familiar sound of his steps a steady rhythm that seemed to harmonize naturally with the cadence of Caroline's breath. He paused just behind her, his presence a silent testament to the distance they had traveled not only across centuries but from themselves to each other. The lines around his eyes deepened with traces of both hardship and joy, and those same eyes met hers in a glance filled with unspoken vows. There was no longer any ambiguity in their connection, no charade to maintain in the village or in their hearts; what had begun as an imposed pretense had blossomed into an authentic bond, one forged in the crucible of shared adversity and nurtured by the slow, steady turning of genuine affection. In Thomas's steady gaze, Caroline found a mirror for her own awakening his every gesture and word a reassurance that the life they had carved out was no mere concession but a declaration of their true selves. The cottage, with its rough-hewn furniture and simple decor, bore witness to their story, holding within its walls the echoes of laughter, whispered confessions, and the quiet strength of hands clasped across the warmth of many evenings. It was imperfect, rustic, and beautiful, much like the love they nurtured full of rough edges smoothed only by the tender patience of mutual understanding.

The small garden that stretched just beyond their door was beginning to bloom in hopeful bursts of color, tender shoots breaking through the soil as if nature itself celebrated their new beginning. Caroline found solace in tending the earth, her delicate hands coaxing life from the ground in rhythms that echoed the growth unfolding between her and Thomas. Each seed planted was an act of faith, a belief in the future despite the shadows of the past they had left behind. The village, too, had shifted around them, its initial suspicion slowly giving way to a quiet acceptance, a grudging respect born from witnessing the couple's unwavering commitment to both the community and each other. Agnes Pryce's watchful eyes, once a source of tension and threat, had faded into the periphery of their lives, the widow's grip loosening as Caroline and Thomas's steadfast presence and integrity reshaped the social fabric in subtle ways. No longer outsiders bound by fear, they had become the heartbeat of Bramleigh a living testament to the power of choice, the triumph of love unshackled by time's relentless march.

Caroline's thoughts often drifted to the mysterious book that had cast them into this past once a source of command and control, now a relic she kept tucked away on the highest shelf, a silent reminder of their origins but no longer their master. The book's final edicts had required honesty and vulnerability, and through that mandate, Caroline discovered depths within herself that no amount of academic rigor could have revealed. She learned that to surrender control was not to capitulate but to open the door to profound connection, that trust was not a weakness but a resilient thread binding two souls in a dance as old as time. Thomas, for his part, had shed layers of uncertainty and guarded reserve, his identity no longer a question mark suspended between worlds but a chosen and cherished place beside Caroline. Together, they had rewritten the narrative that fate had thrust upon them, crafting instead a story of their own making one where love was not the product of circumstance but the conscious embrace of shared destiny.

Their days now unfolded with a comforting predictability, punctuated by moments that shimmered with quiet joys and the soft heat of companionship. Mornings began with the simple ritual of shared tea by the fire, their conversation weaving through the mundane to the extraordinary as fingers brushed and smiles lingered longer than needed. The afternoons saw Caroline engrossed in the modest library she had established in their home, shelves lined not just with dusty tomes but with scribbled journals and letters chronicling their experiences, a tangible testament to the life they had fashioned. Thomas contributed in his own way, his strength and practical wisdom turning their humble abode into a haven of security and warmth. Evenings brought the intimacy of shared shadows and whispered reassurances, where the walls bore witness to the slow unfurling of passion tempered by respect and longing. Their physical union, once a tentative gesture amidst necessity and fear, had matured into a celebration of trust and desire a sacred space where vulnerability was met with tenderness, and love became a language spoken in the silence between heartbeats.

Caroline sometimes marveled at the irony that it was the constraints and dangers of the 18th century so antithetical to her modern sensibilities that had ultimately freed her from the cage of her own making. The rigid social codes, the ever-present threat of exposure, had forced her to confront the fallacy of control without connection, to surrender to a rhythm far more ancient and enduring than any timeline or text. In Thomas, she discovered not only a partner but a mirror reflecting the parts of herself she had kept hidden the parts that yearned for belonging, for acceptance, for the messy, vibrant chaos of human intimacy. Their love had emerged not despite the harsh circumstances but through them, each challenge a forge tempering their resilience and deepening their bond. They had learned that identity was not a fixed point anchored by history or bloodline but a living tapestry woven from choices made daily, sometimes painfully, but always courageously. By claiming their place in Bramleigh, they had claimed themselves not as victims of time or fate, but as architects of a life defined by love and authenticity.

Looking ahead, the horizon unfurled with a promise that was as boundless as their commitment to each other. The village held opportunities yet unseen friendships to cultivate, traditions to embrace, and perhaps even small rebellions against the status quo that Agnes Pryce once so fiercely guarded. They envisioned a future where their home would echo with the laughter of children, where their journals would expand into chronicles passed down through generations, and where the lessons carved from their journey would ripple outward into the world beyond Bramleigh's borders. The very act of looking forward became an act of defiance, a refusal to be tethered to past shadows or fears. They chose instead to live fully in the present, building a legacy not written by the mysterious forces that had brought them here but by the love that sustained them. The intertwining of their lives was no longer a precarious balancing act but a harmonious symphony, each note resonating with the beauty and complexity of two souls who had found their true home in each other.

In these quiet moments, as the sun climbed higher and the world outside began its daily dance, Caroline and Thomas embodied a truth that transcended time itself. Their story was no longer one of displacement or survival but of belonging and blossoming a testament to the enduring power of love to rewrite history, to heal wounds both ancient and fresh, and to illuminate the path forward with a light born of hope, courage, and unwavering devotion. As they rose to face the day, hands entwined and hearts unburdened, the future stretched before them like an open book, its pages waiting to be filled with the stories they would write together stories of passion and peace, of struggle and triumph, and above all, of a love that had passed through the boundaries of time to become eternal.